To my beautiful girlfriend Hayley. Your patience allowed me to write this book. Your kindness, sense of humour and smart mouth, gave me the inspiration for Christian's love interest. To my uncle Jamie and Lee Winter, thanks for taking the time to read a draft and for your input. Time is the most precious commodity and you gave yours to me. Thank you.

CONTENTS

Dedication   1

HUNTER   7

Quiet Time   18

Mikey   23

The Day Job   27

Secrets From Friends   34

The Kid   47

Chat on the Sofa   55

That Place   63

Beautiful Blue Eyes   64

The Sweetest Memory   70

That Beautiful Girl   75

The Kid II   86

The Start Of Something Special   96

Thieving From Thieves   102

The Rat Trap   109

Bullen   112

Turning Wheels   117

The Kid III   122

Past to Present   135

Tipping the Scales   142

What's the Point of it All?   145

Hidden Face to the Voice   146

All Too Much   147

Tickets Please   153

I Want My Money Back   155

Special Delivery   157

Is There a Light at The End?   162

The Kid IV   167

Past Nightmares   172

The Place Where Nightmares Breed   175

All Caught Up   180

Pleasant Moments   184

Sunshine and Showers   191

Wallowing   195

Beginning of the End   199

The Man in Black   204

Life Goes On   220

HUNTER

The man in black

Death travels easily in the twilight hours. It strolls through the shadows that moonlight creates. It takes any form when it hunts for a life. A fox or an owl or a man with a knife.

Focused and eager eyes reflect a dim yellow light. They peer from behind thick foliage that sways gently in the breeze. The air is cool and dry. The night is quiet. Quiet is what this man in black needs. The weather forecast said heavy showers. Luckily, they were wrong. The sky remains clear, thanks to a change in wind direction, and the rain clouds now float above the land more than thirty miles away. He folds his waterproof clothes into a make do cushion and stretches his stiffening limbs. Once comfortable, he peels back the Velcro on his wrist to check the time. It's 12.47am. Time passes slowly when your waiting for something. He lifts his balaclava and scratches his itchy face through its ginger beard. 12.48am.

To kill time, he opens a small rucksack to his left. Sitting on top of a pistol, a small bottle of liquid and a rag is a chocolate bar. He looks up at the house that is thirty-seven meters in front of him. Chocolate and caramel melting in his mouth.

The house has fresh white paint on the walls. It has five large bedrooms. Three at the front of the house, two at the rear. The rear bedrooms have balconies overlooking the impressive gardens and detached garages. Pale blue lighting illuminates large garage doors and semi-nude statues.

The bedroom closest to him is the guest room. At the moment, it's an empty guest room. Attached to it, is a small scaffolding that's being taken away tomorrow. The man in the bush places the last of the chocolate in his mouth. He folds the rapper neatly and places it inside a small compartment on the side of his rucksack. The observations continue.

A single light remains on upstairs. The flicker of a TV can be seen in a window downstairs. The man in black checks his watch again. 12.59am.

A rustle of undergrowth to his right pulls his attention away. Instinctively, he removes a sharpened bayonet from its sheath and rolls upright. Feet planted firmly. Senses on high alert. In the darkness it's almost impossible to find the source. The man leans toward the noise. Bayonet held tight in his hand. He scans around, making sure he doesn't leave his eyes in one position too long. Suddenly a moving shade of black steals his focus. A snuffling hedgehog approaches. His hand relaxes its grip.

The hedgehog brushes up against his foot and defensively curls into a tight ball. He reaches out to touch it. "That's OK, mate. Don't be scared," he whispers. "I'm not going to hurt you."

Suddenly his mind jumps back to a confused and angry time. His eye socket was bloodied. His lip was swollen. His body bruised. He's standing by the side of a river. In one hand he held a hessian bag and in the other he held a brick. The brick and the bag are attached by a single blue string. His younger self is plucking up the courage to act out an experiment. It was an experiment for his mind. To see what, if anything, could give him pleasure, or at least take away some pain. His younger self takes a deep breath and opens the bag. He carefully reaches inside and pulls out a curled-up hedgehog that has the string wrapped around its waist. He walks toward the river, takes another deep breath and throws the hedgehog and brick into the water. He doesn't remember how long the hedgehog struggled for. All he remembers is the feeling that sight gave him. Standing there watching this little spiky creature fighting for its life. Its little nose barely above the water line as its little legs fought with everything to reach the surface. He remembers guilt, grief and sadness. Guilt, grief, sadness and being wet. You see, the experiment was because he had a strong urge to hurt something. To take the rage out of himself and put it onto something else. In a strange sort of way, it did work. That boy did learn something about himself. He learned that he loved animals. But after he'd waded into the water to pull the hedgehog out. Even after he had set it free, that feeling of rage and sadness continued. It continues to this day. Although the man in the black has found a very good way of directing it.

Once the hedgehog has moved away, the man in black realises the house is in darkness. He checks his watch. 01.08am. He picks up his waterproofs and places them into a compartment at the very top of the rucksack. A gentle shake makes sure there's no rattles. Uncontrolled noise in these situations can be fatal. Once he's happy, he crawls out of his hiding place and stretches his stiff body. He places his rucksack on and slides a pair of black leather gloves over his hands.

The man in black sneaks toward the large French doors that lead into the living room and peeks inside. It's empty and dark. He shuffles over to the scaffolding, plans his route up and begins to climb. Seconds later he's at the top and shuffling onto the balcony. Leaning against a wall are several loose scaffolding tubes. He picks one up. The cold hard steal feels good in his hand, but a lump of concrete makes it heavy at one end. He gently places it back down and selects another. This one is about a kilo lighter and four inches shorter. He swings it like a baseball bat. Once, twice and then a final third time to be sure. Then he smiles and places it to one side. After scanning the floor, he negotiates past a dozen broken tiles, a chair and three potted plants. Once he reaches the sliding doors to the guest bedroom, he looks inside. After a minute he's sure it's empty. The handle clicks and the door slides silently to the right. Large mirrors upon fitted wardrobes reflect what little light there is. The smell of flowers fills the air like a meadow in bloom. A meticulously made queen size bed is in the center of the room.

The man in black steps inside. He gently closes the door behind him and removes his rucksack. He attaches the holster and pistol to his right thigh. The liquid and rag he keeps to hand. Then he slings the rucksack over his shoulders. He opens the door to the landing and listens for any sign of movement before going further. There is a noise. He waits and studies it intently. After a minute he's confident it's not coming from any person inside the house. If the man in black knows Bobby Boy at all, the noises were probably made a while ago in a studio of some sort. He creeps toward the noise with the gun raised. The bottle and rag secure in his pocket. The noises become louder and the screams of faked delight become unmistakable. The man in black approaches Bobby Boy's door and opens it a jar. He looks inside, and smiles. The man in black lowers the pistol and slides it back inside the black holster. He opens the bottle, pours some liquid onto the rag and steps into the room.

On a large TV screen to his left, a woman is bent over a chair and being kept busy by three men. The men seem to be enjoying the sexual scene a lot more than she is (although she is putting her bravest face on). Bobby Boy is to his right, laying face up on an enormous bed with a half empty bottle of scotch by his side and his penis in his hand.

Bobby Boy measures about six-foot four and is built like a powerlifter. He has short, dark hair and a tattoo of a dragon eating a bulldog on his neck. It's easy to understands why most people would be intimidated. However, the man in black is not most people. When the man in black takes another step forward, Bobby, starts to stir. The man in black quickly runs over and forces the cloth over his mouth. Bobby's eyes glare at him but the struggle lasts seconds. Bobby falls fast sleep. The man in black takes his rucksack off and opens a small pocket on the front of it. He pulls out a bunch of strong, black cable ties and secures Bobby's hands and feet. He uses his British bayonet to cut the silk quilt cover on Bobby's bed into strips and uses them to secure him to the bed and gag him. Once he's confident that Bobby is bound properly, the man in black can relax. He looks around the room. The enormous bed looks hand crafted. Vines and leaves are carved into the thick wooden posts that reach almost to the high ceiling. A large mirror is fixed to the ceiling, directly above the bed. The headboard is a blood red leather. The carpet is thick and soft underfoot and a light cream colour. Two framed family photos sit upon a table. The backdrop of one is the Eiffel tower. The other is Niagara Falls. The man in black reaches into the pocket at the front of his bag and pulls out a small bottle of smelling salts. He places them under Bobby's nose. "Wakey, wakey, rise and shine," he says in a strong Irish accent.

Bobby's eyes slowly flicker as his senses come back online. When he sees the man in black by his bedside, he becomes enraged. His eyes stare. The veins in his neck bulge as he struggles, making the dragon and bulldog dance. The man in black leans over and puts his whole weight on Bobby boy's chest, starving it of movement and him of oxygen. "Woah there, big man. There's no need for this. Settle down now, there's a good lad. Just settle down." Bobby boy's struggle becomes paltry and his breathing labored. Sweat drips from his forehead. A few minutes pass before he's still. The man in black drags the plush wooden rocking chair from the corner of the bedroom and sits down beside him. When their eyes meet, they stare at each other. "You've a reputation for being quite a brawler, Bobby boy. It's that reputation and your over-confidence that's made it possible for me to put you in this position, so it has."

Bobby regains some of his strength and tries to escape once more. The man in black sits back until this latest attempt fades to nothing.

"Are you finished?"

Bobby boy nods his head.

"Excellent. Now we can get on with the job at hand," the man in black looks around the room." In this house you have money, heroin and cocaine that..." The man in black loses his train of thought because of the moans and groans that are coming from the TV. "I'm sorry but this is very distracting." He checks the remote for any suspicious looking fluids before he picks it up and turns the TV off. "Right then, where were we." He scratches his beard under the balaclava, revealing the slightest amount of red hair to Bobby's eyes. "Oh yes. You've just picked up a kilo of Heroin and cocaine from Liverpool. I'm going to take them, and all the cash you have stashed here. You're gonna to tell me where they are, otherwise, I'm gonna cause you a great deal of pain so I am."

Bobby boy turns his eyes away from the man in black, looks up at the ceiling and starts to laugh. He laughs so hard that the gag in his mouth makes him cough. The man in black sits quietly by his side until silence returns.

"Are you finished?"

Bobby chuckles again.

"OK, now I'm gonna take the gag away, big man and you're gonna talk to me nicely. And we're gonna end tonight in the best possible way, so we are. Understood?"

Bobby nods his head. The man in black leans over, removes the gag and sits back down.

"Ew must be one of the stupidest fuckin' Irishmen alive if you think for one second that I'll tell you a single fuckin' thing." Bobby's voice is deep and gravelly. His Welsh accent becomes stronger the angrier he becomes. Spit balls form at the corners of his mouth. "Do you have any fuckin' idea about what I'm gonna do to you once I get free Paddy? I mean, I'm gonna break every fuckin' bone in your skinny little Irish body." He stares, wide eyed, into his enemy's eyes. "An' I'm gonna take my time doin' it. Do you understand that? Ew skinny little Irish prick! Do ew know who ew're fuckin' with? Nobody fucks with me! Nobody!"

The man in black smiles and shakes his head. Then he stands up, walks through the landing and bedroom and stops at the balcony. When he picks up 'his' scaffolding tube, a sinister voice in his head laughs. The man in black places the bar over his shoulder and re-enters the house.

When Bobby sees the cold steel bar, he tries his best to look undaunted. He fails, miserably. The man in black knows fear when he sees it. He's seen it many times before, on many nights like tonight. "One last chance Bobby Boy. Where's the stuff?"

Bobby looks up at the ceiling. "Fuck you! You, skinny, ginger prick."

"Fair enough. It's your choice." The sinister voice in the man in blacks head laughs hysterically.

He stands beside Bobby's bed, raises the bar high and brings it down with all his force upon Bobby's right shin. Bobby screams. His face turns a pale shade of white. Tears trickle down his face. The man in black leans the scaffolding bar against the bed, sits back down and begins to rock back and forth in the chair.

"I've been doing this a long time Bobby boy. A long, long time." Suddenly vomit explodes from Bobby's mouth and the man in black barely avoids it. He shuffles the chair a few feet to the right. Once Bobby has stopped throwing up, the man in Black wipes the sick from his mouth with a blue cotton pillow-case. "You know there's nobody within a mile of here. Your wife and daughter are spending your drug money in London for two more days and your son is having a sleep over at his friend Chris' house. The only people that can hear your screams are me and you. And..." The man in black leans in. "I don't have anywhere I have to be, Bobby Boy."

Bobby looks down at his leg and the tears return to his eyes. "Ew're fuckin' sick. Why dun ew face me like a real man instead of creepin' into my home when I'm asleep? Ew're a coward. A fuckin'..." The pain gets too much for Bobby, cutting his insults short.

"A coward is someone who lacks the balls to do what he must, Bobby Boy. That's the opposite of what I'm doing. I'm doing what I must to keep the evil at bay." The voice in his head laughs hysterically.

"I'm not an evil man."

"I never said, *you, were*. But you've become too big for your boots, Bobby boy. When you were just a small-time dealer that sold little bags here and there, we could turn a blind eye. But now, Bobby boy. Now you're dealing blocks of Heroin and Co-caine to every low life in south Wales." The man in black shakes his head. "Tut, tut, tut, Bobby boy."

"I do what I do, to put a roof over my kids heads and food in their belly. If people didn't want what I sell, then I'd find somethin' else to do. Until then, I'm a fuckin' drug dealer."

"I completely understand that. A man has to do, what he has to do. Which is why..." The man in black picks up the scaffolding tube and slowly walks around to the other side of the bed. Bobby boy looks up at him as he raises the bar. As it reaches head height, Bobby closes his eyes. The man in black pauses for just a few seconds to give Bobby time. "Tell me what I want to hear Bobby Boy."

"Go fuck yourself, ew skinny little Irish prick."

Bobby closes his eyes. They flicker in anticipation of the fresh wave of excruciating pain that is sure to come. Immeasurable time passes. Bobby's chest rises sharply as he inhales short, sharp breathes. But nothing happens. When he opens them again, he sees the man in black, holding the tip of the steel tube, a foot away from his broken leg. An evil smile on his face. Bobby's heart thumps in his chest. Sick threatens to explode once more. He watches as the man in black slowly inches the weapon toward broken bones. When metal touches skin, a wave of pain follows. Bobby's will holds firm. The man in black puts his weight upon the bar. Bobby's hands grip the bed beneath him, but his mouth remains closed. Undeterred, the man in black uses his free hand to squeeze the shattered bones together.

"STOP!" Bobby shouts. "Stop, stop I'll tell ew."

The man in black smiles and gently places the bar beside the bed. "*He's lying, hit him. Hit him!*" The man in black shakes the evil voice from his head. "Where are they?"

Bobby nods toward the walk-in wardrobe to his right. "In there. Top left cupboard at the far end. Code is 6632#."

Before he leaves the man in black grabs his pistol and places it to Bobby's left eyeball. "Is this a trick? Because I don't like tricks."

Bobby shakes his head.

"It had better not be."

The man in black holsters the pistol, grabs a black plastic bag from his rucksack and goes in search of his loot. He opens the sliding doors and enters the wardrobe. A strong scent of sweet perfume greats him, making him cough. He clears his throat and walks past boxes upon boxes of designer shoes and long dresses of every fabric and colour. "She has expensive bloody taste your wife. No wonder you deal. You're not buying all this shite if your digging holes and building walls for a living."

The man in black opens the black plastic bag and removes a small dust mask. After placing it tightly over his mouth he approaches the top left cupboard and slowly slides it open revealing the safe. He types, "6632#." He covers his eyes and pulls. It opens with a satisfying click and nothing else. "Wow."

After emptying the safe completely, he makes a rough count of the goods before heading back to Bobby. Bobby is close to tears from the pain. "I did tell you I always get what I want didn't I? There was no need for all this violence, Bobby boy. If you'd have just told me in time, you'd still have two fully functioning legs." The man in black shakes his head. "Tough guys never learn." He looks around the room. "You got any pain killers here?"

Bobby looks up at the man in black. A confused look upon his face. Tears trickling down his cheeks.

"Do you have anything here that will help you with the pain?"

"Go fuck yourself, ew sick fuck. Ew got what ew came here for so stop fuckin' with me. Get out of my fuckin' house you ginger twat."

"I'm not being a dick, Bobby Boy. My job is done now, so there's no point is there? I'm being sincere. Do you have anything here that can help you with the pain?"

Bobby boy studies his subduer through glazed eyes. Eventually he nods and swallows the bile that's attempting to leave. "The bathroom cabinet. My wife keeps them hidden from the kids behind a false wall." Bobby winces with pain. "Just open the cabinet, then push and slide the right-hand side to the left."

Bobby boy's head rocks back and his face contorts as another wave of pain shoots from his leg to his brain. His hands fight to reach down to the cause of all this agony.

The man in black drops the big black bag of cash and drugs by the side of Bobby's bed and searches for the other secret stash. He walks over the white marble polished floor, opens the cabinet and slides the door to the left. Half empty bottles and packets of painkillers of every description fall out of the secret hiding place. He grabs as many as he can carry and takes them back to Bobby. "What do you fancy? I have Morphine, Oxy..."

"Vicodin! Give me the Vicodin!" Bobby says cutting him off.

"As you wish." The man in black opens the bottle, leans over and drops a few tablets into Bobby's mouth. "You need something to wash them down with? A whiskey perhaps."

Bobby nods as he tries to choke the dry pills down with an even dryer mouth. The man in black sits on the edge of the bed and pours a small mouthful of watered-down whiskey into his mouth. Bobby swallows them down with a little shake of the head. "Thanks."

"No problem at all, Bobby boy. Glad I could help." The man in black has a quick look around the room. "Right then. This is where you and I part ways I suppose." He picks up the bag from Bobby's bed. "I'm going to make you a deal. Give up dealing forever and I will leave you half your cash, which is about forty-grand. I'm pretty sure there's more here, but I can't be arsed to look, so you're in luck. I'll also leave your wife's jewellery behind. I'm taking all the drugs and most of those painkillers with me though. You've made more than enough money already Bobby Boy, so it's only greed keeping you in this game." The man in black grabs his pistol and places it to Bobby's head. "If you don't agree to my terms. I will come back and kill you and anyone else that's with you. Understood?"

Bobby's eyes have begun to glaze over as the drugs begin to kick in. The man in Black slaps him to regain his awareness. "Do you understand?"

Bobby nods his head.

"So, it's a deal?" The man in black asks to confirm.

Bobby boy nods his head again. "Deal," he slurs.

"OK then Bobby Boy. For your family's sake, I hope you honour it."

The man in black pulls the jewellery and cash from the bag and places it beside Bobby. Then he throws the rest of the painkillers in but leaves a few loose Vicodin by Bobby's hand. After that he double checks that everything he brought to work with him is back inside the rucksack in its correct position.

He looks at Bobby who's beginning to get very spaced out from the meds. He checks the time. 02.53am. He sits down on the rocking chair, pushes his weight back and gently rocks back and forth until the last of Bobby's consciousness departs. Once he's sure Bobby is fast asleep, he checks the time again "03.00am. Perfect." He stands up, cuts the restraints from Bobby's left wrist and makes one final check of the room before putting the rucksack on. Then he grabs the black bag of goodies and scaffolding tube and walks away from Bobby's life as calmly as he walked in.

QUIET TIME

A motorbike stops at the brow of a hill. The engine and lights are switched off. Cycle and rider roll silently down to the bottom of the road. The bike is a modest BMW F 700 GS. It has off road tyres. It has three luggage carriers at the rear and it's completely black. At the bottom of the hill it enters the driveway of house number two. The last house on the right-hand side. The man in black guides the bike around the side, where a small but perfectly discreet garden shed is located under the hanging branches of a large willow tree. The shed is empty, and the doors are open. The man in black dismounts the bike while it's still moving and runs it into the center of the shed. He lowers its stand and removes his helmet. After removing his sweaty, black leather gloves, he runs his fingers through his thick black hair. Hidden under the shed is a thick steal chain. He pulls it through each of the wheels twice and locks it in two places on the shed floor. It's at that moment when the tiredness hits him hard. He yawns and stretches his entire body loose before grabbing his nights pay from the bike's compartments.

Suddenly a noise outside the shed puts him on edge. His hand instinctively reaches inside his rucksack and he spins around with his pistol raised. The bushy red tail of a fox disappears through a hedge. He laughs and places the pistol away. His heart thumps in his chest. When he exits the shed, he places another two locks on its doors and yawns again. The tired rider takes a second to look up at the night sky. The first of the sunlight begins to colour the blackness with its beautiful reds and oranges. He enjoys this time of day. The constant battle between light and dark can create so much beauty. The man in

THE HUNTER'S VALE OF TEARS

black walks past the open gate and high thick bushes at the back of his garden toward his home.

His house is a modest two-bedroom, detached cottage in a quiet little cul-de-sac in the Swansea valleys. The street has sixteen houses and the average age of the occupants is sixty-six. Needless to say, it doesn't have much of a party atmosphere. Which is why it is perfect. Noises draw attention. Attention is bad.

He opens the back door which leads into the kitchen and places his belongings onto the dark blue worktop. The smell is lemony fresh with a hint of lavender, curtesy of a few plugins. His first port of call is the large grey fridge-freezer. He pulls out a slightly frosted glass, a bottle of reasonably priced, but very nice gin and makes himself a well-earned drink. He throws three ice cubes into the half-filled glass, a strawberry and tops with a dash of tonic. He takes a sip as he walks back out to the gate at the back of the garden.

In the short time that he's been inside, the night has begun to look more like morning. The birds have begun to wake and sing, and all seems good in the world. It's a Saturday and the man in black has nothing to do today but rest and play. He takes a few minutes to listen to the wildlife that he loves around him and drink a little bit of what he likes.

Hidden away at the back gate is a soft recliner. The man in black sits down upon it and takes a long drink. His eyes follow a bike track that leads away from his home, down the valley to the lush green grassland below. There are several farm buildings in the area but mostly there is space. Free from people and prying eyes. He has another drink and as the cold intoxicating liquid flows down his throat he can feel the stresses of the night drift away.

A small flock of sparrows fly into the tree to his right and he watches as they call to one another. He can't help but feel that they're warning each other of the potential threat of his presence. He averts his eyes to make them feel more comfortable and enjoys the songs they sing. As more and more of the land below bathes in the morning glow, the people and the animals that work and live there begin to appear. Farmer Pete and his dogs; rocks and star, are the first to appear (they usually are). The man in black watches as the farmer loads up a quad bike and the companions set off to check on their livelihood. A few minutes later, on a narrow country road, Dai the milk man drives past on his way to deliver fresh dairy to his long-time customers and friends.

The man in black finishes his drink, stands up and the sparrows fly away. "Don't go too far, little ones. Breakfast is nearly here." He walks into his kitchen, mixes a few pieces of bread with mixed nuts and dried fruit and places the lot into a bag. Then he fills up a large jug of water and walks back outside. The man in black wouldn't be so confident to say that he has green fingers, but he does think he's done a bloody good job. In the space of a few years, he's managed to transform what was once a lifeless concrete waste, into quite a special place to be. For him and the creatures he shares this space with. A few well-placed Fuchsia's and Beardtongue's for the bees. Two Zinnia's for colour. Hebe that has thrived in its position. A plethora of Geraniums. Periwinkles, Dahlia. A small pond for frogs and newts. It has strong colours, great smells and life within its borders. What more could you hope for? A large bird table and bird bath stand in the center of his garden. He drains the old water away, pours the fresh liquid in its place and empties the contents of the bag onto the table before walking back into the house so they can feel safe. After pouring himself another drink, he looks out of the window and within seconds the first of the bird's land. He smiles, closes the blinds and enjoys the gin while taking off his boots and socks. His sweaty feet stick to the cold tiled floor, but the sensation is refreshing. He allows himself a minute to enjoy it before picking up his belongings and walking upstairs.

His bedroom is large. Nearly 16ft in one direction and slightly larger in the other. Resting near a south facing, double window, sits a Jasmine plant, for its calming scent. Under the window, is a double bed. Two drawers underneath help with storage. Two, framed photos of the Brecon Beacon's raw and rugged landscape, hang upon off-white coloured walls. The photos were taken by himself, on a weekend away with Duke.

He throws the bags on his neatly folded bed and strips off his sweaty clothes. After placing them neatly into the laundry wicker basket, he heads into the bathroom. The bathroom is a modest 8ft x 7ft. It has a bath with mixer taps and a shower head attached. It has a sink, a toilet and a mirror that is slightly too large for the wall it is on.

The reflection of his naked self in the mirror makes him laugh. His thick black hair and ginger beard make him look ridiculous. Although it was a necessary requirement for the job. He picks up the small tube of hair dye on the sink. "Twenty-four-hour hair dye. Washes away with one wash. Well I bloody hope that's right."

He takes a step back so he can see more of himself in the mirror. At six feet tall and thirteen stone he is definitely not a heavy weight. He tenses the muscles on his arms and hits his abs. "Skinny Irish prick. What the fuck was that pumped up wanker on about? I'm ripped mate. Ripped to shit." He turns to his side for another pose. "Anyway. I'd rather be in this shape than be walking around with water in my muscles and have an arse like a dart board."

He checks his watch. 05.56am. "In a few more hours Bobby's little boy will be home." Guilt suddenly crashes into him. "Jesus. That was no way for a boy to see his father." He struggles to force the image of shattered bones from his mind as the voice in his head laughs that evil laugh. He slaps his face twice, but the madness and guilt doesn't shift. He pours bath salts into the water to help with his aches and exits the bathroom.

He grabs his phone from his bed and switches it on. The beeps from messages start rolling in as he sits on the edge of his bed drinking his gin. The first one says: "Hey, Christian. How did it go?" He takes a second to think of a reply: "Not bad. Got a nice bag of treats and some shit off the streets." Christian sends his reply and returns to check on his bath. The steam and heat attack him as soon as he opens the door making him cough. He opens a window, swishes the water around and turns the hot water down. His phone beeps again. It says: I've got a week off now. I'll be round in a bit."

The man in black wipes the mirror clean. "It looks like we'll be having company Christian. You'd better make yourself decent mate." Christian throws his mobile on the bed, takes a bottle of pills from his bag and jumps into his bath.

MIKEY

A voice wakes Christian from the deepest of sleeps. He jerks upright, pushing cold orange water over the edge of the bath. His eyes slowly focus on a figure of a man. He has dark hair. He's about five-foot-seven with the start of a beer belly. He's also wearing a police uniform. The policeman holds a bottle of pills in his hand and is saying something. Christian tries to clear the fuzziness in his head. "Huh...what?" He rubs his eyes and splashes water on his face. "What did you say?"

The policeman rattles the bottle of pills again. "I said, you want to be more careful you dozy bastard. I'm sure that's how Whitney Houston died." The policeman hands Christian a towel and helps him out of the bath. "Is it your back again? You need to go see that chiropractor if it is mun. She'll sort it out for you proper. One or two cracks and you'll be good as new."

"Umm... Yeah, it was my back. Feels better now though. I'm fine I promise. It comes and goes that's all." Christian answers as he gingerly stumbles into the bedroom. "You're earlier than I expected. You bloody startled me."

"Earlier! What fuckin' time do you think it is mush?"

"I dunno. About ten or eleven."

"It's half one, mate."

"Shit. Really?" Christian rubs his eyes. He slumps down on the edge of the bed and checks the time on his phone. "Bloody hell, it is too." He yawns and dries his face and hair. "You wanna pop the kettle on?"

"Yeah sure," the Policeman answers. "Have you eaten? I'll make you somethin' if you want. Some toast or a bacon butty?"

"Sounds nice mate yeah. There's fresh bacon in the fridge."

"I know. That's why I asked. I haven't eaten either." The policeman leaves. Christian dries and gets dressed. Then he follows him downstairs carrying the black bag. The smell of bacon under the grill makes his mouth salivate.

"I'm bloody starving," he says as he walks into the kitchen. Christian picks up his cup of tea and empties the contents of the black bag on the kitchen table. "This is everything." He takes a sip of tea. "Ooh, fair do's. That is a nice brew."

The policeman studies the contents of the bag and counts the cash. "Not bad. You got about forty-five, maybe forty-six grand. Two kilos of Charlie and the same in brown. Not bad at all." He examines the rest of the pills. "Oxycontin, Morphine, Vicodin, bloody hell." The policeman turns his back on the loot and takes the bacon from under the grill. "So, how bad was he when you left him?"

"He won't be walking or threatening people for a while that's for sure. I smashed a scaffolding bar over his leg. Pretty sure I got both bones. It was a bit of a mess like."

The policeman hands a triple decker sandwich with brown sauce and thick cut bacon on thick white bread to Christian. "Well, we knew he wasn' gonna give it to you without some sort of fight. You had to do somethin' mush. How much did you leave him with?"

"Half the cash. I took all the drugs that I could find though." Christian bites off almost a quarter of his bacon sandwich in one go. Mikey watches with amusement as he struggles to deal with the mammoth mouthful. A sip of hot tea helps to ease its passage. "Oh yeah. And I left his wife's jewellery behind." He says eventually. "And a few painkillers to see him through till help comes."

"Smart move. It'll be too easy for him to trace the jewellery back to us anyway. Fuck knows what dodgy contacts that meat heads got."

Christian finishes his sandwich and places the plate in the sink. When the sunlight shines through the window it shows a lingering tint of ginger in his beard. "How many times have you washed the beard mush? You can still see the dye."

"Only once. I'll wash it again later on and then bleach the bathroom."

"You should probably throw away the matt on the floor and your gloves and helmet too, just to be on the safe side."

"Yeah, good point." Christian examines the loot, and he picks up a bundle of cash. "Here's your ten-grand mate."

"Thanks mush."

"Mush? What's with all the mush nonsense? Been down Blaen y Maes again have you?"

Mikey laughs. "Yeah. They're fuckin' wild down there like. I can't help pickin' up my old street slang can I? I fuckin' loves it mush."

Christian laughs. "Well, you're not living there anymore mate. They broke all your windows when you told them you were gonna be a policeman remember?"

"How could I forget." Mikey laughs. "Nothing wrong with the way they talk though. I fuckin' loves it mush. Better than talking like a bloody Englishman." Mikey walks around the kitchen as if he were a thespian controlling the stage. "Hello. My name is Christian Thomas, and I love nothing more than pronouncing every word of the Queens English correctly. It's positively titillating."

Christian laughs and hands the drugs to Mikey. "How long are you staying for, you dick?"

"Oh, I dunno mush. How much booze you got?"

Christian pulls on delicate looking chrome handles and opens two brilliant white cupboard doors. A large assortment of alcohol is revealed.

Mikey smiles. "Looks like I'm gonna be here for a while then. Dun it mush." Mikey walks upstairs to the toilet and flushes the drugs away. When he comes back down, Christian has two large bottles of beer in his hands. Mikey takes one and Christian holds his in the air. "Here's to Bobby boy. May he take last night as the perfect opportunity to change for the better."

Mikey joins in the toast. "To Bobby Boy. May last night's encounter with my best mate Christian, bring you a change for the better. And thanks for the cash, you pumped up, drug dealin' wanker."

"To Bobby Boy," they say as one.

Mikey downs his beer and opens another two. "It's gonna be beer and music from here on in mush."

"Sounds like a good plan to me," Christian says as he takes a big swig of his beer. "What are we doing for background noise? You fancy a bit of nineties Britpop?"

"That is literally music to my ears mate. Get it on."

Christian plays the playlist on his phone and the riff of: The Charlatans; One to another, comes through the speakers in the house.

"What a tune mate. What. A. Fuckin'. Tune." Mikey starts singing along to the words while doing his best impression of the lead singer's Mancunian style. Christian watches his mate and laughs at his poor but dedicated attempt.

"You're off your head mate. Off your fucking head."

"Not yet mate, but I will be. Make some room for me will you. I can feel a Liam Gallagher comin' up and I wanna get into character."

THE DAY JOB

An alarm screeches to life waking Christian from a nightmarish sleep. He rolls over in his sweaty, sticky bed and hits snooze. He rubs his tired eyes. His mouth is dry. His nose is blocked. When he yawns, he makes a sound like a whale under the sea. The time on the alarm is 06.00am. Christian peals the quilt off himself and lies on his back. The struggle is real. The courage and will to get up seems to leave him. His eyes close. It feels like only a few seconds pass when the alarm screeches to life again. Christian slaps his face and forces himself out of bed. The alarm is hit until the noise is silenced. The time is now, 06.20am. He rises to his feet and unsteadily walks into his bathroom like an actor from a zombie film. After he's showered and brushed his teeth, he begins to feel more human. By the time he's dressed, he actually feels ready to start the day. It is a Monday and his working day starts at 08.00am.

He wanders downstairs where the smell of stale beer and farts welcome him. He walks past a naked Mikey and opens the blackout curtains and two windows to allow fresh air to cleanse the room. "What a bloody mess." He picks Mikey's clothes up and folds them neatly beside him. Pulling his phone out of his pocket, he flips open the protective cover to take a photo. When he does, he sees a distinctive white powder against the black case. He checks his thumb and sees it's there too. "Cocaine. What the?" He checks Mikey's trousers and sees a light dusting of white. "Must have rubbed off when he was flushing the shite away." He blows the stuff from the trousers and makes a mental note to remind Mikey to be more careful. Then he wipes the case and takes a photo of Mikey's indecency. He sends it to him with a message that reads: Being greeted with this sight first thing in the morning is an awful way to start the day. And don't even get me started on the smell. He leaves Mikey to sleep off the long weekends shenanigans and heads to work in his modest, slightly beat up, blue, Vauxhall Astra estate car.

After a thirty-five-minute drive, Christian pulls up at a small shop in the Sandfields area of Swansea. The sweet smell of disinfectant fills the air. Brightly coloured temptations, fill the shelves by the counter. He walks in, grabs four pints of milk and a pack of chocolate biscuits. "Hello Christian," the shop keeper says.

"Alright Tariq mate. How are you?"

"Tired, Christian. Very tired. Are you visiting Mrs. Phillips today?"

Christian nods in answer to the rhetorical question. Tariq, like a lot of people in the area, loves a gossip and not much slips by this keen-eyed shopkeeper.

"What a bloody commotion there was last night. It woke me and half the bloody street up. I'll tell you that man is not right in the head. He should be put into hospital or behind bars the crazy bastard."

"I'm sorry to hear that mate. You know some people have a lot more to deal with than others. I'm sure things will die down now that the police are involved." Christian pays the bill and leaves before Tariq begins to dig deeper for juicy gossip. He walks three houses up and stops at a house that has one window covered over with a black plastic bag. The bag rustles as it flaps violently in the wind. An acoustic reminder of the last six hours. He knocks twice on a front door that has several foot marks on its blue paint. After ten seconds with no answer, he knocks again. He looks up and see the blinds in the window sway. Another minute passes with no answer, so he opens the letterbox and shouts through. "It's only me Mrs. Phillips. Christian Thomas the social worker. Remember, I said I'd pop round again to check on you." A window opens above him. Christian steps back and looks up. The woman in the window has a bruised cheek and a cut on her lip. She waves at him.

"That bastard deserves more than locking up for what he's doing to this nice girl." Christian agrees with the voice in his head.

"I'll be down in a minute now. You've caught me in the middle of a feed." Christian notices a croakiness in her usually smooth, soft, voice. Something that comes with lack of sleep or shouting.

A few minutes later there's a rattle of chains and after three pulls on the handle the door opens. Mrs. Phillips stands there in a bright pink dressing gown with her blonde hair held back by a black bow. "Sorry about that." Mrs. Phillips steps to one side. "Come in."

Christian enters the house and tries to close the door behind him. He has little success.

Mrs. Phillips sees him struggling. "Don't worry about that love. Just leave it open. He's been arrested anyway, so he'll be locked up for a while. Plus, the landlord's comin' around to fix everythin' in a few hours." Mrs. Phillips opens the fridge door. "I'd make you a cuppa but the baby took the last of the milk. I'm trying to move away from breast feeding at the moment see."

Christian lifts his arms to show his purchases.

"Well, aren't you a clever boy. And you've bought bickies too. Very nice." She fills the kettle, reaches up and grabs two clean mugs from a cupboard. Christian leaves the door open ajar and follows her into the kitchen. The smell of bleach tickles his nose and he can see that she was halfway through cleaning the floor.

"Sorry about the mess. Can't seem to get one thing finished before another interrupts me."

"That's OK." Christian smiles. "It's a busy life being a mum."

"Ain't that the truth. But if it was just the kids, I'd be fine. It's that asshole of a man that makes my life so difficult." She holds a silver tin in the air. "One level sugar is it?"

"Yes please, and a drop of milk."

The sounds of light footsteps on the stairs, alerts Christian of someone's presence. He turns around and sees bright blonde hair sticking out from behind the bannister. Christian approaches. "Hello again Sarah. Do you remember me?" He crouches down to make himself smaller, but the little girl runs past him to the living room.

"It's been a long night," Mrs. Phillips says holding a plate full of biscuits by his head. He stands up and takes them from her. "Go and have a sit down and I'll bring the tea through in a second."

He walks into the living room and sinks into a soft cream chair. It's so soft that he feels like he's being cuddled. Shortly after Mrs. Phillips sits opposite him. The little girl is sat underneath the dining room table about four meters away. Christian automatically assesses the living room. Apart from the broken window, it's quite neat and tidy, considering the nights events and he can't see any broken glass anywhere. "Must have taken a long time to sort that mess out. Have you slept at all?"

"Not yet. I'll try and have a little nap later when my mum comes around."

"Yeah, that's good. A good family behind you can make all the difference in tough times." He turns and looks at the little girl that's hiding under the table. "Will Sarah be going to school today?"

"I'll get her in for the afternoon hopefully. I've phoned the school and told them what happened, so they're leaving it up to me, whether she goes in or not." Mrs. Phillips turns and smiles at her daughter. "Stop being so silly mun. You Know Christian." She smiles at him. "I'm sorry, Mr. Thomas."

"Christian is fine," he says returning the sincere smile. "It's what my friends call me."

"In that case call me Steph." The warmth starts to slowly return to her voice. She turns back to her daughter. "Come here, you silly little girl and have a cwtch. Stop being so dramatic."

Sarah climbs out from under the table and jumps onto her mother's lap. Her mother wraps her arms around her and lavishes her daughter with kisses until the little girl is giggling and squirming in her arms. Christian smiles at the pair and takes a sip of his tea. "So, what was last night all about?"

"Oh, you know, the usual." Steph rolls her eyes. "He rocks up about half one, shoutin' and screamin'. Sayin' he wants to see his kids. At first, I don't even answer but he tries kickin' the door through. So, I open the window and tell him to get lost."

"That's not what you said. You said a naughty word," Sarah cuts in. "You said..."

Steph places her hand over Sarah's mouth before she can finish her sentence. "I know what I said." She looks at Christian who smiles at her.

"It's fine. If he'd have woken me up at that time of the morning, he'd have the same treatment."

Steph tickles her daughter under the arm and continues her story. "Well, he tries to get into the house through the door and he's shoutin' and screamin'. Lights start to come on in the street so one of the neighbours must of called the police. When I didn't let him in, he picks up a bin and throws it through the window. That's when the police turned up. They gave him a few warnings, but you know what he's like. He just kept on givin' it the big one didn't he. Anyway, they ended up tasering him. Hit him in the ribs and he dropped like a sack of..." Steph laughs. "He was twitching like a fish outta water." She kisses her daughter on her head. "Good enough for him too."

"Daddy's crazy," Sarah adds.

Christian laughs at Sarah's little input. "So, he's refusing to obey the terms of the restraining order. Well in that case, I will get in touch with his probation officer and see what the next steps are. Are you pressing charges for the damage he's caused? To you or the property."

"What's the point? He doesn't work as far as the government know of and whatever he can earn on the sly he..." Steph covers Sarah's ears. "Shoves up his nose or pisses against the wall."

Christian tries not to laugh at her honesty and points to the marks on her face. "Have you given any more thought about pressing charges about the assault then? If you give that to the police on top of what he done last night, it could keep you safe from him for a long time."

"I have and I'm still thinkin'." Steph looks down at her daughter and squeezes Sarah's face. "You know, he's a completely different man when he's sober. We used to be really happy together." She kisses her daughter on the forehead and looks at Christian. "He has a lot of stuff he's dealin' with and I think bein' locked up will only make him worse. He needs counsellin' mun. But if you can get him to go to that then you're a smarter person than me."

"Fair enough. I'll have a word with his probation officer and see what he says." Christian snaps a chocolate biscuit in half. "How is everything else with you then? Are you coping with the littlest one OK?" He dunks the biscuit once and puts it in his mouth.

Steph smiles at the mention of the newest addition to her family. "Yeah she's a little angel. Not so little anymore either. She's ten months now. All she does is eat, sleep and poop."

"She poops a lot," Sarah adds.

"No more than you did when you were that age. You were a poopin' machine. As soon as I'd cleaned you, you'd be cryin' and poopin' again."

Sarah buries her face into her mother's chest to hide her embarrassment. Christian and Steph laugh at her expense.

"That's OK Sarah." Christian says trying to comfort her. "Everybody poops. That's one thing we all have in common." He finishes his cup of tea and stands up. "OK then. Once I speak to his probation officer I'll be in touch." He holds out the empty cup. "That was a nice cuppa thanks. Shall I..."

Steph stands up and takes it from him. "Thanks for swingin' by and checkin' on us. We really appreciate it. Although, it's gonna be nice when you don't have too."

"Yeah." Christian smiles at her. "Hopefully once he sobers, he'll think about what he's done and look to change. I'll keep my fingers crossed for it anyway. But if that doesn't happen then you have my number so just give me a call. Anytime, OK?"

"I will do."

Christian waves goodbye to Sarah and walks out. Steph follows him to the door.

"I'll be in touch," he says, opening the door to his car. "You stay safe, OK."

"We will." Steph waves him goodbye. "And thanks for the milk and biscuits."

"No problem."

Christian sits in his car as the door to Steph's house closes. He turns the radio on and looks through the messages in his phone. His first message is from Mikey. It reads: Rough as fuck. He texts back: Serves you right. You should have stopped when I did.

He's halfway through reading his next message when his phone rings. It's his boss. "Alright Dave. How's it going?"

"Hiya mate. Look, Pete's phoned in sick. Can you cover for him in Townhill? He had a supervised visit and he was meant to be there by eleven and you're the closest we got."

"Yeah, I guess so. I was only heading back to the office to finish some paperwork anyway. Who's the family?"

"The Stevenson's. You remember them?"

"Oh yeah. Couple of dealers right."

"Yeah that's them. Look, I can't tell you too much. Abi will meet you there about ten-forty with the child and she'll bring you up to speed on everything. You shouldn't expect any drama though because I've heard good things that they're now on the straight and narrow. It's just a precaution that we're doubling up."

"OK cool. It's not a problem. I'll head up there now."

"Thanks mate."

Christian hangs up the phone and switches the engine on. As he pulls away, Highway to hell by ACDC comes on the radio. Christian laughs. "Quite a fitting song for the journey."

SECRETS FROM FRIENDS

Christian pulls up outside his house at six in the evening and closes his tired eyes. He takes some time to clear his mind before leaving the quiet of his car and entering whatever state Mikey has left his house. He concentrates on the engine as it gently vibrates the seat beneath him and the white noise from the fan. After several minutes, he opens his eyes. The blinds in the living room window move. Mikey looks out and stares at him. "What are you still doing here?" Christian mouths through the windscreen.

Mikey opens the window. "Why are you sittin' in your car you weirdo? Come in."

Christian sighs and pulls on the temperamental plastic handle to exit the car. A firm shoulder barge helps to further motivate the door into opening. As he approaches the house, Mikey opens the front door. He steps in and sees a room, in a much better state than he was expecting. "You've cleaned!"

"Of course, I've cleaned. Don't I always?"

"No. No you don't. Ever. I honestly think this is the very first time, in fact."

"Bollocks." Mikey scoffs. "I always do my bit. I've just boiled the kettle too. You want one?"

"I'd love one thanks." Christian takes off his shoes and walks across the thick pile carpet to the sofa. He plumps a soft grey cushion, throws it into a corner, then makes himself comfortable while Mikey makes the tea. "So, why are you still here?

Don't you have a home to go to?"

"Well, this is the thing," Mikey shouts from the kitchen.

"Ah bollocks! She's kicked you out again hasn't she?"

Mikey walks into the room carrying two cups of tea and holding a piece of toast in his mouth. Salted butter and saliva runs from the corners of his mouth onto his chin. He hands Christian his tea and removes the toast, minus one big bite. "Yeah kind of."

Christian points to the greasy droplet that about to fall from Mikey's chin onto his plush carpet. "Sort that out will you for fuck sake. You're like a bloody basset hound. Fucking dribbling everywhere you scruffy get."

Mikey wipes his chin onto his sleeve and continues his story. "She said she can't handle my mood swings anymore. And the long hours. I can't really blame her. If I'm honest, I know we need a break from each other anyway. It's been coming for a while like."

"So, you're staying here then?"

"Yup! Do you mind?"

"Course not dude. Mi Casa, Su Casa. I've got work in the morning though, so I can't get messed up again."

Mikey laughs.

"I mean it mate. No more. Not tonight."

"OK, so when a couple of girls turn up in an hour or so and we have a drink or two, you're not gonna join in?"

"Mikey for fuck's sake like. I've got work in the morning."

Mikey holds Christian by the shoulders and looks deep into his eyes. "Look. I'm gonna tell you somethin' that is the complete truth and I want you to do the same." Mikey pauses for a second. "I haven't been laid in three months, OK. My nuts are fit to burst mate. They are gonna blow and take half of Wales with them. Just like the bloody Hiroshima bomb. Kaboom! OK, I'm glad I got that off my chest. Now it's your turn. When was the last time you got any?"

"Couple of weeks ago."

"You fuckin' liar. Who with?"

"Just a girl I met."

"Oh really. A girl you just met. How interesting. What was her name?"

Christian's pauses. His eyes roll into their corners as he tries to think. "Stacey."

"Stacey what?"

Christian's eyes swirl in his head as he tries desperately to think of a decent surname. "Jones," he says finally.

"Wow, Stacey Jones. What a nice name. Where's she from?"

"Umm…" Christian begins to sweat under the bombardment of quick-fire questions.

Mikey laughs. "You're a shitty fuckin' liar Christian. Even if I wasn't a world class copper, I'd be able to tell that your tellin' me massive porky pies right now. Just tell me the truth mun."

Christian sighs. "OK, OK. It's been months. Maybe even a year. Or more. I don't really know how long. Too bloody long."

"OK then. Tonight's the night my friend. Tonight. Is. The. Fucking. Night. I'm pickin' 'em up in." Mikey checks his watch. "About forty minutes. So, you'd better go and make yourself beautiful."

"But what about work?"

"Fuck work. Pull a sicky due to stress mush. You do have a very stressful job like, so you're not really lying."

"I can't. Pete didn't come in today so…"

Mikey shakes Christian. "Fuck Pete as well! Just think of Willy. Your willy. And how he's been neglected for so long." Mikey holds Christian's shoulders tighter. "You need this mate. I need this. Come on. What do you say?"

Christian looks down at his feet and Mikey shakes him again.

"Who are the girls and how do you know them?" Christian asks.

"Ah, yes. He's havin' a little nibble, fair play. It's Paula and Pam. You remember them? They work in that pub we went to a few months ago. The Gate House or somethin' like that. Remember?"

"Oh yeah. Nice girls."

"Really nice. Well, I bumped into Pam today and I asked her out for a drink. She said as long as her friend can come for support. I said that's fine. I'll just bring my mate Christian along. Turns out Paula had a thing for you anyway. So, without you mate this doesn't happen for me. And you wouldn't want that on your conscience, would you?"

Christian takes a few seconds to make up his mind. "Go on then," he says finally.

"Yes! I knew you wouldn't let me down mush. Fuckin' knew it. Right, go and get ready then and I'll nip to the shop to get some nibbles and pick 'em up. We're meetin' here first and then goin' somewhere for a bit of food and drinks."

Christian heads to the shower and by the time he's ready he hears voices coming in through the front door. Paula is about five-foot-six, has bright blue eyes and brown hair done in French plaits. She is wearing a red top, black trousers and black high heel shoes. "Hello again, Christian." Her eyes scan past him to each corner of the room. "I really like your house." She leans in to give Christian a kiss on the cheek just as he's holding out his hand to shake hers. He accidently pokes her in the stomach and his face blushes. Paula does her best to ignore it.

Mikey shakes his head and introduces the other girl. "You remember Pam, don't you? Paula and Pam are like two P's in a pod if you remember? They do everythin' together. Everything." Mikey smiles and the girls giggle at Mikey's comment. "I'm only jokin'." Christian looks at Pam. She is dressed in a longer, black, figure hugging dress. She has brown hair that is brushed straight and green eyes.

Christian suddenly becomes aware he hasn't said anything since the girls walked in. His face becomes a darker shade of red. Mikey and the girls chuckle at Christian's awkwardness, so Mikey has to take the initiative. "What do you girls wanna drink? We have wine, vodka, whiskey, Gin."

"Vodka and coke," the girls say as one.

"Comin' right up."

Mikey leaves the girls and Christian alone and disappears into the kitchen to make the drinks. Christian smiles at the girls but draws a blank at what to say to them. Pam shows initiative and ends the silence. "You have a really nice house. Do you live here alone?"

Christian tries to answer but his voice comes out as a squeak. He quickly clears his throat with a cough. The girls giggle.

"I used to, but I seem to have acquired a lodger these last few days. Not that I mind of course."

"Yeah it's nice to have company. I hate being alone," Paula says. "Mikey says you're a social worker. Is that true?"

"Yeah."

"Must be tough. You know, seeing all that stuff. It must do your head in." Pam says whilst running her fingers through her hair.

"Yeah it is, but you gotta find a way of dealing with it. If families and children need you, you have to just get on with it."

"Aww," the girls say as one.

Christian catches movement out of the corner of his eye and looks out the kitchen. Mikey is giving him the thumbs up. Christian's heart returns to a more normal rate and he goes to put on some music. "You ladies have any particular taste when it comes to music?"

"Not really," they both say.

He puts his playlist on random and the gentle sounds of Ed Sheeran; Thinking out loud, come through the speakers.

"Aww I love this song," Pam says. Her hips swaying ever so slightly.

"Me to," Paula adds.

"Me too," Mikey says as he enters the living room. "There's your drinks girls." He looks at Christian. "You havin' a beer mate?"

"Yes please."

"Well, you'd better come and have a look then mate because we've got a selection out there."

Mikey heads back into the kitchen and Christian follows. When they are out of earshot, Mikey puts his arm around Christian's shoulders and whispers. "See, it's not so hard mate is it? They're nice girls, aren't they?"

"Yeah, I guess."

"Good. Now here's the deal. You're in luck because one of them has been called in to work early tomorrow." He looks at the girls. "I don't remember which one. Anyway, that means that neither of them will be out late. So, we're going to have a drink or two here. Then we'll go up the road to that new bar that's opened and get some food. Hopefully, there'll be enough time left in their schedule to come back here for a nightcap." Mikey winks at Christian. "If you know what I mean?"

Christian blushes and looks down at his feet. "Yeah, OK. A few drinks and nice company sounds good."

Christian grabs a beer from the fridge and returns to the living room with Mikey.

"So, have either of you tried this new bar that's opened up?" Mikey asks.

"No, but it's getting some great reviews." Pam answers.

"My sister went there, and she reckons it was lush." Paula adds. "She said it's like a tapas thing."

"What's that?" Christian asks.

"You know. Loads of little meals. Like..." She looks at Pam for support. "well, like a meal made up of different starters I suppose."

"Oh, right yeah. We had one last year in town. It was nice, I think."

"You think?" Pam says laughing.

"Yeah, it was about Christmas time." Mikey cuts in. "We'd had a few drinks by that point."

"Oh, I see. Well if you can't have a few drinks at Christmas, when can you?"

"So, how long have you two known each other?" Mikey asks.

"Only since I started working at the Gate. Two or three years maybe. What about you two? How did you two meet eachother?" Paula asks.

Mikey's hand curls into a fist at the memory and he forces it into his pocket. Christian sees Mikey's reaction and answers for them. He tells them the same story he tells anyone that asks that question. He tells them that they met through work. It's simple and anything is better than the reality.

"What do you mean?" Pam asks looking at Mikey. "I thought you were a policeman?"

"I am." He takes his relaxed hand out from his pocket and takes a drink. "It's quite common for police and social workers to be called to..." He looks at Christian. "How do I say it? Uncomfortable situations."

"Of course." Pam says giggling. "I don't think I could do either of your jobs. All that violence and sadness and stuff. I'm quite happy being a manager at a pub, thank you very much."

"And I'm happy that you're my manager." Paula says, smiling at her friend.

"You may surprise yourself at how tough you'll be when the time comes ladies. I think there's more to you that meets the eye." Mikey says.

The girls blush and play with their hair.

"Plus, it's not all bad." Christian says. "You do get to meet some nice people too. It's just that, well, they may be a bit down on their luck and struggling, that's all. I've met some of the nicest people ever doing this job. And even when they are not so nice it's great when you see them turn things around."

"Yeah, there's no better feelin' than givin' someone the break they need, to get them back on the straight and narrow." Mikey winks at Christian.

Christian closes his eyes as the image of Bobby's broken leg fills his mind. He finishes his beer and walks out of the room. "Anyone want a refill?"

"I will," Mikey says.

The girls look at their full glasses. "We're fine thank you."

Christian opens the fridge and stares at nothing. His mind filled with dozens of images of broken bones, like a montage from the most graphic horror movies. All the while the voice in his head laughs that evil laugh. It isn't until a hand touches his shoulder that he snaps out of it. "You OK, mate? You've been out here for a few minutes."

Christian grabs a beer and closes the fridge. "Yeah, I'm just really hot that's all." His free hand reaches out to touch the potted Devil's Ivy that's maturing in a sunny spot beside the fridge. Smooth, waxy green leaves help to clear his mind.

"You sure?"

"Yeah, I'm fine." Christian walks away from Mikey.

"Well, where's my beer then, you bloody socialist?" Mikey says.

When Christian gets back into the living room the girls are cooing over the only photo that he has in the room.

"Who's this?" Pam asks.

Christian takes the frame from her hand and smiles. The photo shows an Alsatian dog resting its head on Christian's lap. Rolling hills, fill the backdrop. "That was my dog, Duke. Handsome thing, wasn't he."

"Yeah, he's lush," they both say.

"What happened to him?" Paula asks.

Christian places the photo down and takes a long drink. "He died a few months ago," he says after a few seconds.

"Awe really," Paula asks. "How come?"

Christian adjusts the photo on the highly polished, red-wood table so it's in its favourite spot. Under the sun light from the window and close enough to the fire to feel the warmth. "Umm..." He clears his throat. "He was poisoned."

"What really!" Both girls say shocked.

"Yeah. At least that's what the vets think."

"Who would do such a horrible thing?" Paula asks.

"I can't say too much more about it. It was to do with work."

"Yeah, but we made sure that junkie paid for what he did to Duke. Didn't we?" Christian shakes the laughing voice from his head. "It's still a bit raw," Mikey cuts in. "Anyway, we'd better leave soon if we're going to make that reservation. Shall I phone a taxi for twenty minutes or so?"

"Sounds good. I'm so hungry I could eat an elephant." Pam

says.

"Me too," Mikey says smiling at her.

Mikey walks to the cabinet to get his phone. When he passes Christian, he grabs him by the shoulder and whispers. "What the fucks the matter with you, dude?"

"I don't know. I'm just not feelin' it anymore that's all mate."

Mikey gives him a suspicious look.

"Seriously, I'm shattered. I think the weekend has finally caught up with me. Why don't you three go ahead without me?"

"How's that gonna work? Paula's gonna feel left out then."

"I'm sorry dude. Look, I'm going to head upstairs to splash some cold water over my face. Hopefully that will wake me up. I'll be back down in a minute, now." Christian leaves and Mikey tries calling a taxi but it's engaged. When Mikey hangs the phone up, he can hear Christian talking to himself upstairs. Something that hasn't gone un-noticed by the girls.

"Is your friend OK?" Paula asks.

Mikey listens to the footsteps pacing above him, then looks down to his feet. "I'm sorry girls." he says finally. "My friend's been going through a bit of tough time with things in work recently. And because I like you Pam, I kind of pushed him into this when he really wasn't up for it. I'm sorry, but I think we should call it a day. I really should go and see if there's anything I can do to help him."

"Aww. That's so sweet of you. You really care for him, don't you?"

"Yeah, well he's my best mate like."

Pam smiles at him. "Of course, we can do this another time."

"OK cool. And thanks. I'm sorry you got all dressed up for nothin' ladies. You really do look absolutely amazin' tonight."

The girls blush.

"Come on," Mikey says. "I'll drop you to wherever you want to go."

*

An hour later there's a knock on the bathroom door. "You OK, dude?"

"Yeah, I'm fine." Christian answers.

"Come on, mate. You've been in there ages."

Mikey hears the sound of the last remnants of shower gel being squeezed from a bottle.

"I can't seem to get that orange out of my beard."

"What are you on about you fool? You washed that stuff out ages ago." Mikey walks to Christian's bed and finds an open bottle of morphine. "Are you comin' out anytime soon? I was hopin' we could have a beer and a chat."

"Yeah, give me five minutes."

Mikey places the bottle down and leaves.

Half hour later, Christian, gingerly walks down the stairs. He has a hazy look in his eyes. Mikey is by the kitchen holding a beer. "Don't think we'll be seein' those girls again."

Christian shrugs his shoulders.

"I'd offer you a beer, but I don't think you need it." He walks into the living room and sits down. Christian slumps down beside him on the light brown, suede sofa. "I dun wanna talk about it."

"We don't have to. I just need to know that you're still cool, that's all."

Christian looks at Mikey. "I'm far from cool." He holds up the bottle of Morphine. "But I will be after a good night sleep."

Mikey mulls over the many questions he has in his head. He studies Christian body language and decides to leave it. "Fair enough. We'll just sit and chill here, is it?"

"You dun 'ave anywhere else to go do you?" Christian wipes a little bit of dribble that runs down his mouth.

"What?" Mikey asks confused. What are you on about?"

Saliva gathers on Christian's chin. He doesn't notice it when it drips onto his lap. "Look, these drugs are kickin' in fast, so you won't get much sense out of me in a bit."

"In a bit! Mikey laughs. "I'm not gettin' any bloody sense right now." Mike grabs a cloth and wipes Christian's chin. "Christian, you're my mate like. My best mate. And I'm yours." Mikey sits back down. "I'm worried about you mun, and I think we need to have a chat about what's goin' on in that fragile little head of yours."

Christian mutters something under his breath.

"I'm taking that as a positive answer," Mikey says.

"I said it's the bones. The eyes and the bones. It's always..." Christian's head slips backward, and he corrects it with a jerk. "We are hurting people, to stop them hurting other people. What the fuck! It's so messed up."

"I know that mate. It's crazy. But you know what? We're hypocrites. Massive fuckin' hypocrites. But we have a cause that we feel justifies that hypocrisy. We know first-hand the awful effects drugs have on an individual and in the community. Dealers make money on the weak. They'll take someone with an addictive personality for everything they've got. Even if that poor bastard had nothing to start with. And another thing. We fuckin' know how many times people reoffend after jail. It's bollocks mush, ain't it? Fuckin' junkies and dealers get locked up, get three decent meals a fuckin' day." Mikey's hand movements become even more animated the more agitated he becomes. "They get whatever drugs they need smuggled in. And when they get out, they go straight back to dealin'. Mikey laughs. "With more fuckin' contacts than when they went in." Mikey pauses a second to let his speech sink in. "And look at the things we do to stop it. We've hit what, fifty, maybe sixty, drug dealers over the years. Less than a handful still do it and they do it on a much smaller scale than before. And, I've lost bloody count of how much shit we've flushed away. We do make a difference, mate. We make a positive difference. And it's not just the drug dealers, is it? Look what we do to..."

"OK, OK." Christian stops Mikey from explaining further. "That's enough. I know where you're going."

"OK mate. No more." Mikey grabs Christian's shoulder. "You

know, you can stop anytime you like. We've probably been pushin' it too long, anyway." Christian doesn't respond. Mikey looks at the pills in Christian's hand. "I want you to promise me you'll take it easy on those things."

Christian's head falls back. His eyes are open and he's staring at the ceiling. "I'm fucked." he mumbles.

"I can see that. How many you taken?"

Christian's answer is gibberish, so Mikey takes the bottle from his hand. "I don't think you need any more." Mikey makes himself comfortable, picks up the TV remote and switches to a music channel. Then he places Christian's head in a less painful looking position by putting a pillow underneath it for support.

"You get your head down, kid. It'll all work out I promise, cos you've got your old pal Mikey lookin' after you." Mikey gets up and walks to the kitchen. He grabs a bottle of whisky, a tray of ice cubes and a glass and rejoins his friend by the TV. "Yeah mate." He looks at his dribbling semi-conscious friend. "I'm gonna look after you for as long as you need it." He chuckles to himself. "And not just because I have nowhere else to go. Even though that's technically true." He grabs the remote and switches the TV on. Flicking through the channels until he finds a well-known American sit-com. "Yes, Friends. What a fucking show this was." He quickly looks at Christian to see if he wakes. Christian's inebriated state continues. Mikey pours an unhealthy amount of whisky over the ice in his tumbler. He swirls it around so the whiskey cools against the clear, cracking ice. Then he takes a slow mouthful and puts his feet up. When the introduction music finishes, he looks at Christian again. "Yeah, good friends and good whiskey. What else do you need dude? Hmm?" There's no reply from Christian. "Nothin' that's what. Well, I'll be honest, I coulda done with a rub from one of the P's tonight like, but I'll let that go. Even though they looked amazin' and I reckon it was defo on the cards like. But I'll let it go." Mikey finishes his drink and pours himself another. The ice cubes didn't even have a chance to melt. He looks around the room. Neutral colours. Minimalist in style. Almost empty.

"This room just about sums us up, dun it, mush? There's only one single photo in here, and that's been tarnished with a bad memory. No photos of us together though! Not a single bloody thing that shows either one of us having a good time." Mikey smiles. "We gotta find more colours dude. We're too fuckin' beige mush. We need to expand or...or." He struggles to find the right word. "We need to bloody...sort our bloody lives out. That's what dude. We need more colours and some decent memories worthy of a photo or two." Mikey chuckles. "And maybe a girl or two to tickle our sensitive areas."

THE KID

"Dirty!" they shout. "Dirty! Smelly! Scrubber!" The Kid moves on through the park. Swings squeak as they swing back and forth. His hands buried deep in his pockets. His long, dirty hair blows in the cold, wet wind. His ears feel frost bitten. Water seeps through holes in his trainers, saturating his numb feet. He doesn't look up. He doesn't make eye contact. That offends the older kids that insult him. Offending means a beating. A glass bottle smashes by his heels, sending shards of piercing glitter into his path. He quickens his pace. "Next time, I'll hit your scabby head, you fuckin' scumbag," someone shouts. "Why dun ew and ew'r family fuck off. We dun want drug dealin' scum like ew around yer." screams a girls voice.

The Kid picks up his pace until he's jogging from the insults and falling objects. Without breaking his stride, he hurdles a wall at the edge of the park. A car flies past in a low gear with high revs. Sending spray from the tyres splashing over him. Once it's past, he sprints across the road and slips through a gap in a hedge. Only then does he allow himself a minute to catch his breath. He peers back to see if he's been followed. The older kids, maybe fourteen or fifteen years old, are still in the park. Girls sit on swings and playfully kick their legs into the air. Boys push from behind while swigging on small cans of extra strong cider and bottles of MD 20/20. One boy, in a red baseball cap, smokes a cigarette and stares at the hole in the hedge.

The Kid pushes his hands back inside his wet pockets and moves on. He moves from the cover of the tree line and out onto a quiet narrow street. A mixture of clean and dirty ter-raced houses run along each side of the road. Some have boarded windows. Others have newly painted front doors. Several have football flags where curtains should be. The worst have plywood instead of glass should and vulgar graffiti on the walls.

Sounds of laughter and clapping hands spill from an open window. He's intrigued. Without noticing he's drawn to the noise. The Kid stops and peaks inside. A mother holds a newborn baby in her arms. An older lady claps her hands to the beat of a song. A girl, about the same age as the Kid, dances to the beat. The Kid stares. For over a minute he watches the family play. He smiles. His hips begin to sway to the music. Drizzle rests upon his eyebrows and runs down his face. This happy family life, soaks into him. When the clapping and dancing finish, there's an applause. The Kid inadvertently joins in. The older lady quickly looks around. When she sees the kid, she rises from her chair. "You nosey little bugger! How dare you! Get away from that window you little peeping Tom!" The Kid drops to the floor as a hairbrush is launched in his direction. He rises quickly and darts up the street. The older lady opens the front door and shouts insults at him the entire way.

He follows the course of the road as it bares right and stops at the dead end. A small hole in a wire mesh fence is pulled open. The kid slips in. On the other side, a steep bank, drops down. He slides out of sight. Sitting until the cold sodden earth seeps into his trousers. He catches his breath. His chin, resting lightly on his knees. Leaves rustling all around him. *"It's nice here ain't it?"* "Yeah, it's nice here," The kid said answering the voice. A rat scurries under twisting roots. Squirrels scamper up tree trunks. About ten minutes pass before the kids gets up and carries on. He follows an old dirt track through the wooded area as other curious creatures go about their day. Dried black berry bushes overhang the path. Roots of trees snake out from the ground. The going is tough. Slippery. Slow. Fifteen minutes pass before the sound of civilization filters through the foliage. He steps out onto a gravel forecourt. A large blue sign hangs on the high, rusty steel fence. It reads: Sully's servicing and repairs. Scattered along the perimeter of the fence line are beaten up cars of every year and every description. Taking pride and place next to the large wooden doors of the garage is a blue, mint condition, MK2 Escort RS with a 1977 plate, original wheels and leather trim. Beside that is a 1987 Mini Cooper Convertible Cabriolet with low skirts, spotlights and go faster stripe. The Kid approaches the cars. He looks through the window of the Escort and a voice from the garage shouts. "Boss, that fuckin' kid is back." The Kid ignores him. "Oi!" the voice shouts again. "Stop eyeballing those cars you little shit!" The Kid waits by the side of the car until the boss leaves the office. He is a stocky man with a shaved head and walks with a bit of a limp.

"Alright. Alright. Get back to work lads. I'll take care of him." The Boss limps slowly toward the Kid. The Kid backs away just as slowly. He follows the side of the cladded steal building until the office and car ramps are out of sight. Stooping low, he hides behind a car. Then he waits. A minute later the Boss appears. He's whispering to himself. "Where the fuck did that little bastard go now?"

"Here," the Kid answers just as quiet.

The Boss jumps and turns around quickly.

"Sneaky little bastard you are ain't you?"

The Kid laughs.

"You got the stuff?"

"Yeah," the kid answers.

"Well then. I ain't got all day. Hand it over." The Boss has a strange accent that the kid hasn't heard before. His voice is deep, firm but friendly. The Boss shoves his dirty hands into his oily pocket and pulls out his shiny brown wallet.

The Kid keeps the shell of an old Peugeot between himself and the Boss. "My dad said you still owe him from last time. I can't give it over until ew pay. That's what he told me to say."

"Your dads got some bloody neck, boy, I'll give him that. He's got a long bloody neck and a short bloody memory." The Boss flicks a wad of notes with his thumb. "Here." He hands the Kid a bundle. That's for your old man." He looks the Kid up and down before handing him two more notes. "That's for you. Hide it well now. Go on." The Kid stashes his dad's cash in the usual place and puts his two notes in his left sock. He steps out from behind the car and reaches into his pocket. Inside a clear plastic bag there are dozens of small white pills. He hands them over.

"What are they?" The Kid asks.

"Nosey little shite you are, aren't you?"
The Kid smiles and shrugs his shoulders.

"For my wife," the Boss answers eventually. "The only thing that helps her."

"Is she sick?"

"She's in pain. It's her nerves. Don't really know why though. Not yet anyway."

"Will she be OK?"

The Boss smiles. "Yeah, I think so. As soon as those poxy doctors start believing her she will be anyway. It's probably gonna take a little while longer but she'll get there." He turns to walk away. The boy follows. "What do you think you're doing?" The boss asks.

"I'm leavin'."

"Aye. But not with me you're not. I don't want my boys thinking anything's going on, do I? Bugger off out the same way you usually do."

The Kid turns around and looks at the rusty old fence panel that's pulled away at the bottom corner. The small gap he has to crawl through is covered in spider webs and has sharp, cutting edges.

"But," The Kid begins to protest. He looks at the slice on the side of his hand.

"But nothing," the boss cuts in. He hands the Kid a pair of leather gloves he had in his back pocket. "Put these on. And tell your dad that next time, I wanna be seeing him. A kid shouldn't be doing this nonsense. If he sends you again, he's gonna have a problem with me."

The Kid smiles.

"Ok then. Off you pop." The Boss stuffs the pills in his dirty grey trousers and limps away from the Kid. The kid feels for the notes in his socks, puts the leather gloves on, lifts the heavy, sharp panel and slips into the forest of Japanese Knotweed.

Two hours later, the 'drop offs' are complete. The Kid is jogging along the dancing girl's street, toward the park. He slips under her window unseen and sprints toward the hedge. He stops to check the park. He doesn't move until he's sure the older kids have left. The sky is darker now. "It'll get scary soon." he thinks. It's quiet. The park swings sway gently under the persuasion of the wind. The roundabout is still. He breathes a sigh of relief and steps out of the hedge. Something from somewhere, hits him to the ground. It grabs him by the ankle and drags him back behind the hedge. He kicks at it. Flings his arms wildly. The grip that holds him, holds firm. He sees a red cap. He tries to scream but a hand is forced over his mouth. Then a hood of some kind. He's blinded. Scared. His fists swing about in vain. The assailants laugh as the Kid pees his pants. He begins to sob. Hands rummage through his pockets. Emptying each one. They find nothing. "Where is it? Where's the fuckin' cash?" The Kid stays silent. Three or four hands roughly pat him down. One hand grips his throat. "Where's the fuckin' cash, scumbag?" Something hits him across the face. Something else hits his nose. If he could talk now, the Kid would have told them. Fear has rendered him mute. The hands continue to frisk him until they touch upon a hard object under his armpit. They rip off his jacket. "I've got it. It's here, I've got it." They force the Kid's head to the floor. A foot is loosed into his ribs. The wind is driven from his lungs like an open door on an airplane in flight. He rolls around, gasping. His lungs burn and pull in tight like an emptied balloon. He wheezes, slow, noisy breathes. Desperately fighting to inflate his burning chest. Minutes go by before the Kid can breathe properly. He forces his arms away from his ribs. The pain is fierce. Sharpe. Stabbing. The tears continue. He tentatively removes the hood from his head and looks around. An over-hanging streetlight pokes its rays through the hedgerow, shining its yellow spotlight upon him. He wipes his bloody face onto his boney forearm and coughs a thick red lump of phlegm. Slowly, gingerly, he props himself up to his knees and crawls to his jacket. A large hole has been torn under the armpit where the secret stash of cash used to be. He curls up into a ball with the jacket by his belly and cries. "Mam and dad are gonna be so mad." He remembers the last time they were mad, vividly. It's scarred into his memory and upon his skin. Blood drips from his running nose onto the floor, creating an orange pool in the yellow light. Time, like the car lights less than ten meters away, pass slowly. Eventually, the Kid struggles to his feet, picks up his jacket and stumbles across the road. He reaches the wall at the edge of the park and places two hands upon it. He holds his breathe. Blocks out the pain in his ribs and lifts one leg over to straddle the wall. He waits until the pain has subsided before he dismounts and enters the park. Empty cans rattle as they roll in the breeze. Swings creek as they rock back and forth. Upon the roundabout, a cawing crow watches him. The Kid shuffles on.

Several times on his shuffle he has to stop, because the pain in his ribs became too much. The Kid looks up at two large blocks of flats dominating the area. He pauses for one last time to work out his options. There aren't many. Run away or enter and hope for the best. Both options will involve pain he's sure. The Kid steadies his resolve and sets his feet in motion. He shuffles toward the thirteen-storey block. Wet clothes flap around in the many balconies. Sea gull shit decorates the external walls. A football is hoofed against a wall. The Kid's slow movements cause interest from the gang of youths lingering outside. They turn and stare, but no one came to assist. The football is hoofed in his direction. The youths laugh.

The Kid pushes the heavy fire doors and steps inside, leaving the strong smell of urine behind. He approaches the lifts. The door is jammed open on one and the control panel is ripped out. Multi-coloured graffiti decorates the inside. He pushes the button and waits for the second lift. Patiently he waits. More minutes pass. He thumps at the doors. Even more minute's pass. Eventually he hits the button, swears at everything in "this piece of shit, dump" and shuffles toward the steps. He stands at the bottom and looks up toward the tenth floor. "Ten floors. Two flights of steps on each floor. Nine steps on each flight. That's one hundred and eighty steps." The Kid places his left foot on the first step and pushes his weight upward. His right foot slowly follows.

A long while later the Kid is standing in front of a dirty blue fire door with a sick feeling in his stomach that's as acute as the pain in his ribs. His hand is raised and clenched in a fist, two inches away from the door. He can hear voices on the other side. Angry voices. Suddenly the door swings open. A man, hurling abuse at someone inside is struggling with his jacket. The Kid freezes. "I'll fuckin' kill him when I find him. He'd better have my cash or I'm gonna fuckin' kill him." The man turns and sees the Kid. The bloodied and beaten Kid. He snatches the ripped jacket from his arms and checks the hidden pocket. "Where is it?" The Kid can't answer quick enough. "Where the fuck is it?"

A woman staggers out toward them. Dressing gown, half covering her modesty. A large bottle of cider in her hand. She looks at the Kid. "What happened to you boy?" she slurs.

Tears stream down the Kids face. "They've taken it."

"Who? Who took it?" the man screams.

"I don't know," the Kid answers. "They hit me from behind and took it. They beat me up and took it."

The man grabs the Kid roughly by the arm. Fingertips dig deep into his tender bicep muscle. The Kid is dragged inside. The door slams shut behind him. "What did they look like?" the man yells.

"I dunno. They hit me from behind. They…"

The man shakes the Kid. "You're lyin'! Tell me who did this. Who's got my cash?"

The mother holds the Kid's shoulder. "Tell him the truth boy. Where's our money."

The father shakes the Kid again. "Who's got it? Look boy. We owe some bad people that money. We need it. Who's got it?"

The Kid wipes his eyes. "I dunno. They…"

A note sticks out from the Kid's socks and catches his father's eye. "You lyin' little bastard." He throws the Kid to the dusty carpet and grabs his ankle. "Where's the rest of it? Where's my fuckin' cash?" He rips the notes from his sock.

"They took it." The Kid cries.

"You fuckin' liar." The man hits the Kid across the face. "They took most of my cash but left you a few notes. You fuckin' liar." He hit's the Kid again.

"You've gone and done it now boy." The mother says as she turns and walks away.

The man drags the Kid away from the front door and into a bedroom. The door slams shut behind them. The Kid cries out.

CHAT ON THE SOFA

It's six-fifteen in the afternoon when Christian opens the door to his home. He sees Mikey in the kitchen making toast. By the smell in the air, the toast is slightly blacker than it should be. "So, you made it to work then, mush? How'd you feel?" Mikey asks whilst fanning smoke out the kitchen window.

"Not great like, I'll be honest."

"Same here. This is the first thing I've felt like eatin' all day." Mikey puts the last piece of toast in his mouth. "I'm havin a couple of weeks clean living to try and sort my head out."

"It'll take longer than that, mate. A hell of a lot longer! You finished that whole bottle of whiskey off, didn't you?"

Mikey shakes his head and laughs. "Yeah. Wish I bloody hadn't though."

"Tut, tut, Mikey boy. No wonder your guts are bad." Christian joins Mikey in the kitchen and puts the kettle on. "After this brew, I'm gonna take a shower. And then later on, I'll probably order a takeaway or something if you fancy it? A curry probably. Lamb jalfrezi, pilau rice, naan bread, aloo chat. About twelve poppadoms with chutney and that burny shit they do."

"Ginger?" Mikey asks.

"Yeah, that's it. Ginger. I'm ordering the whole shebang today. You up for it?"

Mikey rubs his stomach. "Sounds great, but I'd better see how this charcoaled toast treats me first. If it stays down, I may just join you."

Christian grabs a small blue cup from the top left-hand cupboard. He looks inside it, then gives it a wipe with a white dish cloth. "What have you been up to today then? Just lazing around the house, I suppose."

"Nope. I've had quite a productive day actually. I woke up late. Had a little play with myself."

Christian fires a look of disgust at Mikey. "You better not of been anywhere near my bedroom or my sofas when your doing that shit you pig. I don't want little snail trails all over the place."

Mikey laughs. "It's fine. I was in the shower mun."

"That's just as bad you dirty bastard. I use that too, you knob. I'm in there with bare bloody feet like."

"Relax mun. I cleaned it all up afterwards. And I squirted it with bleach and stuff. It's the cleanest it's ever been I reckon."

"It had better be. I'm wearing flip flops in there from know on though. And I'm buying a blue light to check it's clean beforehand."

Mikety laughs. "You're such a drama queen. It's just a little bit of cum like. That's all. What's a little bit of cum between friends?"

Christian's unamused face remains fixed. "Fucking animal. What else you get up to? Or don't I want to know?"

"The rest isn't all that exciting. I had an hour with the ex."

The kettle clicks and hot water is poured into the small blue cup. Christian breathes in the green tea aroma. "Really? How did it go?" He grabs a biscuit from a shiny silver tin and sees a small trail of white powder beside it. He snaps the biscuit in half and takes a bite.

"It went OK. I mean it was just a chat and a catch up more than anythin'. Then I went shoppin' in a hired van and dropped a load of stuff off in our lockup."

"Nice. How's it looking in there now?"

"It's looking healthy in there again. Really healthy." Mikey sniffs and wipes his runny nose.

"Bit of a cold have you, mate?" Christian asks.

"I dunno. Maybe, yeah. It's probably the weather or somethin'."

Christian looks at the sun shining through the window. "So,

the lockups getting full is it?"

"Yeah not bad. Got some good stuff in there now."

"OK, cool. We'll have to start finishing that list out soon. I've got a few names already. How about you?"

"I got five or six that are definite. One or two maybes. Depending on our funds, really."

Christian looks at the large bag of cash on top of the kitchen cupboard. "I think we can stretch to seven or eight."

"Cool," Mikey says. "I'll add them in."

Christian leaves Mikey and takes his brew upstairs. He has a bath and puts on comfy fleece pyjamas. When he comes back down, Mikey is curled up on his two-seater sofa. He has the TV on and is watching a film. "What's this?"

"Tombstone," Mikey answers.

"It any good?"

"Yeah it's class. Wyatt Earp and his bro's taking out the cowboys. It's got Kurt Russel and Val Kilmer in it. Cowboy films don't get much better."

"Is it better than Young guns?"

"Ooh, that's a tough call like." Mikey scratches his chin while he thinks. "I dunno." he says finally. "Why don't you just sit down and watch it? You can make an informed decision yourself then."

"Yeah, OK." Christian sits down next to him on his well-worn, soft, grey, suede two-seater sofa. He kicks his slippers off and stretches out. Mikey restarts the film.

Thirty-nine minutes into the film, Mikey turns to Christian. "My nightmares are back and worse than ever."

"What?" Christian sits up, grabs the remote and pauses the movie. "What do you mean, worse? You mean more regular or?"

"More regular. More." Mikey looks down and rubs his sweaty hands. "More terrifying."

"Shit, sorry man. Is that why you're here? Is that why she kicked you out?"

"One of the reasons, yeah. I can't sleep unless I'm wasted. If I'm sober, my dreams will take me back there, and..." Mikey stares at the floor. "I suppose it was inevitable. How could any-one live with someone as messed up as me?" He wipes a bead of sweat that has formed on his forehead.

"Then why don't you tell her? She's a nice girl. Really bloody nice actually. And you've been with her long enough."

Mikey grabs a pillow and stuffs it close to his chest. He looks Christian dead in the eye. "Have you told anyone?"

Christian looks down "No. I think I'm taking it to the grave with me."

"Sometimes, the grave don't sound that bad," Mikey says with a sad sort of look in his eyes.

"Don't say shit like that. We're fuckin' fighters you and I." Christian grabs Mikey's shoulder. "No, we're more than that mate. Much fuckin' much more. We're hunters. So, stop talking like a pussy."

"That's rich, comin' from someone whose smashin' pain-killers like there's no tomorrow. What are you trying to drown with those? How long have you been shovin' that lot down your throat?"

"Probably as long as you've been ramming cocaine up yours."

Mikey's eyes widen before he can look away. "What? What are you on about mun?"

"I found it on your clothes the morning after you came to stay here. And there's powder left in my kitchen. What the fucks going on with you? Is it a real problem? Is there a masssive lump of Charlie stashed away in my house somewhere?"

There's a long pause as Mikey mulls over a response. "Well?" Christian asks.

Eventually, Mikey looks his mate in the eye and confesses. "No, it's just. I kept a small amount back to help me get through the day. The rest I flushed I promise." Mikey squeezes his tem-ple. "Look dude. I'm hardly fuckin' sleepin' anymore. And when I do, I'm stuck in that awful fuckin' place. I can't focus in work. Sometimes I can't even get up for work. My whole life's a mess right now. It's just the odd line now and again to get me up and keep me goin'. That's all. Nothing major."

Christian laughs. "The odd line? The odd fucking line? Are you fuckin serious mate? We know how sneaky that shit can be! We know first-hand. You start off having a line to get up. Then you're having one to keep you going and before long your boshing five grams in through the day, just to feel anything. It's a sneaky drug mate. It'll creep up on you again without you knowing it if you're not careful. Come on mate. You know this shit. Fuck!"

Mikey walks away from Christian. He paces the room with his head in his hands. "I know, I know. But I'm really strugglin'. I don't wanna be sober and have my dreams take me back to that place. So, I drink. Heavily. And in the morning, I'm fucked. I don't know what else I can do."

Christian holds his mate by the shoulders. He stares into his eyes to try and get his point across. "You need to go see a professional or something. There are people that are trained to help in these circumstances. I can put you in touch with a few if you like."

Mikey backs away. "I'm not seein' a fuckin' shrink. I'm not tellin' anyone." Mikey shrugs his shoulders. "Well, I'm talkin' to you now like, but that's cos you're my mate and you already know. But it doesn't go any further, OK?"

"OK, OK." A minute or so of silence passes before Christian asks. "What do you think has brought the nightmares back?"

"I know exactly what it is. You remember that Bullen case?"

"Yeah, I remember." Christian's hands become clammy.

Mikey sees this and stops. "You sure you want to know?"

"Yeah carry on." Christian stands up and starts to pace the room. The soft grey rug under his bare feet helps distract him from the sickly feeling in his stomach.

"Well, I was on the team that arrested that dirty bastard. We practically caught him red handed. As the investigation went on, the detectives found more and more evidence. I mean they had everythin'. There were holes in his alibi. The lab had DNA. They had a witness. They fuckin' had him. They thought for sure they had him."

"But?"

"But two weeks ago, he walked free."

"What? Why didn't I hear anything? Was it on the news?"

"There was a brief minute and a half broadcast on local news but that's it." Mikey stands up. "You know what fuck this. You want a beer?"

"Ah...yeah go on then. So, how did he walk free? What went wrong?"

"The boss said the case was mishandled so the judge threw it out. I mean, I'm not a detective so I don't know the ins and outs of it all, but cops talk you know. It looks as though the evidence was tampered with. Also, the witness they had was deemed unreliable because she'd been drinkin' that evenin'. One small wine and they dismiss her. Complete bullshit if you ask me."

"He walked free?" Christian rubs his sweaty head as the voice within it yells. *"That dirty bastard is out there walking the streets right now. That dirty bastard has to pay."* Christian shakes the crazy from his head. Now is not the time for madness. He needs to be focused. To listen to what's being said. And then, if necessary, to pass judgement. "What do you mean tampered with? Someone tampered with it or procedures weren't followed properly, and it got contaminated?"

Mikey walks back in and hands him a beer. "I know the guys that were dealin' with it and they're meticulous. They were super confident, you know." Mikey drinks half his beer down in one go. The burp afterwards is enormous. "But...somehow the samples they gave were not up to testin'. The seals were broken, and they couldn't say for sure that they were, what they thought they were. It's fuckin' bullshit."

Christian sees the sadness in his friend's eyes. "How come this case has affected you so much? We've dealt with people like that before. What else is there that you're not telling me?"

"There's rumours he wasn't acting alone. That maybe, he's a major part of a paedo ring. They found names of some really influential people on his laptop. Names, places and a hell of lot of photos. The guys, well they were all talking about it. Photos from inside manor houses and boarding schools and..." Mikey pauses. "And care homes. Bryniau Du was one of those homes." The colour drains from Christian's face. Mikey takes a deep breath." You want me to go on?"

Christian takes a second to think. "Yeah, I'm fine."

Mikey continues. "They couldn't prove anything in court because the memory and storage was wiped clean after the lab had accessed the files. Nobody knows who's done it. The copies the labs took, all but disappeared. Only thing that was left were a handful of pics." Mikey finishes his bottle. "My drinkin' got worse as the case went on. It just looked more and more likely that it would fail. And when it did." Mikey looks down at the floor. "It made the whole ordeal," Mikey pauses to think of the right words. "It made it feel real again. Like no time has passed, you know? Like it was happenin' yesterday and could happen again tonight. I get scared. It's stupid I know. I'm a grown man now. I shouldn't be scared of anything like that anymore." He finishes his bottle and goes to get another. "How do you deal with it Christian? I mean, do you ever get like this?"

Christian looks away from Mikey. He thinks about the best possible answers to help his friend in this awful situation. He tells the truth. "Yeah, of course I get scared, mate. Everyone would. It's only natural I suppose."

"Well, you hide it well mate. I'll give you that."

"I may hide it well but I'm not coping well. I mean the only thing different between us is you're using illegal drugs to cope and I'm using legal ones."

Mikey laughs. "What a bloody pair aye?"

"Yeah. We're a fucking mess again." Christian steers the conversation back to the case. "So, do you think someone in your unit tampered with the evidence?"

"I bloody hope not mate, but we can't rule it out."

"So, what are we going to do?"

"I don't know mate. I don't like the thought of him walking the streets though. He's dangerous. Really dangerous."

Christian stands up and walks around the room scratching his beard. The knuckles on his hand whiten as he squeezes the beer bottle. *"We've gotta hurt him. He's a threat. Hurt him to save the others."* This time, Christian lets the voice win. He agrees that the time for action is here once again. "Then we make him less dangerous." Christian says with a detached look in his eyes. "We take away the things he can use to hurt people. And we find a way to out those fuckers that he's connected too. If they've helped him. We hurt them."

"YES. That's it. Take away his ability to harm. Hurt him! Hurt them all!"

Mikey looks at Christian and smiles. "Last night you were ready to throw in the towel. Why the sudden change of heart?"

"We're not talking about drug dealers here. We're talking about real scum."

"I was hopin' you'd say that. He's uprooted because of the press coverage but I actually have an address for him. When do you wanna start planning it?"

"Right now." Christian answers while placing the bottle down. "I'm gonna make another brew. If we start now and get most of the planning done by the weekend, we can hit him then.

THAT PLACE

When the last lights in the long, cold corridor switch off, fear takes a firm hold. Along the corridor there are twelve rooms. Inside each room is a single bed. Inside those beds are twelve young boys hiding beneath their blankets. The boys lie completely still with their senses attuned to every shadow, every flicker and every sound. All of them hoping tonight, it won't be them.

In this old rundown building, time goes by slowly. The days are long when you spend your time trying to be invisible. The nights are even longer.

A rattle of a lock and a twist of a key sends a series of cries along the corridor. The door opens with a terrifying click. Footsteps slap, slowly and deliberately against the cold hard tiles. Echoing through the cold night air. As the footsteps get closer the hearts in the rooms start to thud, as if they were trying to break free. They fail. Hearts, like their bodies, are trapped. Helpless to what is about to come.

The footsteps stop outside a room. Whimpers become terrified screams. The keys rattle again. There is a click of a lock and a squeak from a handle. The door opens and a hand muffles the plea for help.

BEAUTIFUL BLUE EYES

Christian jerks upright in his bed. The thin sheets stick to his sweaty body and his head thumps. He rubs his tired eyes and reaches over to the bedside cabinet. The glass that sits upon it is empty. He looks at the time. It's 03.37am. He remembers he finished the water less than an hour earlier when he last woke up. Just as sweaty and just as scared.

Christian peels the sheets from his skin and throws them on the pile that's started by the side of the bed. He picks up the glass and walks downstairs where the sounds of late-night TV and a snoring friend greets him. Christian turns the TV off and looks at Mikey. "At least someone is getting some shut eye." Being careful not to wake his friend, he walks over to the sofa. He pulls the blanket off the floor and drapes it over Mikey. An empty vodka bottle rattles as it falls to the floor. Christian curses himself and picks it up. "You weren't kidding when you said you need to be wasted mate, were you?" He places the bottle down gently and sees a single tablet lying on the floor. On closer inspection he sees it a strong pain killer. Christian pops it in his mouth, heads to the kitchen to fill his glass with water and goes back to bed.

Five and a half hours later, a very groggy Christian is walking into a shop to get a packet of biscuits and four pints of milk. He dodges stacks of newspapers and several boxes of crisps that were just inside the doorway.

"Hello, Christian. How are you today?" The shopkeeper asks.

"Apart from nearly falling over the assault course you've just installed by the front door, I'm very good mate. How are you?"

The shopkeeper chooses to ignore Christian's sarcastic comment. "I'm tired, Christian. Very tired. That bloody maniac had us up all night again. The police should lock that man up and throw away the key this time. Crazy bastard is what he is. Crazy, crazy, crazy."

"I'm sure the police are doing everything in their power to keep you all safe."

"I hope so. This is a nice place you know. We don't need people like him ruining it."

"Well, hopefully that'll be the last of it now." Christian turns to walk away, but as he does, he sees a lad of about twelve years old, opening boxes of chocolates and placing them on the shelf. "Alright, Sammi. I didn't see you there, mate. How are you?" When the boy turns around, Christian sees that he has a swollen black eye. His head jumps to the darkest of thoughts. The voice within it begins to rage. "What happened to your eye?" "*If he's done somethin' to that kid I'll...*" Christian turns back to the shop-keeper. "What happened to Sammi's eye Tar?" His voice barely disguising the anger welling within.

The shop keeper shakes his head. "Oh, he's being picked on in school again. I gotta go up later on today to see what the teachers are gonna do about it. It's been going on for bloody months now and I've had it up to here."

Christian turns back to Sammi. "Is this true Sam? Are you being picked on?"

"No. Nobody picks on me, cos I'm solid. It was just a fight that's all...and I won."

Tariq laughs. "That's not what happened at all. Your friends said a girl came up to you, punched you in the face and took your money. And I've heard that from a few other people too, so stop lying. We need to stop her picking on you and that's what I'm going to do today."

"You can't dad! You'll just make it worse! Just leave it mun!" Sammi runs out of the shop crying and Christian looks back at Tariq.

"That's a shitty situation Tar." Christian's heart begins to slow to a normal rate. "It's tough knowing what to do for the best, but for the record" He tries to make up for thinking the worst of the shopkeeper. "I think having a word with the teachers is for the best. They should at least keep a closer eye on him."

"That's what I think. Hopefully it'll work anyway. I can't have the boy being beating up by girls all the time. It's embarrassing mun."

"Yeah, I know what you mean, but it does happen." Christian picks up his things. "Well, I'd better be off." He reaches over and shakes the shop keepers' hand. "Good luck at the school this afternoon."

As Christian approaches the house of Mrs. Phillips, he sees a red Toyota Celica outside. Tiny pieces of glass litters the floor around it. There is no window where the driver's side window should be. He looks inside and sees glass scattered on the seats. Boot marks and dents decorate the door. And someone has scratched 'bastard' into its bonnet. When he looks at the house, he notices that it has fared little better. He knocks twice and waits. A few seconds later the handle twists and someone pulls the door. Nothing happens. "Stupid bloody thing," a voice says from inside. "Steph, how do I open this thing? It's jammed again. Steph! Steph!"

"You gotta lift it up as you pull," Steph answers eventually. "Lift, twist and pull."

On the second attempt the door aggressively swings open and a young lady stands in the doorway. She's in her late twenties, has bright blue eyes and brown hair. "Can I help you?"

"Hello. My name is Christian Thomas." Christian reaches for his I.D. "I'm a social worker and I've come to see if Mrs. Phillips and her family are OK."

"Oh yeah, right. She said you'd be comin'. She's upstairs feeding the little one at the moment. Hold on and I'll give her a shout." The brunette turns around and shouts up the stairs. "Steph! Steph!"

"Yeah?"

"Put your titties away. That handsome social worker you told me about is here."

Christian blushes and looks down at his feet. The brunette giggles at his embarrassment and waves him in.

"She'll be down in a minute now. Come in."

As Christian walks in, the brunette holds her hand out and smiles at him. "I'm Katy."

"Christian," he replies, shaking her hand. Her hands feel soft and delicate. They have bright red nails on the fingers and each nail has a shiny little stone in them. There is no wedding ring on her left hand.

Christian goes straight to the kitchen and places the milk and biscuits on the table. The black and white ceramic tiles look damp and shiney. The black worktops are highly polished. The smell of bleach fills the air. Bubbles fill the sink. "I wasn't sure if there were any here, so I brought my own."

"Awe, isn't that sweet of you. Handsome, caring and thoughtful. You must be beatin' the girls off with a stick."

Christian looks down at his feet. His face becomes a brighter shade of red.

Katy giggles. "I'm just playin' with you." She turns, fills the kettle, and places three cups on the table. Christian tries to think of something funny or remotely interesting to say. He fails and looks at his notes instead. When he finally looks up, he sees Katy staring at him and smiling. She hands him his cup of tea and a second later Steph walks into the kitchen in a white, woolen dressing gown. Christian didn't even hear her walk down the stairs. Thankfully she looks unharmed.

"I was really worried about you when I heard he'd come back. Are you OK?"

Steph smiles. "You're so sweet. Yeah, I'm fine thanks. He wasn't here long anyway. The front door took the worst of it."

"He'd of done a lot more though, if I hadn't shown up and started smashin' his beloved piece of shit car up." Katy answers. "He's nothin' but a bully. A bastard and a bully." Katy's warm, playful voice suddenly tinged with menace.

Christian's heart skips a beat. "Did he hurt you at all? You know, when you were outside with him."

"He wouldn't dare." Katy said. A menacing glint shines in her eyes. "My family would chop him up into little pieces if he did. And he bloody knows they will."

Steph laughs. "He's just as scared of you as he is of your family you nutter." She picks up her cup of tea and takes a sip. She looks Christian in the eye. "We're fine honestly. It's nothin' we can't deal with." Steph grabs a biscuit and snaps it in half. "Anyway. I've been thinkin' about what you've been saying these last few weeks. I'm gonna be pressin' charges this time. For everythin'. It's over between us now. And for good this time. He's never gonna change, so I need him out of our lives."

Christian smiles and nods. "I'm sure that's for the best Steph. And you never know. It may even be the catalyst he needs to change." Christian takes a sip of his tea. "How are the girls?"

"Other than being tired and scared they're fine. Daisy's upstairs asleep if you wanna go see her. Sarah's with my mother. We thought it'd be best if she stayed with her for a few days. The police said it was fine anyway. I mean you can check with them if you want to."

"No, that's fine. I've already spoken to them. This was just a swing by to see how you are. Obviously, now that you're taking the brave steps to protect yourself and your children, we will back you all the way, in whatever way we can. And if you need any advice you have my number and you can call me anytime."

"Can I have it?" Katy asks.

Steph laughs at her friend. "You're bloody beyond mun." She looks at Christian. "I'm sorry about her. She can't help herself."

Christian looks at Katy who smiles and winks at him. Christian blushes again and looks to the floor. The two girls giggle together. "OK, then. Umm..." Christian tries to think of something to change the subject. "If you're sure you're OK, then I'm going to the office to check in with my boss and discuss the next steps. Plus, I have a few more calls I need to get to, so..." He finishes his cup of tea, places it in the sink and picks up a sponge to clean it.

"Don't worry about that. I've gotta clean ours anyway," Steph says. "I'll do them in a minute now."

"You really do tick all the boxes, don't you? Handsome, caring, clean and tidy. The list just keeps on growin'." Katy adds.

Christian manages a little smile. "Stop it. You'll give me a big head."

"I'll give you some sort of head." Katy says. She winks at him and smiles.

"OK stop it now." Steph jumps in. "Christian, you should probably leave while you still have your pants on."

Christian places the dirty cup on the side of the sink. "Yeah, I'd better get going. If you need anything, you know where I am." He walks past a smiling Katy and out of the house. When he's outside he turns around and sees Katy stood blocking the front door and waving him goodbye. Steph is on her tiptoes behind her.

"I'll be in touch. Have a nice day won't you," he says.

"We will handsome man. We will," Katy says after she has blown him a kiss.

Christian blushes. As he turns and walks away, he hears a wolf whistle.

"Cracking little arse on you, fair do's," Katy shouts. The two girls laugh and giggle together. When Christian hears the front door close, he takes a deep breath, looks up to the heavens and smiles.

THE SWEETEST MEMORY

Several hours later, Christian is opening the front door to his home. Luckily, the house is clean and quiet. It feels nice. Like a house should feel after a long day at the office. He enters the living room and sees a few small boxes and bags placed neatly in the corner. He walks over and opens them. Inside are several different types of wigs, face paints and a plethora of fancy-dress costumes. "What the fuck is he up to?"

Christian closes the bags and goes to the kitchen to make a brew. As the kettle boils, he walks over to the bread bin and pulls out several pieces of bread. Then he opens a cupboard, pulls out a packet of mixed nuts and fruit and opens the door to his back garden. Once he's outside, it takes his eyes a few seconds to re-adjust to the sunlight. It's a warm day and a tired and thirsty Christian, is feeling it. He places the food upon his bird table and fills the bird bath. After that, he fills several small bowls that he has hidden among the hedges. The bowls supply fresh drinking water for hedgehogs and other small creatures that habituate this habitat. Once the bowls, bath and garden are suitable watered, Christian goes back inside to make himself a sandwich and a brew.

He selects one of two slices of thick white bread and places three slices of honey roasted ham upon it. A dash of salad cream is squeezed on top of the other and spread evenly into each corner. Four piccolo tomatoes from the vine are sliced in half and four slices of cucumber finish it off. Then he grabs a large bag of beef-flavoured, 'hoopy' crisps and walks to his chair at the back of the garden. He finds a nice bit of shade, opens the crisps and takes a big bite of his sandwich. His teeth pierce the cucumber with a satisfying crunch. The tangy salad cream stimulates his taste buds. Christian loves this sandwich. It reminds him of a special person. The only person in fact, that made him feel completely safe. No, more than that...he felt wanted and loved.

He swallows the mouthful of food and takes a sip of tea. Suddenly a black bird lands on a branch above his head and stares down at him. Christian takes a few crisps from his finger-tips, rips off a chunk of bread and throws them onto the floor a few meters in front of him. Seconds later, the bird is happily pecking at the food a few feet away. Christian takes another bite and lets his mind wander back to a time when kindness entered his life. Kindness in the form of a lady. Her name was Christina. She was fifty-three years old and had been a foster carer for over twenty years. She was the last of the carers that Christian had lived with, but the first one that actually cared. He remembers her home intimately. It was a detached stone wall cottage. A thatched roof gave it a fairytale look. Log fires gave it warmth. It overlooked a valley on one side and the dark blue sea on the other. A small stream ran along the gardens edge and led down to a harbour. It had two apple trees, two plum trees, one pear tree and a variety of other things that grew and tasted delicious. It had several bushes of lavender and wild mint growing which gave off the most beautiful smell in the summertime. Insects and birds loved that garden and so did he. He would always see them buzzing about without a care in the world. They seemed happy just to be there and he would watch them for hours. Christian takes another bite of his sandwich and thinks about the day he first began to trust. He was fifteen years old, had run away from a care home and spent nearly two years in between foster care and living on the streets. He was scared, starving and suffering from serious drug withdrawal. While attempting to steal food from a shop, he was seen by the shopkeeper and caught. The police were called, and social workers took him into care once more. Christian didn't hold out much hope that this new home would be any better than his others, so he hatched a plan. He would regain his strength while he could. Steal whatever he could steal and when the beatings began again, he'd hit the streets.

Social workers took him to a small house in a village he couldn't pronounce, in the middle of a countryside he'd never seen. They knocked on the door and into his life this wonderful lady entered (although he didn't know it then). She had silver hair and bright blue eyes. She looked sweet (but Christian's past told him looks can be deceiving). She made the briefest of introductions before leaving the door open and walking inside. The social workers had to push Christian into the home behind her.

His mind jumps forward to a few weeks later. His belly was full, and he had money and clothes stashed away. He hadn't talked to Christina yet. What would be the point? He's going to end up running away anyway. For her part though, she had tried her best to make him feel at home. He remembers standing in her garden by a small bird bath and a statue of a topless lady. At his feet was the football Christina had bought him and a new pair of football boots. Christina was watching him from the kitchen window. He looked back and she smiled at him. "Try them on," she shouted.

Christian kicked his trainers off and bent down. As he placed one of the boots on, he lost his balance, tripped over the football and crashed into the statue. The statue seemed to fall in slow motion. As it inched closer to the floor, he reached out to grab it. He was an inch too short and a second too late. It landed hard. Knocking the naked ladies head completely off. He remembers the panic he felt. He remembers looking up, frightened. Christina was walking toward him with her hands hidden behind her back. He remembers holding his hands up to protect his face from whatever hard object she must be hiding behind her back. He remembers cowering. Then he remembers her sweet voice. "I thought you may be peckish."

Christian looked up to see Christina holding a plate in her

hand. "Are you OK?" she asked.

He looked down at his grazed knee and then at the statue. "I'm sorry. I just tripped. I didn't mean to."

"Oh, I wouldn't worry about that darling. It's been broken and glued back together more times than I care too remember." Christina bends down to his level and shows him the plate. "I've made sandwiches. They're ham salad and my absolute favourite." Her voice was unwavering and her perfectly pronounced words were warm. "I thought you may like them also. If you take a seat, I'll bring you a nice drink and some crisps to go with it."

From that moment on, Christian became more at ease around his carer. They would walk around the countryside or the harbour for hours on end. Talking about their pasts or dreams for the future. He felt that he could open up to her, almost completely. She never judged him or made him feel insecure and she would encourage him always. Occasionally they would stop for food and Christina would hand Christian money and ask him to order. "Manners are the making of a man," she would say. "A simple please and thank you go a long way." So, he would order, and he would be courteous and the people, to his surprise, were courteous back. He would smile and they would smile, and Christina would place a comforting hand on his shoulder. As the months went by, the pair were seldom seen apart and her influence on Christian became clear. He'd watch her closely. Almost studied her. She would walk into a shop and people would stop and talk, not just for a chat, but for advice and those people would take in her every word. She had an air of confidence about her and everybody seemed to respect her. Christian had never seen a person like her before and he made it his mission to be like her.

The black bird flies off and the suddenness of its exit snaps Christian away from his fondest memories. He picks up his brew, takes a gulp and finishes the sandwich off. His mind goes blank. He is relaxed now. The fresh air, comfort food and sweet memories have washed the days grind away. He closes his eyes. Silence. No thoughts of violent acts. No voice telling him to hurt. There's nothing. The memory of that sweet lady has worked it's magic again.

The next thing Christian hears is the sound of his own snoring waking him from sleep. He jerks up and almost falls from the chair. He wipes a trail of dribble that had flowed from his mouth and checks the time. It's 20.43pm and the air is much cooler now. Christian picks up the crockery, rises from the chair and stretches the pain from his neck before heading back into his house.

When he walks into the kitchen, he sees a note on the work-top. It reads; Mate, you looked so peaceful I didn't want to wake you. I'm going to see that person we talked about. I'll be back by the weekend with everything we need. I picked a selection of outfits earlier so you can see what fits you best. Laters x

Christian grabs a lighter from the draw, takes the note outside, burns it to ash and then he heads upstairs to take a shower.

THAT BEAUTIFUL GIRL

The next few days for Christian are relatively quiet. He rises early for work feeling fresh. Does everything he needs to and gets to bed at a civilised time. The days drag, but it's what he needs to relax before what could be quite an active, stressful and tiring weekend.

When the working week finishes, Christian heads for a pint near Mumbles beach in Swansea. He's had zero contact from Mikey since he read that note and the likelihood of anything happening tonight is slim. He enters the first bar he comes to. It's light and airy. Framed posters and signed sports memorabilia decorate the walls. A poster beside the bar states that anyone using drugs will be banned for life. Underneath the poster an old man sits. He's wearing a dirty flat cap and an old wax jacket. He scratches behind the ear of an old black Labrador dog. Either the man or the dog, smell damp. Christian walks to the far end of the bar and orders a lager. He looks around. It's quiet, except for the old man and a group of lads pumping coins into the jukebox and playing pool. The noise they've picked irritates him, so he turns to the barman. "Is this song stuck or something? It seems to be repeating itself a lot."

"I know mate. Every single one they've put on has been shit." The barman looks at the group of young men. "Bunch of wankers." he says under his breathe. "It's alright for you though. You can drink up and leave if you want. I've got another six hours of it."

"Can't you just pull the plug and tell them it's broke?"

"Trust me. If it was my place, I would do." The barman hands Christian his pint. "Three-fifty please bud."

Christian hands the barman ten pounds of Bobby boys drug money, waits for his change. Then he walks outside to swap the noise from the jukebox with the noise of angry drivers. He sits down beside two men that have tattoos on their necks and tight tops that help emphasise their water filled muscles.

Christian chuckles at them, makes himself comfortable and takes a drink. The beer is cold and full of life. He rubs his thumb along the condensation on the glass and stares into its amber glow. "That's a bloody good pint, fair do's."

The men sitting next to him look at up and stare. "You say something mush? You talkin' to us?"

Christian holds his hand up. "No, just thinking out loud that's all lads. Don't mind me."

The men look at each other and one of them calls Christian a "Fucking weirdo."

"Who the fuck are you calling a wierdo? You pumped up pricks! I'll throw you under a fuckin' bus." Christian shakes the voice from his head and has another drink. To keep his mind occupied and the craziness at bay, he takes his phone out of his pocket and starts to flick through YouTube. He finds; Cats do the funniest things, and after a few clips of cats chasing lasers, slipping into toilets and terrorising dogs, he is crying with laughter. So much so, that he doesn't see the angry muscle men leave or the two pretty girls sit next to him.

"People will think you're a weirdo mind. Sitting all alone and laughin' your head off." One of the girls says.

Christian looks up. The tears in his eyes have blurred his vision so he doesn't see properly. "Oh, I'm sorry." He places his phone in his pocket, wipes his eyes and takes another drink of his warming pint.

"They certainly wouldn't let you save any kids," says the other.

Christian looks back at the girls. "Oh, hi. I'm sorry I was miles away then. How are you?" He holds his hand out to shake the hands of Steph and Katy. Katy pulls him closer so she can get a kiss on the cheek.

"Good thanks." Steph answered. "Just out for a couple of drinks and a laugh to unwind. It's been a tough couple of weeks."

"I don't blame you. They do say that laughter is the best medicine, after all." Christian said. *"Alcohol and morphine are pretty close behind though."*

"I don't know about that," Katy adds. "I'm quite fond of the alcohol myself."

Christian laughs and his eyes meet Katy's. *"She's beautiful."* He looks down at his pint and she giggles.

"Why don't you join us?" Steph asks.

"Oh, I don't think you want me interrupting your girl's night out." Christian lifts up his pint. "Besides, I was going after this one."

"Oh, don't be borin' mun. You can have one more at least," Katy stands up revealing her long, toned, tanned legs that lead all the way up to tight denim hot pants.

Christian finishes his pint in two mouthfuls and stands up also. "I suppose one more won't hurt. What are you having?"

"Pink Gin and tonic please." Katy answered.

"Slimline tonic," Steph adds. "With fruity bits."

"OK." Christian laughs. "Doubles or singles?"

The girls look at each other and giggle. "Doubles."

"Double pink gins coming right up." Christian says walking to the bar.

"Hold on. I'll come with you," Katy says. "I'm gonna put some proper music on. I can't sit here listening to that shit all night."

They get to the bar and Christian orders the drinks whilst Katy has a word in the barman's ear. She slips him a note and a few seconds later the music stops. The whole bar looks at each other in the uncomfortable silence. It isn't long before the lads around the pool table become agitated.

"Oh!" one of them shouts at the bar staff. "What's gone on there? I've put a fiver in there."

The barman holds his hand up to apologise. "Sorry lads. It does that sometimes. How much did you say you lost? A fiver is it?" The barman puts the note that Katy gave him on the bar.

"Here you are lads. Sorry about that."

Meanwhile, Katy has slipped around the corner and is pumping coins into the jukebox. Seconds later her musical taste is revealed. Christian knows the song from the very first note that he hears. It was one of his foster mums favourite songs and she played it constantly. Katy walks away from the jukebox strumming her air guitar along to, Romeo and Juliet by Dire Straits. Her eyes are focused on Christian's the whole time. The boys by the pool table begin to protest her choice, but they are quickly silenced when Katy puts her air guitar down and starts to wiggle those hips. Her eyes are locked onto Christian's the whole time. A few seconds later, Steph is putting her glass on the bar beside him and slowly dancing her way beside her friend. Christian didn't even know Steph was there.

The two girls meet in the middle of the bar which they make their dance floor. They giggle and laugh as they move together. All too soon for Christian, the song ends, and the girls stop and join him at the bar.

"That was good," he says when they reach his side.

"If you like that you're gonna love this next one," Katy shouts just as: Beyoncé; All the single ladies, comes through the speakers.

The girls take a big mouthful of their drinks and then, in a much more energetic way, dance toward their stage. Christian notices the lads by the pool table haven't moved since, Dire Straits. The balls and the boys are in completely the same place they were six minutes ago. Even the bar staff are enjoying the show. Christian pulls up a stool and the barman leans in to whisper in his ear. "Is Katy your misses?"

"Oh no. She's a friend of a friend that's all."

"Really?" The barman leans back, looks at Christian and then at Katy. "The way she's looking at you right now I could swear you two are together."

Christian looks back at Katy. Her eyes are once again fixed on him. Her hips and bum wiggle, her hair and head sway, but her eyes are locked completely onto his. She smiles at him and he smiles back. The barman whispers into Christian's ear again. "You may be the luckiest son of a bitch I've ever served. Fair do's."

Christian laughs and fidgets uncomfortably in his seat. When he looks back at the dance floor, he sees the lads at the pool table huddling together. A few words are spoken in between looks over shoulders. Suddenly they break and begin to approach the girls, like a pack of giggling, hungry hyenas.

"Maybe I spoke to soon," the barman says.

Christian gives the barman his best 'Fuck you' stare and the barman backs off. Christian stands up, finishes his pint and walks to the men's room. He washes his hands and catches his reflection in the mirror. "Stop being a pussy and make a move. You'll fucking blow this otherwise. Man up Christian! Man up!" Christian finishes washing his hands, bends down and splashes the cold water over his face. When he rises and his eyes clear, he is shocked to see Katy behind him. He turns around.

"Hi," she says.

"Hi back."

"Dry your face."

Christian grabs a handful of paper towels and wipes the water from his face and hands. He looks back at her. She stands in front of him with the naughtiest look he's ever seen before on her face. She walks up to him, wraps her hands around his neck, steps up onto her tip toes and plants her soft, strawberry flavoured lips onto his. The pair lock lips for what seems like forever but all too soon, a 'knob head hyena' comes barging into the toilet and disturbs them.

"Oh sorry. I um..." the startled hyena becomes stuck for words and turns to walk away, but when he gets to the door he stops. "Wait a minute," he turns back. "I'm in the right place. This is the men's toilet." He points at Katy. "Get out like."

Katy laughs, grabs Christian's hand and leads him out. When the toilet door closes behind them, she turns around and grabs another sneaky kiss before they join Steph by the bar. Steph smiles as they approach.

"Havin' fun?" She asks.

"Yes thanks," Katy answers.

Christian turns a brighter shade of red but says nothing. Katy picks her drink up and whispers into Steph's ear. Christian doesn't hear what's said but it's clear from the response what was asked.

"Oh, shut up mun. He's just a kid. I'd bloody eat him alive. Besides, I'm out tonight to get drunk and that is it. I'm not even thinkin' about boys." She gestures to the barman who picks up the bin. "I threw his number in there." The barman shows the crumpled piece of paper on top and puts the bin down.

"Which is more than I can say to you." Steph says laughing at Christian's colour. "You two look good together though. It's cute."

Katy looks back at Christian then reaches up and pinches his chin. "Cute is right." She picks up her empty glass and shakes it dramatically. "But he's a bit slow with the drinks."

"Point taken." Christian gestures for another round and as he leans over to pay, Katy grabs a bum cheek.

"Thanks, sweet cheeks," she says laughing.

Steph laughs and points to the other side of the bar. "You wanna go and sit over there? I don't fancy being pestered by those little pervs any more tonight."

"Yeah, OK." After the new round of drinks has arrived, Katy grabs Christian by the hand and follows her friend.

They find a quiet corner and pull up some soft cushioned chairs. Christian sits quietly while the girls pull out a small mirror each and see to their make-up. When Katy snaps her mirror shut, she blows Christian a kiss with those soft, red, strawberry flavoured lips. "How come we've never seen you in here before?" She asks.

"I don't know. I suppose I'm not really a regular. I come in early most Fridays, but I'm usually gone before the chaos starts. You two come here a lot, do you?"

"Kind of, yeah. My uncle owns this place. That's how I got them to turn that shit off the juke box," Katy answers. "Me and

Steph used to work the bar here together too."

"It's much better being this side of the bar though. There's nothin' worse than a drunk." Steph takes a long, slow, drink of her gin. "Unless you're the one that's drunk."

"I'll toast to that," Katy adds. The girls giggle and clink their glasses together.

The next few hours are spent chatting and getting to know each other in a much less professional way. Christian learns that the girls have been friends since they can remember, and their parents have been for even longer. He learns that (like him) they have never been on holiday abroad. He learns that Katy works at a well-known supermarket and that she's been single for "too fucking long." She also has a two-year-old Yorkie dog named Pooch. Christian told her that he loves animals and has recently lost his beloved dog. Her response was another kiss from those strawberry lips.

As the night went on, the bar became busy and quiet at random intervals. Punters of every description came and went. A plethora of colours lit up the room. A variety of different languages were spoken and not one single word had ill intent. It was a good night. When last orders had come and gone and the music is finally turned off, Christian and the girls leave the bar and walk out into the fresh, sea-salty air. "OK, well. I guess this is good night. It's been really good seeing you both."

"What do you mean, goodnight?" Steph slurred. "You're gonna leave two hot, drunk girls, walk home alone in the dark, are you? Really?" Steph begins to laugh. "You bastard!"

"He's not goin' anywhere, mun. He's comin' with us." Katy takes him and Steph by the arms and leads the way home.

On their way home, Steph manages to bump into a lamp post that she apologised to, because she thought it was a person. Steph hit a bin that she thought was a dog. She apologised for that also. They also cover Steph by standing either side of her as she peed between two parked cars. When they finally got back to Steph's house, they have to carry her upstairs to her bed.

"Bloody hell. She's really drunk. How come she's so smashed

and you look pretty sober?" Christian asks.

"She was on doubles the whole night and I went on singles. Plus, on my rounds, I was havin' a sneaky water or Lemonade."

"That is sneaky."

"I know." Katy laughs. "Ah, she needed a good blow out, mun. That tosser's had her all stressed out for ages. And, because I'm a sensible person, I needed to make sure I could look after her tonight. I didn't know I'd bumping into you handsome. Did I?"

Christian smiles and takes a step toward Katy. He reaches behind her, pulls her close and kisses her. His hands glide up her side and she grabs his hand to stop him.

"Not here. This is Steph and the girl's home." Katy places her friend on her side and then puts a bin by the side of the bed in case she feels sick.

"Come on."

"Where are we going?"

"To the beach." Katy answers.

Katy takes him by the hand again and leads the way. Within five minutes they are walking along the beach with sand between their toes. The stars shine brightly above them. The smell of sea spray in the air. The taste of salt on their tongues.

"It's easy to forget how beautiful this part of the world can be sometimes ain't it?" Katy cuts the shape of a heart into the soft sand with the tips of her toes. "I mean, obviously it has an ugly grey side to it, doesn't it?"

"Yeah," Christian agrees. "Doesn't help that the council seemed to have spent all their time and money digging up roads and ripping up the greenery for the last thirty years or so."

"Tell me about it. It's all too easy for us to get lost in that grey shit hole." Katy looks Christian in the eye. She smiles then looks up the heavens. "But then on a night like this. When you get the chance to escape from all that concrete, this city really shows you so much more. I pity the people who are always surrounded by the dull and grey."

"Yeah, I know what you mean. I work less than a mile away from here and you can count on one hand how many times I've walked this beach this year." Christian gazes into Katy's eyes. "I'm really glad I'm doing it tonight though."

"Me too," she answers with a smile.

The pair walk the beach until they come to an old brick archway that used to be part of a bridge. Katy grabs Christian by the hand. She drags him under the arch, wraps her arms around him and kisses him. It was a soft, tender kiss to start but quickly got firmer and more intense. He spins her around and pushes her against the wall. Their hands explore each other's bodies. He grabs her hips and buttocks firmly. After just a few seconds, he lifts her up. Her legs wrap around him. She grinds against him. His hand glides along her ribs until it rests upon her firm, pert breast. His thumb teases her erect nipple. She bites his lip. Suddenly, Christian loses his balance and they fall to the floor. Christian face plants into the beach. When he looks up, Katy starts to laugh." What's the matter?" He asks.

Katy pulls of few strands of grass and twigs from his hair and beard. "Nothing. There's just nothing sexier than a man with bush on his face."

Christian laughs at the joke and then spins her on to her back. "Well then. Since you put it that way."

He starts to slowly kiss his way down her tanned, toned body. He unbuttons her shorts. His rough, callused hands titillate her skin. Goosebumps appear, Hairs stand on end. Her hips grind into the sand. Her hands grab tightly onto his hair. Ten minutes later, Christian, is coming up for air. Katy is panting.

"Wow. You were like a thirsty Labrador then." She grabs him by his glistening beard, pulls him up and kisses him hard on his lips. They embrace for a minute and then Katy spins him around. "Now it's my turn." She unzips his trousers and reaches inside. Christian's heart starts to race. His fingers bury themselves in the sand. His legs straighten. His toes curl.

All too soon, a voice creeps into Christian's head, snapping his senses back online. He opens his eyes. Katy is still on her knees but she's looking up at something.

"Oi, Oi," an unknown voice says. "Look at you two dirty bastards. Havin' fun, are we?" Suddenly a man holding a can of lager comes into view.

"Room for one more is there?" The unwanted stranger asks.

Katy rolls toward Christian's arms.

"Oh, don't be shy love," the unwelcome intruder says. "I dun bite mun."

"Fuck off mate, will you! You're ruining the moment." Christian shouts.

"Aww, don't be like that mush. Come on. Let me join in, go on." the intruder looks at Katy. "I got a bigger dick than him too." The intruder reaches into his pants. "Look."

When both his hands are occupied, Katy jumps to her feet and slaps the intruder across the face. The speed and force of the strike knocks him to the floor. Before he can regain his senses, she grabs Christian by the hand and drags him up. "Come on."

The two ran as fast as they could across the beach. As soon as possible, they cross the road and disappear among the maze of streets. Only when they are sure they haven't been followed do they stop to catch their breath. "Remind me never to upset you," Christian says eventually.

Katy laughs. "I don't think you're the type." She points down the road. "You wanna come to mine?"

"Do I ever."

Katy holds his hand and the two walk the streets of Swansea together until Christian stops suddenly. He wriggles his bum and twists his trousers around. Katy gives him a funny look. "What's up?"

"Something's..." Christian unbuttons his trousers and reaches into the back. He wriggles about and pulls out a handful of seaweed. The pair look at each other and burst out laughing. He holds the seaweed out in front of him. "Do you want it?"

"Ewe! No way. That's disgusting."

"Go on. It'll make a nice little reminder of our first day together."

"Shut up you bute!" Katy says as she walks away.

Christian throws the seaweed over a garden hedge and runs to catch up with her. The next few hours together are either spent in the shower, or in a bed, but nearly always in each-other's arms.

THE KID II

The Kid wipes away a thick layer of condensation on the window. Lines of water, trickle down the glass like tears on an invisible boy. The Kid watches as hordes in school uniforms quickly filter their way through to streets. He's in a partly stripped car inside Sully's yard. The rain taps rapidly on the roof. The smell of diesel, cigarette smoke and mould is potent. The Kid pulls a thin, dirty blanket over his head and curls up on the back seat. His fingers explore the sensitive, swollen areas of his face. *"That bastard. I told you we should of ran away sooner. Didn't I tell you?"* The Kid shakes the voice from his head. It's been four days since the robbery and beating. Four days since he left home. He's thirsty and hungry. Empty packets of crisps and empty bottles of pop litter the foot wells. It's been two days since they were sufficient. The Kid knows that if he's going to eat today, he'll have to go further afield to steel. It didn't take long for the shops to get wise to his sleight of hand. And with a face as memorable as his right now, he knows it'll be a while before they forget. He hears the sound of wheels moving over gravel. Then a metallic groan as the yard doors are swung open. The Kid wipes the newly formed condensation away from the window. Sully, the boss, drives his silver Jaguar car into his yard and parks it under the office window. The Kid watches him get out and start patrolling his yard. Hard faced, steely eyed. The limp, seemingly worse on this cold wet morning. Sully the boss, picks up litter and checks the fence line for signs of vandalism. The litter he finds is thrown into a large yellow skip along-side old tires and half-filled plastic oil drums. There is nothing edible in the skip. As he approaches the garage doors, he glances in the

Kid's direction. The kid ducks out of sight. Tense minutes pass, but eventually, he hears locks being clicked open. Large, heavy doors groan loudly as they are wheeled open. The Kid, keeping the blanket over his head, peaks again. Once again, Sully looks over his shoulder in the Kid's direction. "Shit," the Kid whispers. He thinks about running. He thinks about staying put. He thinks about… A face is pressed against the windscreen and the passenger door swings open. Sully stands by the door with a bottle of milk and a saucer in his hand. He takes a step back when he sees the human form in a blanket.

"What the?" Sully places the milk and saucer on the roof of the car and rips the blanket off. The kid buries his face into the seat and holds on. "What the hell are you doin' in here. I've told you before you fuckin'."

The Kid kicks out. "Get off me!"

"You're on my property you little shit. Now get the fuck out." Sully leans in, grabs a leg in one hand and a shoulder in the other. He pulls the kid out with one big heave. Once out, he grips the Kid by the scruff of the neck and pins him against the car. The beaten face, stills Sully's aggression. It takes a few seconds before he recognizes the Kid's features amongst the scabby, purple and brown swelling. "Kid? Kid is that you?"

The Kid nods.

"What the hell happened? Who done this to you?"

The kid's cracked lips stay sealed.

Sully takes a few steps back and raises his hands. "Sorry, I, I didn't know. For a second then, I thought you was that bastard smack head that's been hovering around here, again." He looks at the grey clouds above them. "Come on. It's bloody horrible out here. I think you need to be out of this cold more than my gammy knee does." Sully opens the bottle of milk, pours some into the saucer and leaves it in the car. He cracks a window open and closes the door.

"What's that for?" The Kid asks.

"An old scabby cat. When I seen the windows steamed up, I thought it was back. But I doubt it ever will be now, after you stunk his house out." Sully looks at the kid and laughs. "Come on. I'll make some hot chocolate to put some life back in our limbs." Sully turns and walks away. After a few meters, he realises the Kid hasn't followed. He turns around and sees the Kid looking at the open gates at the front of the yard. "I can guarantee there's no hot chocolate for you out there." he says. The Kid takes a few more seconds to decide. Eventually, he forces his feet into motion. Sully leads him into the garage. The garage is cluttered. Old tyres pile up on the right-hand side of the entrance. Large oil drums fill the left-hand side. An old camper van seals off the rear exit and is either halfway to being stripped or repaired. A large rat scampers about in between the wheels. Sully leads him through and when he opens the office door a wave of heat hits them. Sully sits him down next to a small heater that glows red. "I time it so it's warm when I get in. Nice ain't it? My joints would practically seize up in the winter if I didn't have this."

The Kid stays silent.

"Stay there." Sully says. "I'll put the kettle on." When Sully leaves, the Kid looks around the small office. It's clad in a cheap, wood effect panel. It has a small untidy desk in the corner. A dirty old phone with three numbers written in ink along its base in the middle of the desk. A yellow-pages is on the left-hand side of the phone. A mixture of paperwork, litter and a filthy mug is on the right-hand side. Above the desk there's a calendar that has a lady with her boobs out straddling a sports car. Sully walks in and sees the kid looking at the lady. "Nice ain't she?" The Kid nods. Sully holds the calendar in his hand. "This is the closest I'll ever get to either of these I suspect. But a guy can dream, can't he?" He hands a steaming mug to the Kid.

The Kid blows the steam away and sips the froth that floats on top of his hot chocolate.

"So, you gonna tell me who beat you?"

The Kid closes his eyes and pulls the warmth of the mug closer to him.

"OK." Sully continues. "Well, by the colour of the bruising I'd say it happened a few days ago. And, because I seen you four days ago, I'm thinking pretty soon after that."

The Kid looks at Sully.

"OK' so I'm close to the truth."

Another man enters the office but pauses when he sees the Kid. He has an oily pair of overalls on and a thick woolen hat on his head. He breathes hot breathe into his cupped hands and looks at Sully. "Morning Boss. Everything alright? He asks while rubbing his hands together.

"Yeah. All good Gray. Just a bit of a funny morning, that's all." Sully reaches into his pocket. "Do us a favour. Go and grab us three breakies from across the way." He hands a note to the man. "And keep schtum about this."

The man looks at the Kid again. "Is everything OK, boss? Should I call someone?"

"Yeah, everything's fine Gray. Just go and get those breakies will you. I'll explain everything later on."

"OK, boss. Full shebang is it?"

"Aye. The full monty. This skinny little bugger needs feeding up."

"No problem boss. Any chance I can have a Welsh breakie?" The man asks.

Sully shakes his head. "Why the hell you would wanna spoil your food like that is beyond me. Sea food and pig shouldn't mix Gray. It's a weird combo." Sully looks at the Kid. "You ever tried cockles, beans and bacon together Kid?" The Kid stays silent. "Didn't think so. Take it from me Kid, if you ever get the chance, decline. It's weird. And don't even get me started on Lava bread. Whacking a pile of black sludge in the middle of your plate. Bloody hanging if you ask me. And then they've got the cheek to charge you extra for it. It's a piss take mun." Sully looks at the man.

The man looks at Sully and smiles. "So, is that a yes or a no on the Welsh one?"

Sully takes a second to think. "It's a yes," he says eventually. "But you can eat that smelly shit outside with the seagulls."

"Cheers boss." The man laughs and leaves Sully and the Kid alone. Sully closes the door behind him. "I take it you are hungry right?"

The Kid nods and sips his cooling chocolate.

Sully takes a seat next to him. He looks at the Kids face. "What happened to you Kid? In fact, what's your real name? I can't keep calling you Kid."

The Kid looks into the amber-red glow that warms him. "It's Carl."

"Carl. That's a nice solid name that. I had a mate called Carl when I was a kid. My best mate actually. Crazy bastard he was. Well, he still is in fairness. Loves girls and horses. Probably got about a dozen horses now." Sully laughs. "And probably as many kids." Sully takes a sip of his hot chocolate. The kid's focus remains on the amber glow. "Who did this to you? Carl, if you don't tell me, I can't help." Sully places his arm over the Kids shoulder.

The kid quickly rolls away. Dark liquid chocolate spills onto the dark oily floor. "Get off me," he yells. "Don't touch me!"

Sully stands and takes a step back. "Wow. Sorry Kid. I didn't mean to upset or...or frighten you or whatever. I just wanna make sure the people who dun this won't do it again." Sully holds his hands out in front of him. "That's all. I just wanna help."

The kid slips down the wall and curls up into a ball, sobbing. "You can't. If you try, you'll just make it worse. It always does."

With a wild boar like groan, sully drops down onto one knee so he's at eye level with the kid. "OK, if I can't help, then maybe the police can. But first of all, you have to say who's done this to you. You can't let the bastards get away with this. It ain't right."

"You can't help me. No one can."

Sully backs away from the Kid to give him some space and time to calm down. After ten minutes of silence, the door opens and the smell of breakfast wafts in. A man holding three polystyrene trays stands in the doorway. He looks at Sully. Sully shrugs his shoulders.

The kid wipes his running nose. "I gotta leave. I just gotta..." The kid gets up and tries to run out the door. The man blocks the doorway.

"Please, I gotta go. Please! Everything'll be fine now. He won't..." The Kid tries running at the large frame of the man sealing the escape. The large man, looks for Sully's support. He wears an uneasy look on his face. The kid gives up and backs into the corner again. Tears stream down his face. His breathing, deep, quick and uncontrolled. His eyes flit back and forth.

Sully grabs two cartons of food and bends down to the Kid's eye level once again. Holding the trays out in front of him, he slowly creeps toward the cowering Kid. He smiles. "If you wanna leave Carl, we won't keep you." He places the food by the Kid's feet. "But you need to eat. Please, take these with you." Sully backs away before standing. "OK. I don't wanna cause you any more stress. I just wanna make sure you have some food. OK?"

The Kid doesn't answer. His breathing is just as deep and un-controlled. Sully sighs, takes one last look at the Kid before he and the large man leave the room. Seconds later, the Kid and the food, are exiting the building.

Gray leans his large frame against a car which rocks under his weight. His breathing is also laboured. "What the fuck was all that about?"
Sully looks toward the exit. "Poor bastard's terrified. Doesn't even recognize a helping hand anymore."

"Someone's given him a right old pasting. Any idea who?" Gray asks as he tucks his drooping belly back into his trousers.

Sully scratches his temple with his dirty black fingertips. "Yeah, I have an idea."

"What are you gonna do?"

"What makes you think I'll do anything at all?"

The large man laughs. "We all know how much you like help-ing strays, boss."

Sully laughs. His right hand makes a fist and releases while he thinks. "The woman that drives that blue Beatle. She's a social

91

worker, right?"

Gray scratches his head. "Blue Beatle. Blue Beatle."

"You MOT'd it, last week mun. It failed on brake lights and front pads."

"Oh yeah. Yeah, I think so. It was a service actually but yeah, I remember. Social worker or teacher or something. Something with kids anyway." The large man opens his polystyrene food container, grabs a sausage and bites it in half.

Sully takes a few steps back. "OK. Do me a favour. Grab her number from our books will you. I'm gonna make a few calls to find out where that kid lives. And take that smelly pile of sludge out the front to eat it. It's turning me sick mun!"

The large man laughs. He opens the tray again and spoons a mouthful of the black lava bead. He purposefully makes a bit, dribble from the corners of his mouth. "OK boss. I'll get right on it."

"Hanging." The boss says as he gags. "You're a dirty fuckin' animal. I can't even look at you."

The big man laughs.

Sully walks toward the toilet. "Just get that fuckin' number you pig."

"What's the matter boss? Where are you going," the big man says laughing.

"To the bogs. You've bloody turned me sick mun. Just get that fuckin' number."

*

Written in pencil on a small white, ripped piece of paper is; Tower Coch. Flat 10B. Sully scrunches the paper and throws it out of his Jaguar's open window. Queen; Fat bottom girls, plays on the radio. He looks at his watch. It's 12.33pm. He breathes in the cold fresh air and switches the radio off. In front of him are two large blocks of flats. In front of them, hiding between two wheelie bins, is the Kid. He's been there since 09.57am. The Kid steps out from the bins and walks toward the front doors.

Sully's hand reaches for the door handle. The Kid stops at the front doors. His hands, placed on the glass. The Kid freezes. After a minute, he walks back to the bins and sits down. The Kid has repeated that exercise seven times already. Confirming to Sully that there is something up there he's fearful of. Or more likely, someone. Sully's heart begins to race. He knows the Kid's father well. A man that has never done an honest day's work in his life. Someone who got buy, selling anything he could. That included stolen goods, drugs, and if you talk to some people, even his wife's 'intimate hours'. He is a rogue for sure and a bully. So, adding child beater to the long list of character flaws isn't that far a stretch of the imagination.

Sully crunches his right hand into a fist and smashes it into his left. He repeats until his knuckles and palm are red. His heart beats faster. Twelve minutes later the Kid gets up. This time, he enters the building. Sully waits for a few moments before following. Adrenaline begins to pump through his body and the pain in his leg fades. He's walking fast. Smashing the doors wide open with his free hand. In his other hand, he holds a crowbar. Sully, chooses to ignore the lifts and takes the steps. Each footstep striking concrete firmly and in time with every thump of his heart. In no time at all, Sully is at the eighth floor and hearing cries. The Kid's cries. His pace, like his heartbeat quickens. He reaches door B, floor 10 and Jams the crowbar into the frame. With one heave and an almighty shoulder barge, the barrier is bested. Sully steams toward the sound of violence. He ignores the ladies form that's sleeping on the settee and opens a bedroom door. He sees a belt doubled up and preparing to unleash upon bare buttocks. Sully grabs the belt and headbutts the holder in the face. The man falls to the floor. Blood pours from his flattened nose. Sully rips the belt from his hand and whips it across the man's head. He repeats. Over and over again. The abuser cowers like a terrified creature. He holds a pillow up to protect himself. Sully kicks him in the ribs. The wind and all fight is knocked from the abuser. Sully seizes the opportunity to catch his breath. He looks at the Kid. The beaten, terrified Kid. "I'm sorry you had to see that Carl." Sully throws the belt at the wall and sucks in a lung full of air. "But with some people, words won't do." Another lung full. "This prick needs to know that he can't treat you like this. And if he does, there'll be consequences." Sully launches another boot into the ribs of the abuser. Then he leans over and grabs him by the throat. "Do you understand why I'm here?"

The abuser coughs red and white bubbles and nods.

"Good. Don't make me come back." Sully holds his hand out to the kid. "There's a lady I know that says she'll be able to help your situation. If you come with me, I'll introduce you."

The kid looks at Sully and then at his father. "You can't live with somebody who treats people the way this wanker does." Sully says. "He doesn't care about you Kid. He's never cared about anybody but himself. He's a fuckin' waster." Sully kicks the waster up the arse. "A piece of shit, waste of space, child beating, junkie." Another kick thumps into the child beaters thigh, making him yell out in pain. The Kid wipes his eyes dry and pulls up his pants.

Sully steps away from the cowering figure and looks around the room. Wallpaper, stained yellow by cigarette smoke, hangs loosely on the walls. The corners have come away completely. Shelves hold nothing but a thick layer of dust. A single wardrobe has a door missing. Crumpled clothes pile up at its base. The bed has a duvet with no cover, no sheets and no headboard or pillows. A toy transformer lay broken in two. Sully holds out his hand once again. "You got anything that's keeping you here Kid? I mean, is there any amount of joy or happiness here? D you even have any memories of being happy here?" Sully asks.

The Kid looks around the room and then down at his father. His father spits a mouthful of bloody phlegm onto the floor but quickly curls up into a tight ball when Sully moves a steal toe capped boot in his direction. Eventually the Kid shakes his head. "No," he says. "I dun remember ever being happy here." The Kid takes Sully's hand.

"Well then. Let's get the fuck out of this shit hole." Sully faints one last kick at the figure in the corner before the two friends limp out of the bedroom. When they reach the bedroom door the Kid's mother staggers toward them. "What the fuck do ew think..." She doesn't get the chance to finish slurring her disapproval. Sully's open hand covers her mouth and most of her face. He holds her for a second. A bottle of something falls from her hand. She begins to sob. Sully pushes her backward through the hallway until she falls over on the settee. Then he turns, puts his arms around the Kid and they leave his scumbag parents behind.

THE START OF SOMETHING SPECIAL

Christian wakes in an empty bed. It's ten o-clock. A small flame danced upon a candle. Lemon and lavender perfume fills the air. Bright colours on soft furnishings decorate the room. Yellow curtains frame the windows. Embroidered upon the fabric are delicate looking white flowers that trail the entire length. A healthy mixture of pink and red Roses and pale Lilies fill a pale blue jar on the dressing table. The dressing table is white and clean. Only a small wooden jewellery box and the flowers sit upon it. Allowing its large oval mirror to take center stage. He takes a few seconds to soak up the ambience of the room. Slowly inhaling the intoxicating aroma surrounding him. He remembers last night's escapades and smiles widely. The soft duvet is pulled away and he rises with a spring in his step. Clothes are thrown on or simply picked up and he lightly skips down the stairs. A kettle mid-boil grabs his attention. He follows the sound into the kitchen where two cups sit on the worktop.

"I'm out here handsome," Katy shouts. "Bring the tea with you. Milky and one sugar for me."

The kettle clicks and Christian makes the tea. When he walks outside, he sees Katy lying on a recliner, soaking up the morning sun. A delicate red thong barely covers her privates. A small dog rests by her side. A seven-foot-high wall marks the gardens perimeter but offers little protection against prying eyes.

"Wow! What a sight you are, first thing in the morning. I bet the neighbours bloody love you." Christian hands her a cup. "Well the blokes anyway. Probably not the wives."

"Neighbours aren't home." She points to one house. "They're on holiday." She points to the other. "That one is empty. So, I'm makin' the most of it."

"In that case then. Suns out, plums out." Christian drops his trousers and shakes his hips about in front of a shocked but hysterical Katy.

"You're off your head mun."

Christian bends over and gives her a kiss. The dog growls.

"What's his problem?"

"He's probably after your bone." Katy says pointing to his growing penis.

Christian laughs again. "Well, he can't have it. It's mine." He covers his semi soft penis with a soft cushioned chair and sits down beside Katy to take in some rays.

"Last night was fun," she says.

"Yeah. It really was. Unexpected too."

"Yeah, it's weird that we bumped into each other. Swansea's not the smallest of places is it? I'm really glad we did though."

"Me too."

Christian picks up a small ball from the floor. The dog sees this and is instantly ready to play. His little tail wags back and forth frantically and he spins around in circles. Christian throws the ball against a wall and the dog leaps in the air to catch it. When Pooch returns with it in his mouth Christian fusses him until it's released. The sodden, sticky ball rolls on the floor leaving a damp, translucent trail. The dog looks at Christian. His eyes and wagging tail let his intentions known to Christian. It's play time now. So, throw the bloody ball they say.

"I wasn't too sure he'd like you," Katy says. "But he must do. It normally takes him ages before he trusts anyone enough to play with them see."

"That's good. I'd be gutted if he didn't want anything to do with me. I love dogs."

"Yeah, me too. He's a good judge of character too. So if he

likes you, then that's good enough for me."

"Really? So, this little rascal could of stopped you seeing me again?"

"Definitely. It's happened before." Katy roughs the hair on the dogs head.

Christian throws the ball again. Pooch races after it. Skidding across the floor in his excitement. Christian and laughs. "Crazy creature."

Katy smiles and takes a sip of her tea. "So, what are your plans today then handsome?"

Christian suddenly remembers that he may have business to attend to with Mikey, so he quickly makes up a lie. "Oh, I have a lot of paperwork I need to catch up on. I should of started it yesterday but I got sidetracked." He rubs Katy's leg. "It was the best bloody sidetrack ever though. Totally worth it."

Katy holds his hand and blows him a kiss. "You're very welcome, handsome."

"What about you? Anything exciting planned?"

"I'm gonna check on Steph in a bit now, to see how she's coping. I text her ages ago, but she hasn't even read it yet. She's probably feeling rough as hell. Poor bugger. We did say we'd take her girls out for the day if it's nice, which..." Katy holds her hands up to the sky. "It looks like it's going to be. If she's up for doing something, I can ask if she minds you joining us after your work is finished. If you want to that is. What do you think? We'll probably grab some food and a drink down Mumbles at some point."

"OK, yeah, that sounds nice. I'll give you text if I'm going to be finished early enough."

"Cool. I hope you do."

The couple spend the next twenty minutes recapturing the nights escapades before Christian gets dressed. After that they swap numbers, kiss goodbye, for quite a long time and within the hour Christian is stepping into his home. When he opens the door, he is startled by the sight of Spiderman, sitting on his sofa drinking from a large white coffee cup. "What the fuck are you doing?"

"Wearin' it in," Spiderman answers.

Christian cocks his head and looks at him stupid. "Wearing it in?"

"Yeah. It's like wearin' bloody cardboard mun. Rough as fuck. Really bloody uncomfortable." Spiderman scratches his bum. "My arse crack is sweating like mad. I reckon I'll probably have to choose somethin' else." Mikey says scratching his bum again.

"Probably have to? Probably? Are you for real? You've been sleeping on that sofa for god knows how long. It's going to have your DNA all over it, you bute!"

"Oh yeah." Mikey stands up. "Good point."

"You're supposed to be the smart policeman in this little partnership. You should know that shit."

"I never claimed to be a smart policeman. Just a policeman."

Christian laughs. "That's a good point." He walks over to the windows and wipes a cobweb from the wall. Then he folds the long, light cream curtains properly. Holding them in place with the slightly darker tassels. Christian inspects the window frame. Gliding his hand over the white PVC frame to check for dust. His fingers remain dust free which makes him smile. "So, have you managed to find him?"

Mikey smiles. "Yeah."

"So, it's on for today?"

"Not quite. We got a few things to pick up first."

"Like what?"

"A bike. Preferably one like yours with off roads. We can do that in an hour or two if your free. I know of a gang that go around Swansea stealing cars and bikes. We'll use your bike to lure them."

"No fucking chance mate." Christian cuts in. "Not a chance in fucking hell."

Mikey laughs. "I'll put a tracker on it. It'll be fine I promise."

Christian gives him a suspicious look.

"I give you my word it won't get hurt."

Christian begrudgingly gives in with the slightest nod of acceptance.

"Then, we'll follow them to their lock up and see what they've got. I've checked the records for what's gone missing over the last few weeks and I'm confident they'll have somethin'."

"Why do we need to do that? Why can't we just do it the same as we always do. It's never failed us before."

"Because if we're seen, the bike can't be traced back to us. Plus, the bike thieves ain't gonna grass us up for robbin' them, are they? Trust me on this OK. It's the best plan I got. Plus, those robbin' fucks need to be taught a lesson. They've been taking the piss for too long."

Christian nods. "OK, Spiderman. I trust you."

"Good. I knew you were smarter than you look." Mikey looks Christian up and down. "So, where've you been?"

"Out."

"No shit. Out where? I got home about four and your car wasn't here. I looked in your room and it was empty."

"Awe," Christian smiles. "Have you been worried about me Mikey?"

"Pfft," Mikey scoffs. "I was too busy havin' a quiet beer and a Chinese to care dude. Curious that's all."

"Ooh, a Chinese," Christian says whilst popping his head through the kitchen door and sniffing the air. "Any left?"

Spiderman rubs his belly. "Nope. It took me three sittings, but I finally finished it off a couple of hours ago."

"You, gutsy fat bastard. You know I love a Chinese."

"Yeah, I know, but," Mikey takes a second to find an excuse. "Um, well, I didn't know when you'd be home did I? Coulda been off by the time you did. I wouldn't want you eatin' anythin' that's gone bad like, would I?"

"Whatever, you starving prick." Christian says laughing. "I'll remember that in future."

Mikey chuckles. "Anyway, don't change the subject. Where'd you get to last night?"

Christian smiles at the memory. "I met a girl and stayed at hers."

"Nice! What's she like?"

"Hot. Really hot. Like, unbelievable."

Really?" Mikey looks him up and down. "Fuck off, I don't believe you. You're still in your work clothes. You spent the night in work again, didn't you? For fuck sake mun. You're so sad Christian. I swear life is just passin' you by."

Christian shrugs his shoulders. "OK, I was in work."

"See, why lie to me mate? You got my hopes up for a second then. I was startin' to think there was actually some hope for you."

Christian takes his top off and walks upstairs. "I'm bloody starved." he shouts down.

"Thought you would be. I got eggs, bread and some chocolate biscuits earlier. I was thinkin' scrambled. You up for it?"

"Feeling guilty about not leaving me any takeaway, are you?"

Mikey laughs but doesn't answer.

"I'll have four eggs and three toast," Christian shouts down.

"You'll have three and three, you gutsy bastard. I only bought six eggs."

Christian walks back down the stairs. "You're having eggs on toast as well? Thought you'd just had a Chinese?"

Mikey laughs. "I may have been fibbing about that. I had every intention of grabbing one but everywhere was closed by the time I got back. I was deva' like."

"Ah, you prick." Christian walks back up the stairs.

"I'll put them on now, shall I?" Mikey shouts up to him.

"Yeah go on. I won't be too long."

THIEVING FROM THIEVES

Four hours later, Mikey is in a supermarket car park. He's watching a biker in black gear park his bike by the entrance. Seconds later the biker disappears through the automatic doors. Within two minutes, another bike pulls up with two riders. The rider at the back dismounts and walks toward the baited bike. They hover around it for a few seconds then walk to the supermarket entrance. A quick glance confirms the coast is clear and they return to the baited bike. They check it over, grab the handlebars, kick it off its stand and push it around the corner. Once out of sight, the thief jumps on and the front wheel lifts from the ground. Rider and bike disappear. Five minutes later, the biker in black appears with two bottles of water and a cooked chicken. He walks toward Mikey. Mikey opens the door and Christian jumps in.

"Please tell me we still have a signal?"

Mikey holds up a small tracker. "Loud and clear dude."

"Thank fuck for that." Christian rips a chicken leg from the torso. He bites into it. Fatty juices coat his face.

"See. Didn't I tell you I wouldn't let you down? Didn't I?" Mikey rips the other leg from browned sweating bird. "Shoulda known better than to question my judgement. His teeth tear flesh from bone. "Mikey's got it all figured out mush." He starts the engine and exits the car park. "Yip. Mikey knows best."

"Yeah but…"

"But nothin' dude." Mikey cuts in. "What Mikey says, Mikey

does."

Christian shakes his head. "Talking about yourself in the third person is awfully unbecoming dude."

Mikey laughs and throws the bare bone out the window. "It's true though. People who don't believe me always end up looking like fools." He looks at his friend and smiles. "And that's what you look like right now. A bloody fool." Mikey moves onto a dual carriageway and puts his foot down. "And I'm pretty sure you didn't use that word in the right context."

Christian looks confused. "What word?" He asks.

"Unbecoming." Mikey answers.

"I'm pretty sure I did." Christian answers. His confused look undermining his confident tone. "It means unattractive or inappropriate."

"Really?" Mikey asks "I thought it meant like..." Mikey pauses for a second to think. "I thought it meant like, uncouth or something. Like, not fitting the occasion. Like bad behavior or something."

"Um..." Christian's confused look grows. "I don't even know now. You've bloody spun me out now."

"Yeah me too. Fuck it. We'll just google it later." Mikey says laughing. He points at the red dot moving along a digital map. "Still. My plan is working like a charm dude. These light-fingered fuckers haven't got the slightest idea how bad their day's about to get."

"Yeah," Christian says. A sinister smile appears on his face. "Not a clue."

The pair follow the thief and Christian's bike, north through the Swansea valleys.

"Looks like your bike's leadin' them home mate. What were the chances that they'd be operating right under our bloody noses? Cheeky bastards."

They follow the bike for thirty-five minutes until the signal stops at a quiet industrial site. It's fifteen minutes away from Christian's house by foot. Mikey drives past slowly to confirm which lock up it is." What you think? Are you confident?" Mikey asks.

Christian makes a mental note of the estate, nods his head. Mikey puts his foot down.

"You know we could probably walk back from mine later on. I'm hungry again anyway. Let's go back to mine and have some dinner. We can come back when it's dark."

Mikey looks at Christian suspiciously.

"What?" Christian asks.

"You sure you wanna do this? You know, I can probably do it on my own anyway."

"I'm fine mate. Seriously. If this is what we need to do to get Bullen, I'm well up for it. I promise. I just think it makes more sense to hit them when it's dark. And plus, I'm hungry."

"I actually agree. It sounds like a great plan. Just thought I'd check that's all. The smell of that chicken has made me bloody starvin' again too."

Mikey drives off at a steady pace so as not to arouse suspicion. When they get back to the house Christian makes them a chicken dinner with all the trimmings. A warm treacle pudding with piping hot custard was desert. Then about ten o'clock at night, two dangerous shadows approach the industrial estate from the field behind. They squeeze through a gap in the fence and enter the dark and eerily quiet compound. It is about four hundred meters long, two hundred meters wide and has seven small units inside. Two units have scrap cars outside. One looks like it may have manufactured PVC windows a long time ago. The other four look empty apart from the many rats that run in and out of the small holes that pepper-pot their steel cladding.

The men in black head toward the empty unit at the far end. All the windows are boarded, but the security shutters in front of the large wooden doors are up. Christian checks a door to the left of them. It has half a sign that would have once said entrance nailed upon it. It's locked. He puts his bag down and pulls out a military issue spy cam. He feeds the camera under the door and checks for movement. It's dark and quiet but a dim light is on at the far end of the room.

"What do you think?" Christian asks Mikey in his almost perfect Irish accent.

"Well, we need your bike back and one more, so we gotta get in somehow." Mikey says with his best attempt at an Irishman/Scotsman.

Christian grabs his lock-picking kit from his rucksack. Within seconds there is a click and the door opens. Christian smiles. "Easy peasy." He pokes his head in to check it's still clear. Mikey gets a thumbs up and Christian sneaks in. Mikey opens his bag and pulls out an almost invisible wire that has two hooks at either end. He clips each hook opposite each other at the base of the door frame and closes the door silently behind them. They keep their profiles low and hide amongst the shadows on the outer edge. They move as a team. One moving while the other keeps a lookout. They move in the direction of the only light that shines. Suddenly, noise from a metal tool falling on the concrete floor echoes around the room. The two men freeze and try to find its source. Christian lowers his head down to floor-level and looks under the large collection of vehicles that litter the room. With his senses on high alert and his heart in his mouth, he scuttles around trying to find the source of the noise. Finally, footsteps slap on the floor giving the thief away. He is less than ten meters from Mikey at the outer edge of the light. The thief coughs and spits onto the floor. Mikey and Christian look at each other. They signal the plan in little hand movements and move to their positions. They reach into their rucksacks and pull out one last thing before stashing them under a car. Christian stalks the thief like a well-armed panther from the shadows. Darting from cover to cover until he's four meters away from his back. Christian's heart is pounding. The adrenaline floods into his body and he fights hard to control his breathing. After each step he steadies himself until finally, he's in a perfect position. He takes one last controlled breath, plants his feet firmly and jumps out from his cover, hitting the thief with fifty thousand volts from a stun gun. The thief's body jerks violently, then goes stiff as a board and drops to the floor. Christian puts his knee on the thief's back, grabs one of his arms and breaks it. The thief screams. Suddenly a noise of something falling draws Christian's attention away. He sees a dark shape moving. Christian looks for Mikey but he's nowhere to be seen. Suddenly the front door swings open and the wire snaps. Seconds later, Christian hears the familiar sounds of electricity crackling and a scream. The door swings back open and Mikey drags another restrained thief into the light. The thief holds his right arm as it hangs loose at its shoulder.

"How many others are here?" Mikey asks in his questionable accent.

There's no reply so Christian hits his thief with another fifty thousand volts. "I'll ask one more time. If you don't answer I'm going to break more bones."

The thieves look at each other but their lips stay sealed. Mikey walks to a table and picks up a hammer. He grabs his thief, ties his hands and stands on one of his legs with the hammer raised.

"Only us. There's only us," the thief shouts.

Mikey lowers the hammer but keeps it in his hand.

"Good. Now we're getting somewhere, so we are." Mikey walks around the thieves while staring into their eyes. "Right then lads. Time for my next Question. Why do you think it is acceptable to steal bikes on our turf?"

The thieves look at each other. Confusion clear on their faces. "What? What. I dun understand mun." Christian's thief says. "This is where we've always been. We haven't even..."

Mikey swings the hammer onto the collar bone of the mouthy thief. The crunch of bone is quickly followed by screams of pain. Mikey puts his hands over his mouth to stop the noise.

"This may well be what you've always done and where you've always done it. But it stops now. This is your only warning. Understand? Swansea is ours. Tell the rest of your shitty little gang that the same fate awaits them if we catch them."

Mikey and Christian drag the bodies to a table and cable tie them to it. Then they walk around the garage and do a bit of shopping. "What do you fancy?" Mikey asks Christian.

Christian pulls a cover off a large vehicle. "I think I like the look of this Range Rover."

"That's a bloody good choice I must say."

"What about you?" Christian asks.

"Well it's a nice night for a ride. I think I'll go for two wheels." Mikey stops by a GSXR 750. "Maybe this one."

"Really? Ten to the penny they are pal. I think you'd look better on that." Christian points to the blacked-out BMW F 700 GS in the corner. Now that's a nice bike."

The pair walk over to the bike and pretend they haven't seen it before. They open the fuel tank and give the bike a shake.

"Plenty in the tank sir. Plenty in the tank." Christian says to Mikey.

Mikey laughs. "Well that's me done. I'm taking this one. What about you? You still taking that Range Rover? Or do you fancy a little race?"

"Aye. A race sounds good." Christian stops by a bright green Ford Focus RS. "What do you think? Does it suit me?"

"Green suits you yeah. It's a good job too because that's the colour you'll be when you see me leave you for dust."

"Not while there is a hole in my ass does that thing beat an RS. I'll tell you what. I'll make it interesting." Christian walks over to a similar looking bike with off road wheels and checks it has fuel. "I'll take this to even things out. What do you say? Ten grand for the first back?"

"You're on. This'll be the easiest ten G's I've ever made. Fuckin' child's play."

The two friends turn the keys and both bikes burst into life. "Awe nice," Christian shouts. "This is gonna be fun."

Mikey walks over to the two thieves. He grabs one by the broken arm and squeezes the others collar. They scream in agony and Mikey does his best crazy man laugh in their faces. "Is there anything I should know about these bikes? Any faults?"

The men shake their heads.

"Are the plates good?"

"Yeah," one of them says as tears roll down his face.

"Good." He pats them down for their wallets. When he finds them, he removes their I.D and looks at their addresses. "Shittin' on your own doorsteps lads. Tut, bloody, tut." He taps their I'D on top of their heads. "Now if you're lying to me, or if me or any of my crew have to pay your shitty little gang a visit again." Mikey leans to one side to show Christian standing behind him. His pistol is aimed at their heads. He has his best, evil guy smile on his face. Mikey leans back. "Understand?" The two terrified men stop their whimpering and nod their heads. "We'll stop. I promise we're finished."

"Good." Mikey pats them on their heads again and stands.

He looks at Christian. "Let the race begin."

The two friends pack up their tools, jump on their bikes and rev the engines. They laugh like mad men as they roll them outside. Christian takes one look back, imitates a hand holding a gun to the thieves. Then he pulls the trigger, turns and wheel spins out of the yard.

THE RAT TRAP

A taxi driver pulls up outside an old pub in the outskirts of Hereford. A sign that has a horse and cart painted upon it squeaks above him as the cool wind blows it back and forth. He opens the window and shouts at two people in fancy dress. "Any of you Tom?"

"Aye that's me," the man dressed as a cat answers in an Irish accent.

"Bloody hell, that was quick," added the Irish mouse.

The cat and mouse finish their drinks and jump in the car.

"Looks dead in there, lads." The taxi driver says. "It's been quiet everywhere today. Must be something in the air."

"Yeah, there was only us and a young couple in the corner arguing. Had to get out of there cos it was bringing us down."

"I bet." The taxi driver looks at the two costumes. "If you're Tom, then I guess that makes you Jerry."

Jerry nods his head.

The taxi driver laughs. "So, what's the occasion?"

"No reason. Other than girls love a man in fancy dress."

"Fair enough. Where you heading lads? Town is it?"

"Yeah, but we have to swing by our pals house to pick him up first because he won't get a taxi on his own. He says he feels like a dick." Tom shrugs his shoulders and looks at the taxi driver. "I mean come on. How can anyone look like a dick dressed as Bugs Bunny? He needs to grow up. Anyway, it's a few miles away." Tom pulls a wad of twenties out of his wallet. "There's a hundred pound there, driver. And there'll be another hundred on the way back. It shouldn't take us more than half an hour I reckon. Is that OK?"

The taxi driver counts the cash. "Yeah, that's fine lads. More than fine. Where are we headed?"

Tom looks at Jerry and Jerry raises his hands. "I thought you knew his address." Tom says.

"I know the number. It's number three. Don't ask me the name of the street though. Ah for fuck sake. Hold on. I'll give him a ring now." Jerry takes his phone out of his pocket and rings an old mobile he knows won't be answered. He puts it on loud-speaker and the answer phone kicks in. "I tell you what? He's fuckin' useless that boy."

"What's he said?"

"Nothing. As per usual. He's not fuckin' answering." Just head toward Leominster will you mate, and I'll give you directions on the way."

"Send him a txt to let him know we've left the pub though. You know what he's like." Tom adds.

The driver sets off and Tom and Jerry make themselves comfortable. As they go along, Jerry tells the driver to take a few lefts and rights. Eventually the taxi is driving along a bumpy country road. There are no lights in sight and high hedgerows all around. They pass an abandoned barn and Jerry tells the driver to pull over so he can pee. The driver stops and Jerry jumps out. To pass the time, Tom chats to the driver about his hobbies.

"Do you like football mate?"

"Yeah, I do."

"Me too. Who's your favourite team then?"

The taxi driver hits the Manchester United smelly that is swinging on his rear-view mirror.

"Oh, you're a United fan, are you? I'm a Liverpool fan myself. On a scale of one to ten. How much do you love United?"

"Ten," the taxi driver says in a heartbeat.

"Ten? Oh blimey. That's a lot." Tom pauses for a second to think of his next question. He turns and looks the driver dead in the eyes. "So, do you think that's more or less than you like raping thirteen-year-old girls Bullen?"

The taxi driver looks at Tom. Fear, clear in his eyes. Tom's eyes remained focused. Bullen starts to mumble something, but he's interrupted by Jerry's hand as it sneaks over his mouth. There's a brief struggle before Bullen the monster falls fast asleep.

BULLEN

Tom the cat, studies the man in the front seat. Sweaty, pale, chubby. Late fifties, maybe sixties. To look at him you wouldn't think that he's capable of the things he's done. Suppose that's why he got away with it so for long. Jerry, the mouse, pokes Bullen in his closed eyes and holds his nostrils shut. Bullen's head moves from side to side. His mouth opens. Jerry forces his mouth shut once more to seal off his air supply. Bullen's head twists and turns. Slowly at first but as his oxygen levels drop the struggle becomes wild.

Eventually, Bullen wakes from a bad dream into a terrifying reality. He looks out through the windscreen and sees his car has been moved. As far as he can tell, he and the vehicle are inside an old barn. He moves his hands off his lap and checks for marks. They are free and unhurt. He looks down at his feet. His shoes are missing but they are not bound. He wipes his brow.

"Hello again."

Bullen jumps at the unexpected voice. He looks behind. The cat from his nightmare is laying on his back seat holding a gun. Bullen's hand instinctively goes to the keys at his ignition. They are missing. He hears a rattle and looks back to see Tom holding them up. Bullen's next instinct is to pull on the handle. When the door opens, he sees Jerry, standing with a gun pointing at him. In his other hand is a ten-inch carving knife. Jerry puts the knife to his own throat and imitates slicing it. Bullen lets go of the door and sits back quietly.

"If you try to escape, we will torture you before we kill you. Understand?" Jerry asks.

Bullen looks at Jerry and nods his head. He looks down and

sees that Jerry is wearing his shoes. Bullen's eyes follow footprints that lead away from Jerry and stop at a pile of half burnt photos and clothes.

"We've been to your house," Tom says. "We know everything about you. We know you are guilty of the most horrendous acts and that the system failed to punish you. We are here to rectify that failure."

Bullen begins to panic. He tries to plead his innocence, but fear makes his high-pitched voice stutter and slur.

Tom holds the pistol to his lips. "Sshhh. We know everything. Don't waste your breath, Bullen." Tom opens the window to let fresh air in and rests his head on the door frame. "Like I said. We know everything about you, Bullen." He emphasises the name. "What we don't know, is everything about your accomplices."

Jerry takes a step forward and bends down to Bullen's eye level. "And that is your way out of this situation."

Bullen's eyes light up.

"That's right Bullen. We're giving you a way out. If you tell us everything you know about the people that helped you escape jail, plus everything about the people that are in your perverted ring of monsters. Then we'll free you and continue our hunt with them."

Bullen starts to cry. "I promise you, I'm not who you think I am. I swear, if you let me go, I won't tell the police. I haven't even seen your faces, OK. Just let me go and I'll forget everything. I promise."

Jerry pulls a piece of paper from his pocket and unfolds it. It's a newspaper cut out and in bold letters the headline reads: Justice at last; Paedophile gets what's coming. Under the headline is a picture of a man that was beaten halfway to death before being handed in to the police with evidence of his crimes.

"Do you like our work?" Jerry asks. "My favourite is when I cut off his penis and taped it inside his mouth." Jerry pauses to let that thought sink in. "This is your fate Bullen, if you do not do as we ask."

Bullen starts to sob uncontrollably.

"It's your only way out." Tom adds.

"OK, OK. I'll do it. I'll tell you." Bullen says in between deep breaths to try and calm himself.

"Good. Inside your glove box you have a notepad, don't you?" Tom says.

Bullen nods.

"Take it out and start to write a confession to us. Start with your full name and then list all the details of your crimes. If I notice you have forgotten any of those crimes, my friend over there with the knife will remind you. Then, I want you to list everybody that helped you and the parts that they had in either the assaults and grooming or how they helped you escape jail. Is this understood?"

Bullen begins to cry. "They'll kill me."

"If you don't, then you die tonight." Jerry says holding the tip of the knife to Bullen's throat.

Bullen wipes the tears from his eyes. "OK, OK. I'll do it," he screeches.

"Good. Then you may start," Jerry says.

"I don't have a pen."

"You can use the Parker pen that you have in your inside pocket. You know, the one you got from town on Thursday afternoon."

Bullen reaches inside his pocket and pulls out the pen. He looks at Tom in the rear-view mirror.

"We've been watching. We'll always be watching."

Bullen clicks the top and when the pen touches the pad it doesn't stop until all of the dirty details are down. When he's finished, he hands it to Tom in the back seat to check it over. Tom's hands begin to shake with rage as each page is turned. "Are you sure that's everything and everyone?" He asks.

"Yes. I'm sure." Bullen wipes his eyes and clears his throat. "I'm a dead man now. The names and details in that book will get me killed?"

Tom and Jerry look at each other but no words are spoken. After a minute of silence, Jerry pulls out Bullen's mobile phone and switches it on. "What's the password?"

"United1902," Bullen answers.

Jerry types in the password and begins to write a message.

"What are you doing?" Bullen asks.

"I'm writing a message to a journalist for the Daily Telegraph. She'll help you shine a light on all of the people you've named. Once the spotlight is on them, they'll find it very difficult to hurt you. They'll probably put you in protective custody until you're sentenced. I mean you are definitely going to jail, Bullen. But you've committed horrendous crimes. It's only right that you do. The only other option you have right now is me and Tom over there take a hammer to your limbs and call the police on you anyway."

Tom reaches inside a bag and pulls out two hammers. "It's up to you."

Bullen looks at the hammers and then looks at his phone. "Send the text," he says finally.

Jerry hits send and switches the phone off. He removes the sim card, the battery and throws them and the phone in different directions around the barn.

"Right then. Now it's time for us to say goodbye." Tom says.

Bullen turns around to look at Tom. When he does, Jerry sneaks up behind him and puts his hand over his mouth. Seconds later, Bullen is fast asleep. Tom and Jerry get to work covering their tracks.

"How long do you think we've got?" Christian asks as he places Bullen's shoes back on him and puts on a pair of standard issue police shoes.

"Well, she's down here reporting on the Special forces cutbacks so not too long. But it should be enough for us to do what we need to."

Tom and Jerry start to clean up, making sure the only footprints are from Bullen's or police shoes. Christian places photos that Mikey gained from Bullen's flat around the fire while Mikey makes copies of Bullen's confession on his phone. The flash from Mikey's phone makes the barn look like a crime scene. Illuminating the friends while they work. To finish off they grab a hose pipe from their bag and run it from the exhaust of Bullen's car, into his window. They half seal it shut with a waterproof jacket they found in his boot and switch the engine on. Once they are sure everything is done, they head to the back of the barn where the stolen bike is hidden. They remove their fancy-dress costumes and stuff them in a large rucksack. They take one final look at their handy work before Christian rolls the bike away. Mikey switches the Taxi's engine on and picks up the rucksack. They walk a small concrete path for one hundred meters to a stream where Christian starts the bikes engine. Mikey jumps on and they follow the stream until they reach the top of the hill. A minute or so later, headlights from a car stop at the barn. Mikey grabs a pair of infrared binoculars from his rucksack. He sees a female climb out. Cautiously she approaches the barn. She has a flashlight in her hand and a phone by her ear.

"It's her." Mikey says.

"Good."

"She's on the phone to someone."

"Do you think it's the cops?"

"It'll be her boss knowin' her."

A few seconds later they see flashes of light coming from the barn. "Good girl." Mikey says.

"Take as many photos as you can. Make sure you get it all now. Don't you dare trust the bloody cops."

"Do you think she'll see the notepad?" Christian asks.

"She could hardly miss it. It's right next to him on the seat."

They sit on top of the hill for ten more minutes while the flash from a camera continues. When the familiar blue lights appear in the distance, the flashes stop. Christian starts the engine. They take one final look at the barn before the two friends speed off into the night.

TURNING WHEELS

It's the middle of the day when Christian wakes from the deepest of sleeps. He grabs his phone and checks the news reports. The first article reads: Child abusers confession sends shockwave through Britain's high society. Christian reads on. The article states that, a previously accused paedophile reveals he was part of a well organised ring that exploited the most vulnerable children in our society. Most of whom were in care. The man who the police name as; Mr. X, revealed this in a confession he left during a failed suicide. Mr. X is now in police custody and is being questioned.

Christian jumps out of bed and heads downstairs. Mikey is sprawled out on the sofa, watching the news with a brew.

"Kettle's just boiled, lazy arse. Have you seen the shit storm we created? It's amazing! Heads are gonna roll mush."

"Hope so. Have there been any arrests yet?"

"A few people have been brought into questioning but they're lettin' their lawyers do most of the press stuff."

"That's brilliant news. I think this calls for a celebratory biscuit." Christian makes himself a brew and comes in with a pack of dark chocolate digestives. He cracks one in half and dunks it in his tea. The reporters on TV reveal more of the story.

"Do you think he'll mention us?" Christian asks.

"Maybe. If they make him say it's all made up because he thought his life was in danger, then yeah, it could hurt the case. But ultimately, this should get the ball rolling and give the other victims more power to come forward. The police will have to investigate thoroughly. They just have to. The press will make sure of it."

"Hope you're right." The phone in Christian's pocket beeps. He picks it up to check the message. It's from Katy. It has only one word in it, but he smiles when he reads it. It says; Hi. He replies; Hi back. A few seconds later she responds with; Do you fancy a dinner? I'm starved.

Christian replies; Sounds bloody great. Where and when?

A minute later his phone beeps again; Soon as you can. I'm heading to that pub now. How long will it take you?"

Christian does the math in his head and replies; Forty-three minutes.

Katy replies; Lol, accurate. See you in a bit then. Xxx.

Forty-seven minutes later, Christian is walking into the bar. It's busy. A long table along the far-right hand side of the room, seats seven adults, six children and three teenagers engrossed in their phones. The Children play and jostle with each other in their seats. Adults try to in vain to control them. The teenagers are blissfully unaware. One kid throws a plastic toy car from his chair and it narrowly misses Christian's head. The laughing boy is immediately reprimanded by the adult to his right. Christian guesses it's his father. The father puts his hand up and sincerely apologises to Christian. Christian smiles and hands the car back. "Don't worry about it mate. Kids will be kids." Christian leaves the crazy table to their not so happy meal. He narrowly avoids two waitresses carrying four plates of meat, roast potatoes and gravy and goes in search of Katy. He finds her in the only quiet corner left in the pub. She sits beside a radiator that's painted brown and a single pained wooden framed window that's painted red. She checks her watch. "You're late."

"Not a bad guess though, I'm only four minutes out. The traffic's crazy out there beautiful. Sunday bloody drivers every-where." Christian kisses her tenderly on the lips. She has her hair done up and held back by a black bow. Her ears carry big, circular, silver earrings and small blue studs. She is wearing a blue woolen jumper, that hangs over her left shoulder. After a long embrace, Christian sits down. "You look beautiful."

Katy smiles. Her eyes twinkle.

"Have you ordered yet?" He asks.

"Not yet," she says picking up the menu. It consists of a single sheet of laminate. A picture of a perfectly glazed chicken, rotating on a spit, is the background. "How hungry are you, because they do two or three courses and it's only a pound difference. I think I'm goin' for three."

"Three sounds great," Christian says picking up the menu. "I'm having the soup, beef and chocolate fudge cake with cream."

"Bloody hell, that's quick." Katy taps her fingernails on her teeth while she thinks. "It does sound good though. I think I'll have the same."

Christian stands up but Katy grabs his hand and pulls him back. "What are you doin'?" she asks.

"Going to order." Christian replies.

"No, you're not. I asked you to come here, so sit down. Now what drink do you want?"

Christian tries his best to change Katy's mind but fails. Five minutes later she is placing a lager in front of him and sipping a pink gin with fruity bits.

"What's that like?" Christian asks.

"What? Pink gin? Awe, it's lush mun. Try a bit." Katy hands him the glass but he pushes it away and looks around.

"It's not the most-manliest of drinks is it?"

Katy laughs. "You men are crazy creatures aren't you. It's a drink mun! Just bloody try it. I promise it won't make you any less of a man." Katy hands Christian her glass again. He has one more look around before taking the quickest of sips.

"Ooh, yeah that is good. It's got a nice summery flavour to it."

"Told you. So is your penis still attached?"

Christian plays along with the mockery and reaches down to his privates. "Just about."

"Good." Katy winks and smiles. "You're gonna need it later."

Christian laughs and over the next hour or so they sit and enjoy each other's company, while eating some good pub grub with a few more drinks. Afterwards, they decide to make the most of the sunshine and take a walk along the beach. As soon as the warm sand touches Katy's feet, she reaches out and holds Christian's hand. It makes him smile.

"I can't remember the last time we had so many nice days in a row," Katy says.

"Me neither. Normally it pisses down for five days out of seven, but this year's been fantastic. It's like we actually have a proper summer. It's crazy."

Christian bends down and picks up a pebble. He rubs the sand from its surface with his thumb, revealing the bright blue colour with white and red lines running through it. "It kinda looks like a heart, don't you think?"

Katy takes a closer look and smiles. "I think that gin may have affected you after all."

Christian laughs. As he is about to throw the stone away, Katy grabs his hand. "Can I have it?"

He smiles. "Of course." He opens his hand up. "It's yours."

Katy goes on her tip toes and kisses him on the lips. "Thanks, handsome."

The lovers walk along the beach doing the things that lovers do and talking about things that lovers talk about. They find out some interesting things about each other and also some uninteresting things. Like for instance; Katy believes in ghosts. She believes that her grandfather is looking after her because whenever she feels upset, strange things start happening and usually to the person that's caused her the pain. Christian doesn't believe in ghosts but made a mental note to never upset Katy just in case. Also, Katy is a Virgo and that means that blah blah blah. Christian tried but he just could not even feign interest in that topic. When he yawned for the tenth time, Katy took the hint and stopped. Then they grabbed an ice cream and watched each other's backs while the opportunistic seagulls circled above them. A few hours later, with the sunlight fading and tired legs carrying them, they made the long walk back.

Over the next few weeks the pair spent more and more time together. They would meet in Christian's lunch break or on the odd night that Katy's shifts would allow. So eventually, they had the 'conversation'. It went a little bit like this. Katy finished work and Christian was waiting at her door with a bunch of flowers and a bottle of pink gin. "What are they for?" She asked.

"No reason. Just thought you'd like them that's all. Do you?"

"Yeah, I love 'em. Thanks." Katy smiled at him and smelled the flowers. "My god, you're proper into me, aren't you?"

Christian blushed but tried his best to act cool. Katy smiled and pulled his beard. "It's OK. Just say it."

Christian looked at his feet. "Say what?"

"You know what."

"No, I don't. I'm just giving you flowers that's all." Christian's colour took on a brand-new shade of red.

"Just say it you knob." Katy said laughing.

"OK, OK. I really like you. I'm really into you."

"Really into me. Wow, that's romantic." Katy said rolling her eyes. "That's what all the girls want to hear from their man."

"OK, I love you."

"See! Wasn't so hard was it?" Katy said laughing. "I love you too handsome." She stood on her tip toes and kissed him. "Now get in there and take your pants off."

After that conversation the pair would spend most nights together. For the first time in a long time, Christian's mind was at ease. His heart was happy and the voice in his head had gone silent for the first time since he could remember. Everything it seemed, had worked out. Until a news broadcast shattered the silence.

THE KID III

Soulful sounds vibrate through the air in waves, creating a relaxed party atmosphere. The sun beats its glorious rays upon the shimmering earth. Freshly cut grass floats on warming water inside an inflatable pool. A cat moves from the shade of a table to the shade of a tree. Hiding from the heat of the day or the firm grasp of the Kid. It stares at the Kid. The Kid subconsciously scratches the claw marks it left behind when his hands wrapped tightly around its throat. Beside the claw marks are several nasty scars left behind from lit cigarettes and a razor-sharp blade. Most of them were created by the Kid. Something else steals his focus. He watches her run her fingers through her long blonde hair and tuck it behind her shoulders. Her big red lips glisten. She looks up at him. The kid quickly, looks away. The girl is a little older than him. She is also the daughter of the family he's staying with. She places a hula-hoop around her. He watches her move.

It's been nine months since the Kid last seen his parents. Two months since he's seen Sully. The big man with the limp had held true to his word. He protected him. Put a roof over him. Made him feel warm. The Kid stayed with him for a few weeks until the social worker had time to find a more permanent solution. A teary-eyed Sully had said, if he wasn't so pushed to take care of his ailing wife, the Kid could have stayed there permanently. The Kid understood. Sully had already done more than enough. More than anyone had before.

A steak sizzles and spits when it's put onto the blackened steal grill. Drops of liquid fat, drip from the contracting meat. Flames dance upon red-hot coals. The Kid picks up a half-eaten burger from the table and takes a bite. Red sauce and melted cheese colour the corners of his mouth. He wipes his face with the back of his hand. Cold orange squash washes it down.

"Hope you're still hungry."

The kid looks around. Beside a red brick barbeque, a man is holding tongs. He's wearing an apron. A cave man, cooking over a fire, is printed upon it. A birthday gift from his wife. The Kid gives him a thumbs up and finishes his burger. The man turns the meat over and takes a sip of his beer. His name is Pete. He's forty-two years old, slightly over-weight and works in a bank. His wife is Kim, short for Kimberly, but she doesn't like Kimberly, so people call her Kim. She's younger than Pete. Seven years younger and much prettier. Their daughter, Gwyn, has her looks. Kim walks back from the kitchen holding fresh buttered rolls and a vodka and tonic. The ice, clinks as she walks. She places the rolls down on a white plastic table and smiles at the Kid. "Hope your still hungry," she says.

The Kid gives her a thumbs up. Kim pushes the large umbrella up at the center of the table. She smiles and walks away to stand beside her husband. They make small talk. The Kid watches them. Kim laughs as her husband talks. Her hand rests gently on his shoulder. She looks into his eyes and smiles. They seem happy. Genuinely happy. He'd never seen a family dynamic like this before. Not in real life anyway.

The hula-hoop drops to the floor. Gwyn steps over it and glides her blonde hair away from her eyes with her blue fingernails. As she approaches the table, her mother Kim joins her. "Why don't you show Carl how to do that. He might enjoy it, go on." Kim looks at the Kid. "It's good fun, go on." Kim smiles. "And good exercise, why don't you try it."

The Kid smiles back and looks at her daughter. Gwyn doesn't acknowledge them. She picks up her drink and joins her father amongst the smoke and sizzle. Her mother sighs and sits down. Her back remains straight. Her legs held tight at the knee "She'll come around. She can't stay mad forever, can she?" Kim shuffles uncomfortable in her seat and looks at her daughter. "I mean, it's not like we never included her in our decision to foster. She seemed happy with it." Kim suddenly realises that she's talking out loud. She looks at the Kid. "She'll come around, Carl. You're a nice boy. She'll come around, I promise." She pats the Kid on the leg, places her drink on the table and walks toward the hula-hoop. The Kid grabs a handful of onion rings from the table and moves his seat clockwise. The change of temperature from sunlight to shade is instant and gratifying. Tangy, orange crisps, crunch.

The Kid reflects on his situation. Even if one of the three people he lives with, doesn't want him there. The two that do, are feeding him well. The Kid has never been so heavy. His gaunt, pale face has plumped and coloured. His Jeans now possess a bum you can see. His shoulders have broadened. A steak is placed in front of him. Another hand is placed on his shoulder.

"See if it's cooked enough for you mate. It may be a little bloody still." Pete says.

The Kid rips the steak in half, gives him a thumbs up and bites into it. Pete roughs the Kid's hair and walks away. The Kid's eyes follow. They lock onto long blonde hair and eyes that return a hostile stare. Her young face doesn't smile. The Kid's stomach churns, and he looks away. He places half of the steak into his mouth and takes a bite. Juices run down his cheek and neck. He ignores the uncomfortable feeling and concentrates on the food. Each mouthful makes him stronger. Being stronger gives him options, should things go wrong. He notices a trail of ants foraging among the many crumbs scattered on the table. His finger hovers above one of them. Casting it in shadow. It follows the unsuspecting creature from above. Like a dark cloud above the doomed. Eventually, the cloud drops, squashing the ant into a dark black stain. The cloud and shadow move on to find another. And another. Something at the edge of his vision catches his eye. A butterfly flies toward him. It's colourful wings direct it, unconfidently through the air. It comes to rest upon his hand. Beautifully coloured, delicate wings come together as it settles. Antennae twitch. The Kid lifts his finger from the remains of several ants. The shadow moves up his arm until it finds its target. It hovers for ten seconds and falls.

*

Two days later the Kid, is standing at a vandalised bus stop, in his neatly pressed school uniform. The morning is cool, and the sky is blue. By his side, is Kim. She smiles at him and gives him a thumbs up. Behind them, her daughter Gwyn, is chatting to a friend. Kim puts her arm around the Kid as a beaten old school bus rolls up the road. It stops with a screech and the doors open. The Kid hears loud voices from within. He holds Kim's hand tightly. He hates this bus and all the kids that sit within it.

Gwyn and her friend push past him and step upon the bus. "Excuse me," Kim says. "Don't I at least get a goodbye?"

Gwyn turns around. Her eyes roll into the corners and she puts on an exaggerated, fake smile. "Goodbye Mom." Then she strolls into the bus, giggling with her friend.

Kim looks at the Kid. "Honestly, that girl. She's becoming more like...like." She smiles at the Kid. "Well, to be honest, she's a lot like me when I was her age. But don't tell her I said that." Kim runs her fingers through the Kids hair to tidy it up and folds his collar neatly over his tie. "There. Much better. Now you look even more handsome." She looks at the bus. Children jostle about in their seats. Paper airplanes fly through the air. The volume of noise goes up as the seconds tick bye.

The bus driver coughs to get their attention. He is a fat man with spikey hair that's going bald. A gold cross hangs upon his pierced left ear and he has a yellow stain on his white shirt. "Any time today, love. It's not like I have ten more stops to do or a school to get too."

Kim gives him an unpleasant look and he quickly looks away. "Now you listen to me," she whispers in the Kids ear. "You are good boy with a good heart and a good head on your shoulders. This school is better off with you in it, OK? So, don't you let anybody tell you any different." She holds the Kid's shoulder firmer and looks him in the eye. "OK?" Then she looks around at the bus. "And, if those kids become confrontational again, you must tell a teacher. You can't go around fighting." She looks through each window of the bus. As if daring anyone to confront her. "Even if a few of those little shits deserve it." She said rather too loudly for the Kid's comfort. She pinches his cheek. "Promise me. No more fighting."

The kid smiles. "OK. I promise."

Kim steps aside and the Kid walks onto the bus. As soon as he's in, the driver closes the door and puts his foot on the accelerator. The bus lurches forward. The Kid grabs a handrail to steady himself and sits on the first empty seat. It's behind the driver and has blackened chewing gum interwoven with the dirty brown seats. A smelly ashtray is somewhere close. The cigarette smell tickles his throat. The Kid makes himself comfortable between the blobs of gum and looks out of the window. He watches as big, posh homes and nice cars whizz by. He wonders how many children live in those homes. He wonders if those kids are happy. If the families are happy.

The bus slows down and the doors open. A girl and two boy's step on. One boy has a black eye. The Kid separates his feet for balance and makes a fist in his right hand. His eyes remain on the world outside the bus. His peripheral vision, watches for sudden movements near his vulnerable blind side. Only when the voices and insults beside him move on, does he relax for a second.

Outside the windows are big green trees that partially cover his view of a white walled house. Electric gates open and a silver, BMW convertible, exits the grounds. The person driving has sunglasses on and a grey suit. The doors of the bus close and he's pushed back into his seat. The Kid closes his eyes and waits for what's about to happen. Seconds later he is hit in the head by dozens of pieces of paper. Some have been ripped, chewed into spit balls and blown out through empty pens. They hit his neck and head with a wet slap. Others are scrunched into balls. The worst ones are folded into planes. The planes have words written on the wings. The words are pretty similar. They read; Fuck off back to the council estate. Or; Smelly council rat. Go die in a sewer. The Kid takes a deep breath and looks back through the glass. Tall trees. Neatly cut hedges. Bushes in the shapes of animals. Fast cars. Faster bikes. Big houses. A swimming pool or two. He fights to stop tears from seeping out.

Twenty minutes later, the bus rolls into the school grounds. The Kid quickly gets out. A teacher, wearing a horrible, brown, sweater and grey trousers, is waiting at the bus stop. He's in his mid-fifties and has a silver beard and thick, brown-framed glasses. The Kid approaches him.

"Go straight to your form tutor lad. Go on," he says.

The Kid carries on walking. When he hears the teacher talking again, he turns around.

"Everything alright Master Williams?" The teacher asks the boy with the black eye.

"Yes sir," the boy answers. Beside the boy is Kim's daughter, Gwyn. It was their writing on the airplanes.

"Good, good." The teacher says nodding his head. "Would you like me to walk you two into the school this morning."

"I don't think that will be necessary sir. I don't think he'll do anything again."

The boy and Gwyn smile at the Kid. The Kid looks at his feet and walks away. A bell rings and he quickens his pace.

The school is a newly refurbished building from the industrial era. It has brown brick walls and six floors. As well as the multi-million-pound refurbishment it acquired an Olympic sized swimming pool. Currently, a female team is training inside the pool. Scores of boys gather at the windows. They jostle for the best places to look inside. The Kid hears them talking about bushes and spider legs and saying crude, dirty things to each other. He walks through the main entrance, into a light-blue corridor and over grey, square tiles. On the walls are photos of all of the schools, current and passed sports teams. Above and at the center of the photos, is the school moto in capitals: O NERTH I NERTH. The Kid was told it means, FROM STRENGTH TO STRENGTH. It seemed to strike a chord with him instantly. He likes it a lot. In a very large cabinet next to the photos, are several shelves filled with all the trophies that the teams have won. It's completely full. A group of boys see him looking at the trophies and walk toward him. He moves on. Past groups of giggling girls and hordes of testosterone filled boys. His head is kept low. His pace quick.

Eventually he reaches his form room and walks in. He's the first one there. Not even the teacher is present. He finds a seat at the back, next to a window and sits down. Upon the black board at the front of the class, math equations are written in white chalk. Along the top of every wall are symbols and equations that the Kid has never seen before. Written upon or carved into his table are the memories of who's loved who and what sexual preferences some kids may or may not have had. The Kid adjusts his seating position in the hard-wooden chair. The bell, rings again. Seconds later, the door opens. The teacher and several pupils enter. The pupils settle themselves upon their pre-selected seats, alongside their usual company. A large smelly boy sits in front of the Kid. His hair is cut short and patchy. When the bell rings for the final time, only two seats remain, out of the thirty in the room. One beside the Kid and one by the smelly boy. The teacher takes his seat and opens his register. "OK, OK. Quiet down, quiet down." The chatter and giggling stops. "Andrew Davies?" The teacher asks.

"Present, sir." a boy answers.

"Hayley Morgan?" The teacher asks.

"Here." the girl answers.

The teacher looks up. "Present, sir!" he corrects.

"Sorry sir. Present sir." The girl says giggling.

"Gareth Henry?"

There's no reply. The teacher looks up. "Anybody seen Gareth today?"

The pupils look about, but nobody answers. The teacher moves on. "Mathew Jones?"

Suddenly there's a knock and the classroom door swings open. A ginger boy walks in. "Sorry I'm late Sir."

"That's OK. Take a seat Gareth," the teacher says.

Gareth walks through the lines of chairs and settles at his two remaining options. He looks at the Kid. Then he looks at the smelly boy and back at the Kid. Eventually, he pulls out the chair beside the smelly boy and sits down. The boy with the Black eye smiles.

After about ten minutes, when the record of everyone present is complete, the class is dismissed. The noise levels build quickly as conversations continue where they left off. Table and chairs squeak along the floor. The Kid waits until the room is empty before he gets up. "Everything alright today Carl? Have you had anymore instances like the other day?" His form tutor is a small man with a scruffy grey/ginger beard. He has a hint of playfulness in his voice.

"No sir," the Kid answers.

"No what?" the teacher says laughing. "No, you're not alright, or no you haven't had any more trouble."

The Kid smiles. "I'm OK sir. No trouble today sir."

"That's good to hear. And if he does give you any, you come and see me straight away, OK?" The teacher lowers his voice and looks over his shoulders. "His Dad may have the headmaster in his pocket, but I know a tosser when I see one. And that little shit, is a massive tosser."

The Kid chuckles. "Thank you, sir."

"Ok. You'd better get to your first lesson. Do you know what it is?"

The Kid removes a green, thin piece of card from his pocket. On it, is his weekly planned lessons. "English," he says. "With Mr. Gracia."

"Do you remember where that is?" His teacher gives him a second to think.

"Um, sixth floor?"

"That's right. Sixth floor. All the way to the end of the corridor."

"Yeah, I remember now. Thanks Sir."

"Ok" The sound of rowdy children starts to come in from the corridor outside. "My class is getting impatient by the sounds of things." His teacher stands up. "I'll see you after dinner, OK."

His teacher escorts him to the door. He opens it quickly. The noise dies down, just as quickly. "I tell you what! You lot must be really eager for the numbers today. You just can't wait for the numbers. Making all this racket, just to get my attention. What wonderfully eager pupils you are. It's just fantastic." He grabs the Kid by the shoulders and leads him to the steps. Pupils stroll past them to get to their seats. The Kid carries on upwards. After a few steps, he hears his teacher talking. "Not so fast you three. Mark, tuck your shirt in. Stacey, put your tie back on. Steven, get those bloody earrings out. Every time it's you three. What do you think? That one day I'll suddenly forget? It's everyday mun! Every bloody day!" The teacher turns to look at the kid. He smiles and gives him a thumbs up.

The Kid reciprocates the gesture and carries on upwards. Fourteen steps later, he hears the sound of someone clearing his throat. He stops and pokes his head in between the flights of steps to look upward. A boy with a black eye and Gwyn stand above him. The boy has his mouth open. Phlegm, dripping from his lips. It drops and hits the Kid in his eye. The boy and Gwyn run off laughing. "You dirty fuckin scrubber," the boy shouts. It's at that moment when the Kid's form teacher pokes his head around the corner. "What's happened? Are you Ok?" The Kid drops his book bag and cleans his eyes with his sleeve. When his form tutor sees the green and yellow slime on his blue jumper and face, it makes him gag. The Kid ignores him. Anger swells within. He pulls the jumper over his head and scrunches it into a ball. He can still hear the footsteps. The laughing. Taunting him. He follows. Like a raging bull, he storms through the corridors. The teacher calls after him but the Kid moves fast. Step by step, the Kid, hunts for the aggressors. Up to the top floor. All along the two-hundred-meter corridor. Smashing through double doors. His tutor calling after him but he's too slow to interfere.

Down six floors and a hundred and twenty steps. By now, a female voice had joined his form tutor's. But they are still too slow. The Kid has the scent now. He's closing. He follows them along the ground floor and out through a fire exit. Thirty meters in front of him, standing beside a red brick bike shed are Gwyn and her black-eyed boyfriend. He sprints toward him. Jumper held tight in one hand. The other, in a fist. Twenty-five meters. Twenty meters. Two more boys walk out from behind the bike shed and join the taunting couple. Fifteen meters. Ten meters. The confident look on the black-eyed boys face, dissolves. Five meters. The Kid throws the jumper at the closest boy. A skinny lad with a tooth missing and his head shaved. While he's temporarily blinded, the Kid, leaps up and kicks him in the stomach. The boy crumples to the floor. Next up is a large boy that's built like a rugby player. His ears, like cauliflower. His shoulders are broad. The second boy swings a half-hearted, slow right hook. The Kid ducks under it and retaliates with a well-timed uppercut. Foe two, crumples beside the foe one. Without breaking his stride, the Kid rugby tackles the black-eyed boy to the ground. "Get off him! You bastard, get off him." Gwyn yells. The kid ignores her and thumps the boy in his nose with his right hand. Then he smashes him across the jaw with his left. Right. Left. Right. Left. Right. Blow after blow. A voice inside his head laughs hysterically. Suddenly, he's lifted from the ground. His arms are held by his side. His form tutor has him in a bear hug. His scruffy beard, scratches against the Kids neck. "Calm down boy! Just calm down!" The Kid kicks out. He twists and turns. He tries everything that could release him from this vice like grip, so he can vent the anger inside. Nothing works. The grip holds firm. Within minutes an audience has gathered. A tearful Gwyn is taken away by the deputy headmaster. The two 'back-up' boys were picked up and carried away by the PT teacher. The headmaster crouches beside an unconscious form on the floor. The raging inferno inside the Kid, is quickly extinguished. His limbs, like his struggle, become limp. He stares at the bloodied face. The flat nose that points to one side. A large gash above the left eye. The jaw, open and adrift.

The headmaster looks at the Kid. "Get him into my office now! And somebody call an ambulance."

The form tutor lowers the Kid, grabs him tightly on the wrist and pulls him away from the scene of his crime. "God damn it boy. What's wrong with you? Huh?" He kicks a door open with his right foot and pulls the Kid along a corridor. Unsupervised pupils look out from classroom doors. They stare at the Kid and whisper. One or two pupils shout their approvals at the Kid. The form teacher yells at them as they pass. "Get back inside you lot. And shut those bloody doors, you nosey little bastards." He leads the Kid past the trophy cabinets and photos of excellent achievements. They turn right at the end of the corridor and stop at a door that has footprints outlined in white paint outside. A sign is screwed into the center of the door. It says: Please knock and wait. The form tutor barges the door open and drags the Kid inside. He walks in behind him. "God damn it," he says when the door is closed. "Didn't I tell you that if you get anymore shit from them two, that you're to come and see me? Huh? Didn't I tell you that?"

The Kid doesn't answer. He looks at the floor instead. His shaking, bleeding hands are stuffed tightly in his pockets. The form tutor paces the room. "God damn it. You played straight into their hands, boy." It's a few minutes until the form tutor has regained enough self-control to be stationary. He looks at the Kid. "You don't beat people like him by using your fists boy. Not in the long run anyway," he says. "Look at me when I'm talking to you."

The Kid looks up, but shame makes him avoid eye contact. "I'm sorry," he whispers. Tears flood his eyes. "I don't know why I did it. I just." His sobbing over rules his language.

"I know, I know boy." The form tutor places a comforting hand on the Kid's shoulder. "You got a hell of a temper on you boy. A hell of a temper." He pushes the Kid backwards until he's against a chair. Then he sits him down.

"What's gonna happen now?" the Kid asks.

"Don't know boy." The form tutor looks out of a window at the schools enclosed garden. Ducks and chickens peck at grasses and insects. Large, green leafed plants sprout from the ground. Rows of vegetables, colour a square patch of loose earth. "I think it's safe to assume you'll get at least a suspension from school." The Kid hears an ambulance siren in the distance. "But, if I was a betting man, I think you're more likely going to be expelled." The form tutor, turns and looks at the Kid. "Even with me saying you were being provoked. There's only so much it'll do. This is your second strike in as many months, boy. Under normal circumstances, you could plead the victim and get the benefit of the doubt. But, as I've told you before, that lad's father and the headmaster go way back. If it comes between keeping you in this school and a bunch of new sports facilities, I know which one the headmaster will choose." The sirens are loud now. The Kid can see blue lights reflecting through the window. Suddenly the door flies open, and the headmaster comes barging in. His face is red and sweaty. His wooly jumper is riding up around his rotund belly. The shirt underneath is light blue and trying to escape from his corduroy trousers. "Leave us alone please," he says to the form tutor.

The form tutor stands his ground. "Before I go headmaster, I'd like to say that I saw this young lad being provoked. It's the fourth time I've seen it happen over the last few weeks and the fourth time I've reported it. I seen it. They spat in his fa..."

The headmaster interrupts. His red sweaty face becomes redder. "Are you trying to tell me, that what this violent yob has done today is justified, Mr Lovell?" His voice is raised and angry.

Mr. Lovell looks away. He takes a second to think. "Not justified, no. Not exactly. But an impulsive reaction to torment. He's being picked on, Headmaster. Bloody well spat on actually. And, I thought in this school, we don't stand for bullying. Isn't that what we tell parents when they come. Zero tolerance on bullying of any kind." The form tutor seemed to grow in confidence with every word he spoke. "Or do we turn a blind eye if it's not financially beneficial?"

The headmaster takes a step toward Mr. Lovell. He towers above him like a giant over an infant. Mr. Lovell steps back. "Do not stand there and try to tell me about the integrity of this school and my policies. I have a pupil out there with what appears to be a broken jaw, a broken nose and possibly an eye socket or two. Now it is my duty to punish those responsible." He looks at the Kid. "That is, after the police have dealt with you, young man. I'm sure his father will be looking to punish you with the full extent of the law. What you have done out there is a serious crime. A very serious crime."

The Kid begins to sob. His eyes fog over as the tears refract the light. The room becomes a blur of mixed colours and shapes, like an oil painter's wet canvas. The Kid shakes his head, but that only makes the room spin. His stomach churns. The colours in the room begin to fade. Reds and blues become greys and blacks. The Kid stands and holds out his hand for help. It grasps at thin air and the room turns black.

PAST TO PRESENT

Christian's alarm woke him for work at his usual time. It's Wednesday morning and the pitter patter of rain on his window told him the weather had changed. As usual he woke with the smile on his face and a pretty girl in his head. It's a strange feeling and he loves it. He loves her more. He got up, made himself a brew and sat on the sofa. Mikey wasn't there anymore. He and his girlfriend are trying to patch things up and the last thing he'd heard, Mikey was taking her away on his boat for a few days. So, for the last week or so, Christian's house has been quiet. It's been nice. Really nice. He loves Mikey like a brother, but after weeks of drunken chaos and waking up to a naked, hairy arse every morning, Mikey's really started to get on his tits. Christian had a sip of tea and turned on the TV. That is when his mood changed. No, it was more than that. Everything changed.

A female reporter stands in front of a jail, reporting on the death of a prisoner. Christian's heart skips a beat and he drop's his cup. She had not even named the man that died yet, but Christian knew who it would be. He knew she would report on this. She was the reporter they text, and she was the first on the scene that night. "Bullen." The man that could close the noose around that ring of perverts is dead. *"They got to him. The bastards have murdered to him."*

Christian picks up the cup with shaking hands and heads to the kitchen to find a cloth. When he finds it, he holds it over his face and screams. He drops to the floor and screams again. "Bastards." He sits on the cold floor for over ten minutes, screaming into the cloth to keep the neighbours from hearing his moment of madness. Only when his anger is quelled does he get back up. He washes handfuls of cold water over his face and takes one deep breath after another. His control lasts until he sees his reflection in the window. He stares at it. It appears as just an outline. Like a distant memory that has most of the details forgotten. *"That's what you are to him. That's how you appear in his mind. Just an outline of a boy alongside countless other invisible boys."* Christian's hands grip the sink and his anger returns. *"He doesn't even remember you."* Christian walks to the fridge and grabs a beer. He hits the top off and drinks the whole thing down. Then he grabs another and does the same. *"Look at you. Oh, the pity. You're feeling sorry for yourself while they're getting away with ruining lives. No, it's more than that. It's murder. They've murdered the life you were supposed to have. They murder every life they touch with their filthy perverted hands. They commit murder while you wallow here feeling sorry for yourself. What a waste. What a pathetic waste of a man you are."* Christian runs into the living room, kicks the sofa over. He picks the TV up and smashes it against the floor. His hands scratch at his face and pull at his hair. The pain helps to stop the voice in his head and for a brief moment, it's silent. He stomps around the sofa in clockwise circles until he feels calm enough to remove his hands. He takes deep, controlled breathes. After a few minutes he feels calm enough to stop. He looks around. The carnage he's created makes him chuckle. "Bloody hell I'm as bad as Mikey." He leans against a wall and looks down at his shaking hands. Black hairs from his beard stick out from under his nails and blood stains three fingers. He wipes them clean and dries the sweat on his pants. "OK, Christian, get your shit together. You need a cool head mate. Stay calm and you'll figure this out." He picks up the sofa and TV, gets a cloth to dry the spilt tea and runs a hoover over the carpet. Once the room is tidy, he runs upstairs to shower and calls a taxi to come and pick him up.

A few hours later, Christian is sat with a work colleague. They are preparing themselves to supervise a couple with their children. The parents they are supervising have a history of drug abuse and between them they've spent over ten years in prison.

Mostly for possession of class A drugs, but with a bit a violence in between. His colleague's name is Martha. She is fifty-two years old and has been doing this job for over twenty-five years. She's also a very sweet Scottish lady and Christian, will not have a bad word said about her. They arrive near the address and park next to a car that has bricks where the wheels should be. They walk past a lamppost that has no light, but the shell of a push bike and a horse tied to it. They navigate passed a variety of different animal poo and arrive at a house that has a brand-new BMW M4 parked on the garden. Martha knocks on the door. The little boy and girl hold her hand tightly. When the door opens, they hide behind her completely. Their mother answers and the kids show a little bit more of themselves. Martha guides them in.

The interior of the house is clean and tidy. Light blue carpet is underfoot. The walls are plastered and painted to a neat finish. In a golden frame hanging on the wall is a photo of a boy in boxing gloves holding his arm up. Next to him is a referee and another boxer with a solemn look. Christian closes the front door and follows at the rear. The mother takes them into the living room where a man that resembles the boxer is sat. He doesn't acknowledge anybody or get up from his seat. He just stares. The living room is clean and tidy. It contains a large, blue, L-shaped sofa with a soft cream throw over the back. A TV that is too large for the room it is in, hangs above a plasma screen fire. The room smells of smoke and air freshener.

Christian takes a seat on the arm and watches the mother as she sits with her daughter. She picks up a brand-new doll and encourages her daughter to play. The daughter sits just out of reach. As if she's unsure, but not entirely scared. Her brother sits at Martha's feet and rolls a car across the floor. He interacts with neither parent and makes eye contact with no one apart from Martha. Both children have a look in their eyes that Christian knows well. He studies the mother. Her interactions, her body language and the children's response. The little girl seems unsure but not scared of her. But they are scared of someone. "*No, it's not her. Not entirely. Maybe she's unable to help them when they need it."* The drugs she's addicted to have ruined her looks and she is little more than skin and bone. Her scattered, crooked teeth are yellowish brown and her eyes are sunk. Christian's notes say she has enrolled herself in a program to get clean. It's because of this that she has been allowed supervised access to her kids.

Christian looks at the father. The father looks at Christian. His bright red face and bent, bulbous nose, typical of an alcoholic/junkie. His mouth contains less teeth than his wife. It makes him look years older than he actually is. At first glance you would think he's in his fifties but in actual fact, (and Christian had to look at his records twice to believe it) he's only forty-two. The father fidgets in his seat. His feet tap on the floor. Both hands tap against his knees. Christian makes eye contact with the father for a few seconds and then looks down at the mother and daughter. His mind goes blank and he unconsciously doodles on his paperwork.

"What the fuck are ew writin' now?" The father asks in an unnecessarily angry voice.

"Hmm?" Christian looks up at the father. "Sorry, what?"

"I said. What. The. Fuck. Are. You. Writing now?"

"Excuse me sir, but there's no need for that language is there?" Martha cuts in with her diluted Scottish accent and sweet tone. "There are children here and they shouldn't be hearing that sort of thing. Please, lower your voice, or you'll scare them."

"Dun tell me what to do ew fat old slag."

"Stop it Paul, please. You'll ruin everythin'." The mother stands and tries her best to calm her husband.

The father stands up and pushes the mother back down. The kids hide beside their mother who holds them close by. Martha gets in front of the kids and holds the fathers stare. She may look like Mrs. Doubtfire, but she's ballsy enough to work the doors of most nightclubs. She holds her hands up in front of her to stop him coming forward. "Sir, please, calm down. You're not going to help your situation by becoming angry and aggressive toward us. We've tried our best to come up with a solution that suits everybody and that is what we're doing now. So please, calm down or we will have to review our plans."

"Please Paul. Calm down. They'll take my kids away again otherwise," the mother pleads.

"Shut up you silly bitch! They'll never let 'em live with us anyway. They think we're scum." He points his yellow stained finger at Christian. "Dun ew? He's been lookin down at me all day. I've seen 'im. Lookin' down his nose at me and writin' shit in his book. Wankers like ew love the power dun ew?" He steps toward Christian. "I bet ew was bullied in school, wun ew? Ew faggot! I bet ew couldn' wait to get some power so ew could fuck up ordinary people's lives."

"Sir, please calm down or we'll terminate this meeting right now." Martha says a little more firmly.

"Shut up, ew fat bitch. Dun think ew have the right to tell me what to do in my own 'ouse."

"OK sir, have it your way. Come along children."

The mother bursts into tears when Martha reaches out to take the children's hands. While her back is turned, the father takes a step forward and raises his hand as if to strike. Christian sees this, steps in front of the father. The 'toothless tool' becomes enraged. He swings his right hand at Christian's head, hitting him above the temple. Christian stumbles to his side and protects his face from another strike. The fist misses by inches and his momentum tips the junkie off balance. Christian is quick to react. He grabs the father's arm, twists it behind his back and places his foot between his legs to trap them. They wrestle for a few seconds but eventually, Christian pushes him over. Just before the pair hit the ground, Christian forces the junkies arm up further and pushes his elbow into his shoulder. Christian hears three, very satisfying snaps. Almost instantly, screams of agony follow. "That's what you get for hurting those kids. Next time, I'll break your fucking neck." Christian whispers in his ear.

He rolls off and looks at Martha. "We need to call the police and get them to safety."

"Ew've broken my arm. My arm. My fuckin' arm. Ew've broken my fuckin' arm," the father shouts. Tears roll down his bloated red face.

Christian places a hand on the father's shattered shoulder and uses it to push himself up. The father screams, but no one goes to help. Martha, the mother and the kids are running to safety outside, leaving Christian to stay with the injured man.

Christian sits down on the chair and watches the junkie roll around in agony. He does not help. "Pricks like you shouldn't have kids. You should be sterilized, you junkie fuck."

A few minutes later, Christian hears the sirens. He waits until the very last second before kneeling down beside the injured man. The junkie shouts every obscenity he can think of at Christian, but Christian is doing his best 'concerned citizen' impression when the police walk in. "He won't let me help him. He said his arm is hurt but he won't let me help him."

"It's OK sir. We'll take it from here." The police officers crouch down beside the junkie and Christian gets up and walks outside. Martha is comforting the crying kids by her car. Another police officer is talking to the sobbing mother. As Christian walks past she bends over and throws up over the officer's shoes. Christian gives them a wide birth and continues to Martha's side.

"What a mess," she says.

"I'm really sorry. He just come at me. I didn't know what to do."

"I'm not talking about you. I'm talking about that." Martha points at the sick on the officer's shiny black shoes. "It's going to take a lot more than a wet wipe to clean that up."

Martha holds out her hand to shake Christian's. "You done good today lad. He would have hit me, I'm sure of it." She looks down at the kids. "That's the last time you'll see your father until you say otherwise. I promise." Martha eyes the front of the house as the police officers lead the father out. "I'll make sure to put your brave act into my report. I'll make sure they know I was very scared. Like I feared for my life." Martha winks and Christian smiles at her. "How's your face? Did he hurt you?"

"It's fine." Christian remembers the marks from his own fingernails." Just a glancing blow."

"That's good. He's a big bloke. That's probably why he hurt his arm so much. You know, falling so awkwardly with so much weight." Martha gives Christian another wink and a smile. "OK. Let's give these guys a statement so we can be on our way."

TIPPING THE SCALES

A little after five in the evening, Christian is stood outside his boss's office. He knocks twice and Dave calls him in. The room smells like coffee and a body that has done too many hours in the same clothes. Dave stands up, hits the table with his rather rotund belly and knocks over a framed photo of his children, (the only thing that is on his desk, other than his laptop). He picks it up, gestures to a chair opposite him and sits back down. Christian makes himself comfortable on the hard-plastic chair. "You asked to see me?"

Dave looks at him with his usual serious expression. "Yeah...umm. A little over an hour ago I got off the phone with the police." His monotone voice gives nothing away. "They told me the father's pressing charges against you for the incident that happened earlier today. I've spoken to Martha and the police and I have their version of the events. Now I have to hear yours."

Christian laughs. "Is this a joke Dave?"

"I can assure you I'm quite serious. This a serious matter. The fathers collar bone is broken in two places, and he has a dislocated shoulder. His lawyer is pushing for ABH."

"Really? He was swingin' haymakers around the room. I caught one in the face so I restrained him as best I could. Look." Christian shows Dave the scratches he made with his own fingernails earlier that day. "That's it. That's the whole story. If he wasn't so crazy, then none of it would of happened."

"He's saying you were intentionally aggravating him. He said he never threw a punch and that he was only gesturing. He's saying that you confronted him with aggression and stepped forward, and that's how he struck you. Then you wrapped his arm behind his back and tripped him over. He's also saying he could smell alcohol on your breath. This is also his wife's version of events."

Christian feels his face reddening. His heart begins to race and the adrenaline flushes around his body. There is a moments silence that feels like an age before Dave speaks again.

"I've got no doubt that what you're saying is true because Martha's story is the same as yours. However, these are very serious allegations and while there's a police investigation going on, I think it's wise that you're not on the job. This sort of thing will put a lot of pressure on a person, who's job, by its very nature, is already very stressful, so..." Dave pauses and looks Christian in the eye. "I'm gonna have to suspend you on full pay until this thing blows over. I'm sorry Christian. I think it's our best move."

"Are you serious? Some junkie child beater attacks me, and I get suspended. You gotta be kidding me."

"Hold on Christian. Those are very serious allegations you're making about the father and to date, we don't have any evidence of this. I'm sorry. It's for the best. Think of it as a forced holiday. Once we get this over and done with, you will be back with us."

"Will this be on my record then? I've never put a foot wrong here. I've always been professional."

"Unfortunately, yes, there'll be a record of this, but I have no doubt that the investigation will clear you. You're a wonderful servant to families around here. Once the courts hear so many great things about you, they'll realise how silly this whole thing is. You'll be back before you know it."

The kind words don't help to lighten Christian's mood. "Well, it doesn't look like I have much choice in the matter."

"Unfortunately, not. We'll be in touch as things progress." Dave holds his hand up and Christian rises to shake it. "Keep your head up kid. It'll be fine. We're a family here and we fight for each other all the way."

Christian's eyes start to water as the kindness and sincerity of

Dave's words sink in. He clears his throat, shakes Dave's hand and thanks him. Then he turns around and walks away.

WHAT'S THE POINT
OF IT ALL?

A few hours later, a taxi pulls up behind a blue Astra estate. The door opens and Christian falls out. "You OK mate?" the taxi driver asks. "You need a hand?"

Christian looks up. Two drivers float around in a symmetrical dance. He closes one eye to help his focus. "No, no. I'm good," he slurs. "The bloody floor…" Christian hits the floor with his hand. "It moved that's all. It's always bloody movin'. Do…do you feel it? Round and round and round."

The taxi driver thinks about the question for a second. He responds by closing the door and pulling away from Christian's drive. Christian rolls around on the 'moving floor' and tries to get up. He fails and falls on his arse. As the world around him spins faster than ever, he decides the best course of action is to stay low and crawl to his house. After a minute, he gets to the front door but can't balance enough to stand. Holding tightly to the door handle, he manages to get onto his knees. He removes his keys from his pocket and looks at the swirling, hazy mess of cut metal. He picks one at random, misses the keyhole and falls hard. The impact beats the wind from his lungs, and it takes a while to recapture his breath. He holds his chest while he thinks about a third attempt. Very quickly he decides against it. Instead, he curls up next to the front wheel of his car. Hoping it will stop his world from spinning. It does. The world slows and only for a second, he rests his tired eyes.

HIDDEN FACE TO
THE VOICE

Christian finds himself alone, in a dark room. His hands are not bound, but they will not leave his sides. An invisible force pushes against his chest. He tries to get up, but he cannot pull himself from the bed he is lying on. He looks around the small square room and sees only dark corners and darker shadows. He tries to shout but nothing comes out. Frantically, he struggles with all his strength. His invisible binds get tighter. Digging deep into his skin. He begins to panic. He tries to remember how he came to be in this place, but his memory has gone. He wriggles, kicks, pulls and pushes with all his strength but he does not move an inch. His breathing becomes laboured. His heart pounds. Suddenly a black figure appears from the darkest shadow. He's wearing a black stove-pipe hat and a black suit. He glides toward Christian. Fear overwhelms him, freezing him still. His heart feels like it could burst. The figure in black leans over Christian's petrified form and whispers. "Don't be afraid. It's not your time yet."

ALL TOO MUCH

Christian coughs and splutters back into reality. He sees Mikey, pushing his fingers into his mouth and removing lumps of vomit from his airways. He gasps lung full after lung full of life-saving delicious air. Mikey places him on his side and slaps his back. "You fuckin' idiot. What 'ave ew done?" Christian's head and heart are too preoccupied with survival to entertain an answer. They thump, burn and beat as fast as they can until the oxygen levels are recovered. After four minutes, when Christian's breathing becomes more controlled and his face becomes less blue, Mikey places his head on his lap and sits with him.

"What have you taken?"

"I don't remember."

"Don't be a fuckin' idiot Christan. Tell me, what 'ave you taken?"

"I dunno! Bit of this. Bit of that."

"What were you thinkin' you stupid bastard? You could of died."

Christian can see the pain he's caused his friend. "It wasn't what I wanted mate. I swear. I just needed to forget for a while that's all. I got suspended today." Christian's Adam's apple moves up and down and his eyes wince. "My throats killing me mate. I need a drink to flush it. Give me a hand to get up will you." Mikey helps him to his feet, walks him into his house and sits him down. "I'll get you a drink." When Mikey returns, he hands a bottle of ice-cold water to Christian and opens a beer for himself. "What the fuck are you up to mush? It's not like you to stress about this kind of stuff. You're normally the cool one."

Christian drinks half the bottle. Seconds later, brain-freeze kicks in. "Jesus Christ that's cold."

"Well it would be wouldn' it. It's just come out of the fridge you bute."

Christian holds his breath and shakes his head until the brain-freeze thaws. "Sorry dude. I didn't mean to scare you."

"Well, you did you prick. You're fuckin' lucky I swung by when I did. I just happened to speak to one of the lads in work today and he told me about a social worker breakin' some junkies arm. I had a feelin' it was you, so I thought I'd check. I tried phoning but got no joy. So, I decided to just come and see if you were about." Mikey shakes his head. "Fuckin' dick."

"I'm sorry man."

"That why you're suspended then?"

"Yeah. That smack head and his zombie looking, junkie wife are pressing charges. I'm suspended until it's dealt with. It's fucking bullshit dude."

Christian explains all the details to Mikey and Mikey agrees that it is in fact, "fuckin' bullshit." Then Mikey goes back to the fridge to get another bottle for the pair of them. Christian places the water by his feet and takes Mikey's beer off him. He drinks the whole thing down and tries his best to deal with the next wave of painful brain-freeze.

"I dun think you should be doin' that mate. Your bodies already told you it's had enough for one day." Mikey says.

"And I'm telling my body to man up or fuck off."

"Fair enough. Just thought I'd act like a concerned friend that's all." Mikey grabs himself a beer.

"You sure you're alright mate. I'm really worried about you. It's not like you at all. Is there anything I can do to help? Anything at all?"

Christian can see the worry in Mikey's eyes. "I'll be fine dude. I promise. Just a bad day at the office that's all. I suppose it was bound to happen sooner or later with all the wankers we work with."

"I suppose, but if you do think of anything, then let me help, OK? Other than that, all I can say is try not to dwell on it too much. Like your boss told you. You're a good social worker and I know for a fact that Swansea will be worse off without you around helping people."

Mikey's kind words actually bring a lump to Christian's throat and a tear to his eye. Christian swigs from his beer to hide the effect it had on him. "Thanks mate," he says eventually. "So, what's happening with that Bullen case now? Have you heard anything?"

Mikey studies Christian for a few seconds before sitting down. "Yeah, I've heard bits and bobs. Just before he died, he went down on record about the names and details in his confession. I mean he's named top lawyers, judges, politician's, some police as well as your average Joe paedo. He's name dropped a shit tonne of the UK's elite." Mikey pauses and takes a sip from his bottle. "However, the accused are trying to dismiss it as slander. Their saying he's a mentally unstable man that's trying to destroy the reputations of honest, god-fearing people."

"And now he's dead."

"Yip. Dead as fuck."

What happens to the case now?" Christian asks.

"Well, the reporter made copies of his confession. Rumour has it, she's threatenin' to reveal it publicly in all of its dirty details. But, at the moment there's not a paper in town that's gonna print it. That's the problem we face."

Mikey takes Christian's empty bottle. "You want a brew?"

"No, I want a whiskey."

Mikey, compromises and grabs two more beers. "Take your time on this one please."

Christian places the beer by his feet. "Yes, mommy."

"Anyway." Mikey continues. "I'm not sure what else we can do. I mean the thought of them getting away with their crimes sickens me. It's all I think about."

"You're back in work now, Mikey. Surely there's a lot of talk about this. Surely the cops are looking to nail these bastards."

"Of course, but it's not easy. These are powerful people, Christian. They're gonna do everythin' they can to try and quash this. I mean look at Bullen. He was meant to be protected but I've heard a serial rapist was able to get into his cell for the last five days of his life. He was probably bummed every night for the best part of a week before he topped himself. If he did kill himself. I mean who knows what these guys will do to protect themselves."

Christian chokes on the beer he's drinking. "A rapist..." he clears his throat and looks at Mikey to see if it's a joke. Mikey's face says it's not. "Well, good enough for the sick bastard. I hope the rapist was hung like a donkey. What goes around comes around mother fucker."

"Yeah, he got what he deserved but it's also made this case much harder. His confession is just ink on paper without him there to back it up on the stand."

"So, what are we going to do? You made a copy of his confession. You have that list of names. Can we snatch one of them and make them squeal?"

"It's too much risk right now. The cops are all over them and a lot of them are in hiding and speaking through attorneys."

Christian stands up and starts pacing the room. He swigs the last of the beer and wipes the froth that spills down his cheek. "There's gotta be something mate. There's no fucking way they're getting away with this."

"I know mate, I know, but we gotta be smart. If an opportunity shows itself then we strike, but other than that. I say we let this reporter lead the charge. She's relentless mate. She won't give up on this."

Christian goes to fetch another beer. "OK. We'll leave it to her for now." When he gets to the fridge, he holds a beer up. "You staying or what?"

"Yeah, I might as well. Got nowhere else to be."

"What do you mean? I thought you and her, were good?" Christian smirks. "What did you do?"

Mikey nearly chokes on the last of his beer. "What do you mean? What did I do? Why's it automatically my fault?"

"I know you Mikey. I've known you for a long time."

"Ah, it's nothin' really. You know, just the usual. Nightmares, boozin', mood swings. To be honest I think we're pretty much done now anyway. We can't keep arguin' all the time. It's no good for either of us. She deserves better than me I think."

"Well, that's a shame mate. Really." Christian reaches into his pocket and pulls out two bags of different sizes. "I've got green and mushrooms. You up for it?"

Mikey smiles" I thought you were dead against drugs now. What's happenin' to you dude."

"What's happening is, I've had a tit full of trying to be a good guy all the time when life clearly wants me to be bad. From the moment I was born it's been beating me down. Life can suck my dick and choke on my balls."

Mikey laughs.

"Seriously dude. Suck it and choke. Have I ever told you what my first memory is?"

Mikey shakes his head. "Dun think so."

"It's being slapped across the face by my mother. That's my very first memory. It's like she literally slapped all my senses online. What the fuck like. I've had enough mush. It's bollocks."

"So what? You're just givin' up now? Is that it?"

"No," Christian rubs his tired eyes. "I'm just switching off from everything for a while. For a long while if I can. Fuck it. You remember when we were on the streets with no one to look after us but ourselves. We were cold, hungry but we had each other."

Mikey smiles. "And drugs. We had lots of drugs and drink. We were off our tits for most of it I think."

"Exactly. For the briefest of moments and before that shit really took hold, we could forget about all the madness that we'd been through and all the stuff that was happening at that time. Right now, I just want that. To be with my mate and forget for a while." Christian shakes the bags in his hand. "Are you coming with me on this trip? There's room for one more."

Mikey takes the bag with the cannabis in and smells it. "Wow. You really are makin' the most of your free time, aren't you? It's a good thing I'm on holiday now and I can keep you company ain't it?"

"Jesus. You have more time off than the Queen. No wonder this country is going to shit. The coppers are all off their tits on holiday."

Mikey laughs and grabs a handful of mushrooms. "Not all of them mate. There's some good ones out there."

"But not you though?" Christian says as he begins to roll a joint.

"No, not me. I am not a good cop. Not good at all."

TICKETS PLEASE

Christian is lying on his back, staring at the ceiling while white artex shells dance around him in perfect symmetry. His head feels light. His body, heavy. Mikey has followed tiny colourful creatures behind the sofa. He's laughing as they blow multi-coloured hearts in the air and he pops them with his multi-coloured feathered hands.

"You're just so beautiful. Can I keep you? Can I?" Mikey whispers. He crawls after them while they frolic around the room. "Don't run away. Wait for me, little ones."

The shells on the ceiling begin to melt and slip down the walls. Christian gets up and tries to stop them. He pushes against the wall with his hands, but the shells keep falling. They melt onto his hands and become like scales on his skin. He starts to panic. He shakes his hands, but the scales are too sticky. They creep toward his face and start to devour him. He jumps back on the sofa and closes his eyes. "It's just a trip. It's just a trip." He looks at his hands again and the shells have gone. He tries to regain his grip on the trip but when he sees Mikey crawling around the floor laughing, paranoia kicks in. *What's he laughing at? What's he doing. He can see them, can't he? He can see those bloody scales. They're on me, aren't they? Shit. Get them off. Get them off."* Christian jumps to his feet and rushes to the kitchen. He grabs a knife and scrapes it across his skin. When a trickle of crimson appears, he panics even more. He runs upstairs to his bedroom and barges the door open. Light from the landing reflects onto a mirror and he catches a glimpse of someone inside it. It stops him in his tracks. He recognises the person. It's the man from his dream. It's the shadow man in the stove pipe hat. Christian approaches cautiously. The knife held tight in his hand. He sees the hat and the cloak but no face. As if the man has his back to him. Christian touches the mirror. The shadow man doesn't move. "Who are you?" Christian asks.

"Me?" The shadow man asks. "I am nothing and everything."

"Why are you here?" Christian shouts.

"I am here because you are here, and I will leave when you do."

"Are you an angel?"

The shadow man laughs his evil laugh and the mirror starts to shake.

"Who are you?" Christian shouts.

The shadow man turns around. Christian sees his own face, with the flesh torn or eaten away. He yells and stabs the knife into the mirrors frame. The shadow man doesn't flinch, but an eel slithers out from his open mouth. Christian jumps into his bed and cowers beneath the sheets. The shadow man in the mirror, laughs his evil laugh.

I WANT MY
MONEY BACK

Christian wakes in a pool of sweat. Daylight shines through the weave of the duvet. Birds are singing outside. He feels... weird. Like the feeling you get when you know you've done wrong and you know you've been caught doing it. It's anxiety and paranoia with other emotions mixed in. Last night's antics are a blur. While he tries to remember, he lifts one side of the duvet to let some fresh air in. His mouth is dry and sticky. He reaches over to the glass that's beside his bed. It's warm to the touch and has bubbles on the inside of the glass. He checks it for floaties and drinks the lot down. Something unseen in the glass hits the back off his throat and makes him gag.

Suddenly a noise from close by startles him. He turns around to see Mikey slapping the knife in the mirror from side to side. "Bad trip was it?"

"Bloody awful mate. If I could, I'd ask for my money back." He clears his throat. "How was yours?"

"I laughed so much I peed myself a little bit." Mikey points to the stain in his crotch. "Was worth it though. Got carpet burns on my knees too, from chasing little smurfy, womble like animals around all night." He lifts a trouser leg to show the evidence. "They're really sore mind." He gently shuffles the trousers back around his ankles. "What the fuck happened to you?"

Christian tells Mikey about his trip and the reason he flipped out. Mikey laughs. "Told you it wasn't a good idea takin' everythin' you did, less than an hour after I found you chokin' to death."

"I'll make sure I contact the manufacturers and tell them. They should probably put that on their labels."

Mikey laughs. "Good luck with that." He pulls the knife out of the wooden frame and rubs its blade across his thumb. "You know you'll get through this mate, don't you? You're good at your job. Very good. Your boss knows that too."

"I hope your right mate. I don't know what I'll do otherwise."

Mikey flips the knife in his hands a couple of times. "It's got a nice balance this knife. It feels good in your hand."

"Yeah, I know. I thought the same thing when I held it."

Mikey stops flipping the knife and looks at Christian. "What's the plan for today?"

Christian thinks for a few seconds. "I think I need to do some good."

"What kind of good? Good as in smashing up bad guys or another kind? Because, I'll be honest. I'm really not in the mood for anything violent Christian. I feel a bit emotional like."

Christian laughs. "Yeah, me too mate. Don't worry, I don't mean the violent kind of good. I mean like, good in the community sort of good. We still have twenty grand of Bobby boy's money. We could do a bit of shopping again. See what's about. The list I've got is pretty big now anyway and if we leave it any longer, we'll never get it done."

"Oh, yeah. OK man. That sounds like a great plan. Let's have a bit of breaky and start to plan it all out. I really fancy pancakes."

"Ooh, pancakes sound amazing. Pancakes with banana and chocolate spread. I'm gonna make a joint too. I need something to take the edge off."

Mikey laughs. "Already have mate. They're downstairs."

SPECIAL DELIVERY

A few hours later the lads are fed, watered and still a little bit stoned. They've hired a van, put false number plates on it and are driving into town. They stop at a large store and Christian pulls out his list to check the items he needs. He puts on a disguise and jumps out leaving Mikey, to park the van. Mikey picks a spot near the loading bay, pulls his hat over his eyes and stretches out. The best of nineties Britpop plays quietly through the speakers. A half-eaten bag of onion rings sits on the dashboard.

Over an hour later, Christian is sneaking up to the window that Mikey is leaning against. He looks in the mirror. Mikey is dead to the world. He has his orange stained mouth open and his eyes closed. Christian creeps forward until he's beside the door. He's close enough to see Mikey's breath steaming up the window. Christian bangs hard on the window and opens the door. A terrified Mikey jumps up and falls out of the van. Christian laughs so hard that he's unable to catch Mikey as he intended too. His unamused mate falls hard onto the concrete floor.

"You dozy bastard. What you do that for? You're gonna give me a heart attack one day."

Christian fights to control his laughter. It's over a minute before he can help Mikey up. "I'm just trying to keep you on your toes mate. You let your guard down for one second and this world will eat you up."

"Well you can call it a success then mate, because I am officially, on my fucking toes now." Mikey's holds his chest. "Jesus. I think my heart's gonna burst."

"Stop being so dramatic." Christian says laughing. It takes

them a few seconds longer to gather their heads. "OK, are you good?" He asks Mikey.

Mikey dusts off his trousers. "No, I'm fuckin' not."

"Good. Now for my next test, I'd like you to reverse the van into that loading bay." Christian points to the two boys in Hi-Viz vests and well over two dozen boxes of different sizes. "Make sure you have your disguise on." Then he walks back to join the lads on the loading bay. When the van is in place, Christian double checks the items are correct before he and the assistants load them. "Three cookers 500mm wide. Two cookers 600mm wide. Four fridge freezers. Two fridges. One microwave. One freezer. Five TV's (of different sizes and specifications). Five PlayStations and five Xbox's (with dozens of games)." The list went on.

Mikey puts on his disguise and joins in with the loading. "Top of the morning to you lads," he says in his best Irish accent.

The shop assistants give him a nod and about twenty minutes later the van is loaded and the assistants are walking away with a healthy tip from Bobby boy.

"Where to first?" Mikey asks.

"Well, we should start at the nearest point and work our way out I suppose. So, I'd go to..." Christian taps a pen on his teeth while he thinks. "Bonymaen. Mrs. Davies' fridge-freezer broke and she can't afford another. Last time we spoke she was going to get one of those short-term loans to pay for one." Christian shakes his head at the thought. "I'm telling you those fuckers will keep her in debt for a lifetime if they get hold of her. So, I'd say she is the first customer. Plus, I bought a TV and Play-Station for her boy David. He's a good kid and he's had to grow up fast and help out around the house a lot since her illness. So, I thought it would be nice for him to be able to switch off from it all from time to time."

"Aww see." Mikey scruffs Christian's hair. "It's not true what they say about you is it? You're not a complete wanker, really are you?"

Christian shoves Mikey's hand away and sorts out his hair.

"No, not all the time. Just most of it."

Mikey laughs. "OK, cool. Bonymaen it is. I still think we should of got two vans. We could of picked the rest of the stuff up from the lock up and done it all today then. Now we'll probably have to double back on ourselves."

"Well, we can see how we get on with these. To be honest mate, I think lugging this lot up to some of these houses will be more than enough work for today. Especially considering I still feel a bit ropey from yesterdays antics."

"Yeah, you're probably right. You're not really built for manual labour either. Are you?" Mikey says squeezing Christian's bicep.

Christian shrugs Mikey's hand away again. "Speak for yourself mate. I'm a machine."

"We'll see. First one to drop something loses and has to get the pints in later is it?"

"Deal. Let's get moving then. The sound of a free pint has made me thirsty."

Fifteen minutes later the lads are carrying a 'stupid, heavy piece of shit' fridge-freezer up twenty-three steps that have brambles hanging over on one side and slippery moss under foot. When they get to the top, Mikey drops his end to the floor and sits down next to it gasping for air. Christian rings the doorbell and laughs. A few minutes go by and nobody answers. Christian looks at Mikey who is still sat on the floor. His dark hair has begun to stick to his sweaty red face. "We probably should have knocked to see if anyone was in first."

Mikey looks like he's lost the will to live. "Doesn't matter if she's in or not. This lot is staying here now."

Another minute passes before they hear a rattling lock and the door opens. A lady in her late thirties, with bags under her eyes, stands in the doorway. Christian tips his cap to her. "Good afternoon Miss. We are here on behalf of the 'People that help' charity. We are pleased to tell you that you have won this top of the range fridge-freezer." He points to the TV and PlayStation that is hiding behind it. "And this games console and TV."

"What do you mean? I haven't entered any draw or raffle. How have I won anything?"

"You didn't have to enter anything. We've heard good things about you and your family and that's all we needed. And every now and again we get gifts from superstores to reward families like yours." Christian gives her his warmest smile. Suddenly a boy of ten appears by Mrs. Davies' side. Christian grabs the PlayStation and hands it to him. "This is for you David. For looking after your mummy so well. And you have a brand-new TV to play it on too." A huge smile appears on his face. He looks at his Mum and she bursts into tears. "Is this true? Are these really for us?"

"Yes, they are. Think of it as a thank you for all the help you've done around the community."

Mrs. Davies becomes inconsolable and Christian gives her a hug. "It's the least you deserve." He looks down at the young boy. "The two of you deserve this. Good people deserve good things."

Once the tears have gone, Mikey and Christian carry the fridge-freezer into the house and bring the old, "heavy piece of shit" fridge-freezer back down the steps and dump it on the roadside.

"One down, lots more to go." Christian says as he picks a tired Mikey up off the floor again.

"I've always said that this is the stupidest idea you've ever had. Why do I always help you? Next time I'm definitely makin' sure I'm in work." He wipes his sweaty face. "These disguises are boiling hot as well. Why did I ever agree to this?"

"Because you're a good guy Mikey. Well, sometimes. I tell you what. Once we are done, I'll get the beers in. Even though you dropped the fridge."

"I fuckin didn't. I placed it down."

"You're such a liar. Your soft, baby fingers couldn't hold it anymore and you dropped it, you minge."

"Bollocks. I'll take you up on the beer offer though." Mikey checks his watch. "Is it too early to have one now?"

"Once we finish, I said." Christian checks the time. "If we get them all done by four, I may even treat you to a nice steak and chips too. So, you better put your foot down, driver."

Christian jumps in, puts his seat belt on and takes one last look at the house. He sees the nets in the window move and Mrs. Davies holds an envelope in her hand. She waves for him to return. Christian shakes his head. She opens the envelope revealing the one thousand pound he left for her inside the fridge.

Christian smiles at her and gives her a thumbs up.

Mrs Davies wipes her eyes. "Thank you," she mouths.

"You're very welcome," he says, waving her goodbye.

Mikey puts his foot down and Christian beams from ear to ear. He feels an enormous amount of pride that he has helped to take a little bit of pressure away from an already struggling household.

IS THERE A LIGHT AT THE END?

Seven hours and sixteen minutes later, the lads have dropped the van and disguises off. An exhausted Mikey is being helped into a seat by Christian, who has tears streaming down his face.

"It's not funny you prick! I've really hurt it mun!"

Christian pulls up a seat beside him and sits down. He tries to talk to Mikey but he's laughing too much.

"If I never see a bloody fridge again it'll be too soon. I'm tellin' you. I've got a new-found respect for delivery men. Doin' that shit all day is tough like." Mikey fidgets in his seat and winces from the pain. Christian laughs even more. "You're a heartless prick mind. Go make yourself useful and get the beers in will ew."

Christian wipes his tears, gets up and walks to the bar.

"And don't forget the food. I want steak and chips with all the trimmings after what's happened to me today. It's the least you can do."

A minute or two later, Christian is placing two pints of lager down on the table when a lady walks past and says hi. Christian takes one quick glance at her, says hi back and sits down next to Mikey. The lady stands a few feet away from him and stares. She has silver/purple hair and... "Oh shit," Christian says standing up. "Katy, hi. I'm sorry, I didn't recognise you. You've changed your hair?"

Katy glides her manicured nails through her hair. "Yeah, do you like it?

"It's purple."

"It's lavender grey actually. Do you like it?"

"Oh, yeah, yeah. It looks really nice." Christian smiles at Katy. Katy smiles back. "I'm sorry you've kind of thrown me. You look beautiful."

Katy's smile gets bigger and she leans in for a kiss. "I was beginnin' to think you were ignoring me?"

"Yeah, I'm sorry I..."

Christian's apology gets interrupted by Mikey, who clears his throat really loudly. Christian and Katy look down.

"Shit, sorry. Katy, I'd like you to meet my friend, Mikey. He's an old friend. Mikey, this is Katy. She's the girl I told you about."

"When?" Mikey asks. "When did you tell me about her?"

Christian blushes and Katy gives him a very accusing look. "The weekend I saw you and I still had my works clothes on. Remember?"

Katy places her hands on her hips. Christian can feel Katy's eyes burning into him. He starts to panic.

Mikey laughs. "Oh, right that girl. I thought you were making her up." He holds his hand out to shake Katy's hand, but the movement hurts him. He quickly pulls it back down. "I'm sorry. I don't mean to be rude, but I've done my back in."

"No need to apologise Mikey. You sit there and rest."

"Thanks." Mikey smiles at her and looks at Christian's bright red face. "Yeah, I thought he was making you up because he's usually rubbish with girls. Really rubbish actually. But he seems to be changing that, fair do's." Mikey winks at Christian. "You know I was wondering why you had the sudden urge to come here. I mean, we must of passed about five decent boozers before we got here. And normally we woulda gone in any one of them, but you insisted on coming here. Now I know why."

Christian shrugs his shoulders and laughs. "Don't know what you're on about dude. It's just a coincidence." He looks at Katy. "Will you join us for a drink or two?"

"Oh, no I'd better not. I'm meeting Steph for a bite to eat and a drink. We wouldn't want to intrude."

"Don't be silly. You won't be intruding." Christian pulls out a seat. "Please."

"Yeah please join us." Mikey adds.

Katy sits down and Christian goes to get her a drink. When he returns, Steph is approaching the table. He introduces everybody, takes the food orders and goes to get Steph a drink. When he returns, he hears Mikey telling the girls a little bit about himself.

"Oh, you're a policeman are you?" Steph leans toward Mikey and plays with her hair. Katy notices this, looks at Christian and smiles. Christian looks back at her with a confused look on his face. "What?" he whispers in her ear.

Katy nods at Steph and Mikey.

"What about them?"

Katy rolls her eyes. "You're hopeless."

Christian sits down none the wiser about what is going on with Steph and Mikey and places his hand on Katy's. "You really do look beautiful. Sorry about not texting. I've had a lot of things to deal with."

"No worries handsome. Is everythin' OK now?"

Christian looks into Katy's bright blue eyes. He wants to tell her about his job and the suspension, but he fights the urge. He smiles at her. "Yeah, everything's fine." He takes a mouthful of his beer and looks down. Katy's smile fades. She strokes Christian's hand with hers as they sit in silence. Mikey sees Christian's sad face and kicks him in the shin. Christian winces in pain. "What's that for?"

"Muscle spasm mate. Sorry. My back's really giving me grief." Mikey fidgets in his seat to try and confirm his lie. Christian looks at him suspiciously.

"So, what brings the two of you out tonight? Business or pleasure?" Steph asks.

"Pleasure," Mikey answers. "I had holidays to take, so I give Christian a ring to see if he fancied a few. What about you two?"

"Pleasure." Steph answers. "I dun have my kids tonight, so we are 'out out'. You two fancy a few in town after this? There's a band on down the vaults later. They're meant to be really good like. They're called the riff."

"I would, but I dun think my back would let me." Mikey answered.

"Is it really that bad?" Steph asks.

"Yeah. It's bloody killing me."

"Awe. How'd you do it?"

"Two days ago, I tackled a thief to the ground after he robbed an old people's home." He looks at Christian and smiles. "It's been bad ever since."

Christian shakes his head in disgust.

"Aww, you're so brave. You're like a real-life hero, aren't you?"

"Well, maybe" Mikey said, failing to hide his smugness. "But I'm just doin' my job. You know police officers have to put the wellbeing of civilians before themselves on a regular basis."

Steph's fidgety fingers become tangled in her hair and she fights to get them loose. Katy laughs and Steph blushes. Christian sits there wondering what on earth is going on.

A little while later the food is brought out and the four of them tuck in while the conversations continue. They talk about crime. They talk about pets and kids. They talk about traffic. They talk about everything that people talk about when beer and food is flowing, and the atmosphere is pleasant. Then, out of nowhere, the atmosphere changed, and Christian became quiet. Something out of the corner of his eye distracts him and he stops talking midsentence. His head turns and the colour drains from his face. Katy asks him if he's OK, but he ignores her. He stands up and walks to the TV. His eyes fixed on the image of a man.

Katy walks up behind him and touches his arm." Are you OK handsome?"

Christian jumps at the touch. "It's him," she hears him whisper.

Mikey and Steph are quick to follow behind. Mikey grabs Christian's shoulder for his own support as much as Christian's. "You alright mate? You look sick."

"It's him," he answers. A tear falls down Christian's cheek and Mikey looks at the screen. He reads the words that are running along the bottom of the TV and pulls Christian's shoulder harder. "Not here mate. We gotta go. Come on." Mikey makes an excuse and as quickly as he can manage, ushers his friend out the door while the girls look on confused.

THE KID IV

Hard soles hit the highly polished floor and echo along the cream and gold corridor. Upon the walls, hang pictures of beautiful scenery and important looking people in scarlet robes and white wigs. Latin words and Roman numerals are scattered here and there upon gold coloured tiles. Dozens of people in suits walk past him. None make eye contact. Some are carrying clip boards. Others carry files filled with paperwork. The Kid sits quietly on a hard-wooden bench. The new shirt and trousers he's wearing are itchy and restricting. He fights the urge to undo a button or two. On his left side is a person that's supposed to help him. Someone who knows law. Her voice has a tone of authority, like a teacher. Her eyes and smile are warm and friendly. Sat on his right-hand side is Kim. She is much slimmer than she was when they first met. Her eyes are bloodshot. Her make-up barely disguises the bags they carry. Every night over the last few weeks she's been in the Kid's corner, fighting for him. Her opponents, the man she married and the girl she gave birth too. The Kid would sit in his room as the family would scream at each other below. Gwyn, the daughter was usually the instigator and aggressor. She would fire insults at her mother for sticking by the Kid. Her mother would counter in defence. Like amateur fencers, but the fight would last for hours. Gwyn would lunge with her usual; he's a psychopath. I can't believe you want him to stay. Her mother would parry with; we made a commitment to help him. We don't just give up on people. That's not the type of family we are. Gwyn would riposte with; but he's not family though, is he? You practically picked him up off the streets six months ago. "Exactly," her mother would reply. "He was a young boy living on the streets. He was probably terrified. And you want to send him back there do you?" On and on and on and on. Louder and louder until finally, Pete, the referee, would call time on the bout. Both opponents would storm off to their individual rooms to cool down. Kim's room was normally the kitchen. She would grab a bottle of red wine and a large glass and would only been seen again once it was gone. Sometimes, she would be carrying a second bottle by then, or even a third. Gwyn's room was her bedroom. Loud music and tears were her remedy. The rematch would be scheduled for about twenty hours later.

A door to his left opens. The Kid watches as a teary, red-eyed boy, not much older than him, is led out by a policeman. A lady in a black dress exits a few seconds later. Her eyes are red too, but not from tears. She is uncomfortable on her feet like his mum used to be. She looks around, pulls a hip flask from her purse and follows.

Kim sees the Kid watching the doors and holds his hand. She smiles at him. Her smile doesn't hide the worry in her eyes. She hasn't spoken much these last few days. Nobody in that house has. Although Gwyn has been happier. Her looks have held a certain smugness.

A man in a black suit opens the door, looks at the Kid and calls him in. Kim takes a napkin from her bag and wipes her eyes. The legal lady and the Kid stand up and approach the man. When he's at the door, Kim grabs the Kid and hugs him. It's a long, tight hug. Her tears roll down his neck. "I'm sorry," she whispers. "I'm so very sorry."

"Don't be silly." The Kid pulls away, just far enough to see her face. "You got nothing to be sorry for." A small, golden pendent hangs from a delicate gold necklace around Kim's neck. It's in the shape of a heart. Inside the pendent is a photograph of a baby boy. Kim would say that the boy would have been about the same age as the Kid. She always had a tear in her eye when she said it. He would watch her, sitting beside the window in the kitchen with a glass of wine, staring at it for ages. "You've been really good to me." The Kid says with an honest smile. "Better than my own mum ever did." They embrace and shed a tear or two together for one last time. Then they enter.

The room is big. It has rows of wooden benches along each end. Some are filled with people. Long purple curtains, frame several, stained glass windows. It reminds the Kid of a church, only lighter. In the center, at the far end, a man in funny clothing stood. The Kid remembers him from last time. He's the judge. Below him, sat a lady with a typewriter. The Kid follows the woman with the clip board to a seat. Kim stays at the back of the room. While standing at the dock, the Kid has a chance to look at the faces on the seats opposite. One man in particular, catches his eye. The man that's staring at him. A man that looks similar to the boy he beat. The Kid looks away.

When everyone is ready, the judge asks the Kid to confirm his name and other details. The Kid does as he's asked, and he's allowed to sit. Then his lawyer takes to the floor. She pleads to the judge for leniency. She tells the Judge that the Kid has pleaded guilty because he knows that his actions were wrong. That much is true. The Kid knows he should have stopped beating him sooner. However, he disagrees that he should never have beaten him at all. He just couldn't stop himself at the time. His lawyer says that the Kid's the product of a broken home. She emphasises, that he's been working with his foster carer to deal with anger issues. That much was not true. He's never been angry with or around Kim. She was always so kind to him. When the Kid's lawyer had finished, another man took the floor. "The prosecution," his lawyer whispers. The Kid remembers him too. He uses words like: Psychotic episode. Loner. Angry. Violent tendencies. Broken home. Drug abuse. When he's finished, the Judge silences the room to give his verdict. He says something the Kid has never heard before. He says the words; psychological evaluation. The Kid hears sobbing from behind him. He looks back and sees Kim crying.

He smiles at her and whispers, "It's Ok. I'll be OK."

The judge goes on to say that the Kid will be sent to a care home for a minimum of twelve months. The name of the care home is Bryniau Du. There, he will be evaluated until the doctors say that he is no longer a threat to society. Throughout the whole of his sentencing, the men in the seat opposite were smiling. No more than that. They were beaming from ear to ear.

Once the Judge had finished, the Kid was led outside by a police officer. Kim was no longer in her seat and she was not outside the room either. The Kid new she wouldn't be. He could tell in her eyes that she had no fight left for him. She could no longer alienate herself from her own flesh and blood to fight his cause. It was the right choice of course, for her and her family. The Kid understood completely.

The Kid and the police officer walked through the busy courthouse side by side. His lawyer was five feet at the rear looking through the file of her next case. She also, had done all she could for the Kid at Kim's request. "Ultimately," she said, "he was getting off lightly. By pleading guilty he was excepting the charges. Those charges could have meant juvenile detention and those, she stipulated, can be tough places to be. A few months in a care home, being treated by doctors should be a breeze compared to it. She smiled when she said that.

The police officer stopped at the back of the building and opened the thick wooden doors. A large white van with mesh over the windows was on the other side. Its back door is open and a large prison guard holding a truncheon is leaning against it.

"This the last one?" The prison guard asks. He's a big man, broad shouldered and a well-kept beard. His accent is like something from the gangster films his dad used to watch.

"Yeah, this is him," the police officer answers.

"Dun look so fackin' psychotic to me. Looks like a scared little kid. What he do that they sending him up there for?"

"Violent assault."

"Violent fackin' assault. What, with those stringy arms?" The prison guard looks him up and down and chuckles. "You're havin' a fackin' laugh ain't yah. Seen tougher looking toddlers than this one."

The Kids lawyer clears her throat to remind them of her presence. The prison guard tips his cap to apologise and opens a steal gate inside the van. Before the police officer can hand the Kid over, the lawyer takes the Kid's hand. She holds it tenderly. "You make sure you keep your nose clean in there." She says with warmth in her voice. "You are nothing like they say you are. You're a good Kid, with a bright future. Don't let those crazy bastards up there make you think you belong. OK? Six months and out. You can have a bright future ahead of you. I've seen way worse lads than you turn it around. A lot bloody worse."

The Kid smiles and nods his head. "Six and out. Piece of cake." He shakes the lawyer's hand. "Thanks." Then he turns around and enters the van. His next stop, the care home named Bryniau Du.

PAST NIGHTMARES

Back at the house, Mikey is trying his best to calm Christian down as he paces the living room floor. His head is down, his shoulders hunched, and his fists clenched tightly. The new TV is smashed in the corner from the kick Christian gave it.

"That's him, I'm telling you. I'll never forget that filthy fucking perverts face. It's fucking him Mikey, definitely."

Mikey tries to get out of the chair to stop Christian throwing the plant pot. He's too slow. It crashes against the wall, sending earth and shards of hardened clay across the room.

"Please mate, calm down. We can figure this all out. We just need to think about it with cool heads. Please sit down. I'll grab us some beers and we can sit and talk. Smashin' your house up isn't gonna help. If there's any more noise the neighbours are gonna come snoopin' or even worse the police will. Please mate. Calm down."

Christian stops pacing and looks at the damage he's caused. His hands scratch at his face and he takes long, deep breaths. After a minute he looks up. "OK. OK, I'm calm."

Mikey struggles to his feet and grabs two beers. He hands one to Christian and slowly, painfully sits back down.

"Your back still bad then?" Christian asks.

"Yeah, it's killing me. I'm gonna need some painkillers. Do we have anything left."

"Don't think so." Christian smiles.

"Really wish you weren't such a gutsy bastard the last few weeks. Fuckin' pill popper."

"Fucking rich coming from a coke head." Christian laughs and Mikey makes himself as comfortable as possible. "I'm glad my agony makes you happy."

"I'm far from happy Mikey. But it is rather amusing." Christian makes himself comfortable as well and takes a drink. After drinking half the bottle, he places it by his feet, crouches over it and puts his head in his hands. "Ahh, what am I gonna do mate? I mean there's no way I can live with myself if I do nothing. Now that I've seen his face again and got a name, he has to pay."

"There's every chance he will pay mate. Someone's already accused him of sexual abuse and the likelihood is there will be others. That reporter chick and dozens of others are all over this story. If she's got one victim willing to make a statement, then you can guarantee she'll find more. One by one they'll come forward. Mate, you remember what is was like in that place. Fuckin' hell it was everywhere." Mikey takes a big drink of his beer. He squeezes his temples to push his own demons away. After a few seconds he opens his eyes to the room and his friend. "The police are investigating it mate and he will have to answer to them. Just because he's a politician doesn't mean he's above the law. They'll investigate no matter what. They'll bring him down mate, I'm sure of it."

"What if it's not enough? What if I need to be the one to make him pay for what he's done? What if a prison sentence isn't enough for me? And to be honest mate, I really don't think it will be."

Mikey looks into Christian's eyes more serious than he's ever done before. "We can't go after a politician mate. They'll hunt us down, find us and throw away the key. We have too much to live for. Let the police do their work and then the courts."

Christian stands up, finishes his beer and starts to pace the room again.

"Stay calm mate. Christian! Christian!" Mikey slaps his hands to get his friends attention. Christian turns to Mikey. "I am calm. I'm just thinking."

"Good to hear. What are you thinking?"

"I'm thinking a few things. I'm thinking about what I'm going to do to that sick bastard if the police fail me. But... I'm also thinking that I'm going to struggle to sleep tonight. Which leads me on to my next thought." Christian smiles.

"Which is?" Mikey asks.

"I'm pretty sure there's a bottle of something from Bobby Boy's stash under my bed."

Mikey crosses his fingers and looks to the heavens. "Please let it be pain killers. Please let it be pain killers."

Christian laughs. "OK Mikey. I'll do it your way. I'll wait to see what the police do. But if they fail me and everyone else he's abused, then I'm going after this fucker. I'll make him pay the old fashioned way."

"If that happens Christian, then I'll help you. I give you my word." Mikey tries to stand again. He gives up with a sigh and sits down. "Providing you bring me those drugs and also a bottle or something to piss in."

THE PLACE WHERE NIGHTMARES BREED

Rattling keys scratch around a keyhole. A handle squeaks and a lock clicks open. Pleas from a frightened child echo along the corridor. The door closes. The Kid lay in his bed, looking up at the blackness. The blood thumps around his body and he fights the temptation to vomit. As quietly as he can, he rolls over in his bed. He holds a pillow firmly over his head to drown out the struggle in the room next door. It works until the bed's wooden legs, scrape over the cold tiled floor. The child in the room next door, screams.

The Kid knows what that means. It's happened to him once before. His stomach boils as his mind takes him back in time to every form of abuse he's ever had. From the broken arm for answering back to the blackened eye because he didn't eat his food. His parents were big on punishment. They hurt him, at every opportunity they could. Now this place is doing it, and not just to him. The place is filled with joyless children. There are no smiles on faces. No carefree playing. No shoulders to cry on. Their childhood is being stripped away from them for the pleasure of sick bastards. The light in their eyes has gone. It has been replaced by the darkest of thoughts as their souls are dragged into a bottomless void. As the minutes pass by, his memories go deeper and darker. Eventually his mind is drowning in the faces of all the people he hates. Suddenly he's standing by the river again watching the hedgehog swim for its life. That helpless feeling that the poor little animal must have felt, adds to his sickness. Why did he do it? What was he searching for? Then something in him snaps and he's back in the care home but his mind has changed. *"No. No, not tonight. I won't allow it."* He throws the pillow onto the floor and reaches under his bed. The feel of cold hard steel tingles upon his heightened senses. Sickness and fear leave him. Courage overwhelms him.

He walks through his dark room to the outline of a slightly darker door and feels around for the handle. The noise from the room next door becomes louder. More intimate. More invading. The cries from somebody in need, steadies the Kid's resolve. He is no longer scared. He will do what he must. He glides his thumb against the cold hard blade and walks toward the noise. His heart beats, faster and faster, but he feels like he's in complete control. He does not tremble, he does not shake. He is a hunter. Once he's at the doorway he turns in without breaking a stride. The terrifying scene assaults his mind. His footsteps continue forward. He feels the knife in his hand for one last time. Then there's a scream. A loud and satisfying scream. The beat of the Kid's heart slows as he watches the predator turn into pray. The pray rolls onto the floor. It reaches frantically for the knife in his arse. The perverted monster has been all but slain. The satisfying screams continue. The Kid grabs a pillowcase, rips the case in half and gags the mouth of the monster. A whimpering figure in the corner grabs his attention. He holds out his hand. "He can't hurt you anymore, Mikey. Come on, we gotta get outta here. Grab his keys."

Mikey looks at the Kid, but fear holds him to the base of his bed.

"He can't hurt you now. He's not hurtin' anyone, ever again. Come on. We can't stay here. We gotta leave." The Kid picks the blanket up from the floor and places it over Mikey's shoulders. "Please, we dun ave much time. Be brave."
Mikey nods his head and gets to his feet.

The Kid starts collecting supplies from the room and Mikey wraps the blanket tight around him. He looks at his abuser as it rolls around the floor. After a few seconds he takes a step back, wipes the tears from his eyes and with all his force, kicks the knife's handle. It screams so loud that Mikey thought the whole world would wake up. He bends down and holds his hand around the monster's mouth. "Now ew know how it feels, dun ew? Ew sick cunt." Mikey stands up, walks around the back of the monster and yanks out the blade. The monster screams out in agony. Mikey laughs as a pool of thick red blood spreads out around his feet. He looks at the blade in his hand and revenge fills his mind. He kicks the beast on its back, reaches down and with one swipe of the razor-sharp blade, he cuts off its genitals.

The last scream brings the Kid to Mikey's side. "You finished?" Mikey nods.

"Come on en. Let's get the fuck outta yer."

The two boys run out of the room and make their escape. They run through darkened corridors and through heavy wooden doors. They check for open windows, but thick wire mesh is bolted on the outside of each frame. They search for any way to escape. They use the keys they have to open doors to all of the children's rooms. Some stay for fear of being caught and punished. Others run with no idea of where they're going. Eventually, and by more luck than judgement, they reach a room full of TV screens and video tapes. The Kid smiles. "What are you smiling for?" Mikey asks.

"We've just found our way out." The Kid answers. He picks up a random tape. It's dated for two months earlier. Then he finds a written register with the records of all the visitors that have come to the care home over the past year.

"I don't get it." Mikey says scratching his head.

"Have you ever wondered why there are no security guards here when the monsters come for us in the middle of the night?" The Kid asks.

"No. I just wish that they were."

"Because they don't want witnesses. Look, we're gonna be in a lot of shit for what we done today Mikey. But if we take these tapes and this file and hide them somewhere. We have something to barter with. We have video witnesses. If we don't have proof, those fuckers that are hurtin' all these kids will put us away forever."

Mikey starts to look through the tapes. After flinging four to the floor he finds what he's looking for. The colour drains from his face.

"You Ok mate?" The Kid asks.

"Yeah. I'm fine." Mikey points to the register in the Kid's hand. "Is there anything in there that matches the date on this tape?"

The Kid opens the register. He flips through several pages and stops. "There are ten names on that day."

Mikey pockets the tape and continues his search. A dozen more are flung to the floor before he stops. He's holding two in his hands. "What about these?"

"Seven names on the first one. Thirteen on the other." The Kid puts his hand on Mikey's shoulder. "I'm not going to ask why these dates are so important to you mate, but we need to start moving on. Are there anymore you need to find?"

"Yes." Mikey's eyes tear up. "But I've forgotten the dates."

The Kid gives Mikey a hug. "That's OK Mikey. You've got three and…" The Kid looks at the tapes. "I'll tell you what. Let's just grab as many as we can carry and be on our way. Hopefully the ones we grab are the ones we need."

Mikey agrees and the lads quickly empty half of the warm clothes and supplies they took from their rooms and replace them with as many tapes as they can carry. Lastly, the Kid grabs the file of visitor names and the tape that's in the recorder. They fling the lot over their shoulders and run out of the room. Only one door remains at the very end of the corridor and there's only one key that they haven't used. Carl has to use two hands to twist it, but eventually, after some tense and long seconds, it opens. They look back.

"What about the others?" Mikey asks.

"If we found this door, then they will too, Mikey. Look, the coppers will be all over this place in a few hours mate. If some kids were stupid enough to stay in their room's, then that'll be their time to save themselves. Right now, we ave to disappear."

Mikey agrees. He hits the fire alarm and the two friends get on their heels and run for the woods. When they reach the tree line, they look back for one last time. The old building is lit up in bright yellow lights. Gargoyles decorate the brickwork like demons protecting their evil masters. Welded upon the enormous metal fence that surrounds the grounds are large thick black letters. They say, BRYNIAU DU CARE HOME. Mikey and the Kid spit on the floor, and then run like hell itself was on their heels.

ALL CAUGHT UP

Christian wakes to the sound of his phones alarm. His head is thumping, his mouth is dry. His memory, sketchy. He looks around to get his bearings. He is on his living room floor surrounded by pillows, crisp packets and bottles. Some of the bottles are filled with a suspicious golden liquid. The faint red light of either dusk or dawn shines through the windows.

"You lied to me," says a voice from somewhere.

Christian crawls along the floor toward the direction of the voice until he sees a pair of legs on the other side of the sofa.

"You lied to me."

"What do you mean?" Christian asks.

"You've been talkin' in your sleep mate. You were havin' a nightmare about that place. You told me you don't have nightmares anymore."

"That wasn't a nightmare. Not for me anyway. My nightmare in that place was eleven days before. That was a dream about becoming the man I am."

"Oh. So, it was my nightmare." Mikey spins around until he is eye level with Christian. "Well one of my nightmares. I had so many in that place. You're lucky you weren't there that long."

"Lucky's not what I would call it, but I know what you mean." Christian rests his head on his arms. The two friends lie in silence for a while thinking about their time in that place until Christian shuffles to his feet. "I'm getting a drink of water. You want one?"

"I'd love one mate. I'm spittin' feathers here."

Christian helps Mikey to his feet and goes to get a glass of water for each of them. When he returns, Mikey has the news on.

He hands him his drink then sits down beside him to catch up with what's going on in the world.

"Look at it," Mikey says. "Nothin' but doom and gloom. Wars in far off countries. Gang wars on the streets of Britain. Money problems. Trade problems. Job problems. Immigration problems. Terrorist problems. It's enough to drive you crazy. Where the fucks the good in the world and why don't they show more of it?"

"I know dude. It's fucking bollocks. You know what I think? I think they do it to control us. If we fear the outside world it makes us more compliant. Well, that's what I think."

"Maybe. I just think it would be nice if they balanced it out a bit more. Show some love like, you know? There's plenty of it out there in the world and I think people would appreciate hearin' about it more often. Speakin' of which." Mikey looks at Christian. "This girl you're seein'. She seems nice. Are you serious about her?"

"I don't know. I mean, I like her a lot but..." Christian looks down at the floor and rubs his hands.

"But what?"

"But I'm damaged goods mate. I don't know how close I can let her get. Take last night for example. When I'm really stressed, I start talking in my sleep. What am I gonna say if she starts asking questions about it? I don't think she could handle knowing my past."

"Yeah, I get that. I've never opened up to anyone about it either. But I've never been with anyone I've had much of a connection with. You two really get on. I mean, she seems to really care about you."

"Yeah, I suppose. What would I say though? Oh yeah, I forget to mention that I was abused in a care home as a young boy and so was Mikey. And then one night, me and Mikey stabbed and cut the dick off one of the abusers and the only reason we escaped jail was because the authorities made us swear not to talk about what went on and who was doing it. Oh yeah, and by the way, Christian isn't even the name I was born with. It's Carl.

I changed my name in memory of the woman that changed my life. That good enough for you?"

"Yeah, you could say that. Just leave my name out of it."

"Shut up you bute. If I'm going down, you're coming with me."

"OK, well maybe it's not wise to mention anythin' about that night specifically until you know her better. But you gotta say somethin' about yesterday. You should text her or give her a call at least. She looked really worried about you mate and you don't wanna blow it do you? Not to mention she's really hot. I mean you're really punchin' above your weight mate. It's not even funny."

"Alright mate, lay off will you. I'm feeling a little bit fragile today as it is. I don't need you knocking me down too."

"I'm just sayin' that's all. She's really fit. Her friends not bad either. She's got a hell of an arse on her, fair do's. It's like a peach. What's her deal?"

Christian laughs. "Her deal is she is too good for you. That's her deal mate."

"How insulting."

Christian laughs and gets another water for the pair of them. "Her deal is she was in an abusive relationship. I can't really say much more than that."

Mikey's eyes light up. "Was? I knew she was into me last night. I could tell. How long has she been single for?"

Christian gives Mikey his refill and sits back down. "You'll have to ask her mate. It's confidential and her story to tell. If you like I can ask Katy if she wants you to have her number, but she didn't seem that interested to me last night." Christian sighs and rubs his head. "For fuck sake. How am I going to explain last night's behavior? She probably thinks I'm a right freak now."

"I don't think so mate. She just seemed concerned that's all. Have she text you?"

Christian reaches into his pocket and pulls out his phone. "I've got five missed calls and eleven messages."

"All from her?"

"Yip."

"What do they say?"

Christian starts to read the messages in his mind and Mikey throws a pillow at him.

"What do they say you prick?"

"They say that she's worried and wishes I'd talk to her. All pretty much the same. The last few ask if she's done anything wrong."

"See, I told you she likes you. Text her to let her know it's not her fault. And then, maybe ask for her friend's number for me."

Christian laughs. "Yeah, OK. I'll do that now. But not the number bit."

Mikey sighs. "You're a heartless prick."

PLEASANT MOMENTS

Several hours later, Christian is stood outside Joe's ice cream parlour in Mumbles. He's wearing his finest grey pinstripe suit with highly polished brown leather shoes. Even he will admit he looks dapper. The air is cool but a menacing wind whips around and scatters sand across the road in waves. Mikey walks out of a corner shop looking just as dapper and cleans his shoes with the wet wipes he's just bought. "Do I look OK?"

"Yeah, you look good mate. Stop panicking will you."

Mikey checks the time on his phone. "What time did they say they'll be here? Half six was it? They're late already. Do you think they'll turn up?"

"Yes Mikey! For fucks sake, stop panicking you weirdo. You're making me nervous."

"I'm not panickin'. I'm just askin'."

"Well stop asking. Yes, they are late, but they will be here. They promised."

Seconds later a black cab pulls up and Katy waves at them. When the door opens, the lad's eyes light up because girls look stunning. Katy's wearing an all blue dress that stops just above the knee. She has light-blue high-heels on and just enough cleavage on show to set the heart racing. Steph is wearing a similar style dress that's black. It's also cut low at the front but she has a variety of colourful jewellery on to keep eyes occupied.

"Wow," Mikey says a little bit too loud. "Suddenly I feel very underdressed."

Steph smiles at him, closes the door and the taxi pulls away.

"Hi and wow!" Christian says. He kisses Katy on the cheek. "You look stunning."

"Thank you. I thought I'd make the effort." She smiles at him and her brilliant blue eyes sparkle making his heart skip a beat. "You look very handsome too."

"Thanks." Christian takes Katy by the hand. "Hope you're hungry because I'm starving."

"Me too. All I've had is a piece of toast all day. I've heard good things about this restaurant so I'm going for it tonight. I've really wanted to try it for a while see."

"Me too," Steph cuts in. Christian had forgotten that her and Mikey were even there. "Shall we go in then?"

Inside the restaurant the clash of cutlery and the smell of freshly cooked food fills the air. The look is modern. The walls have strong colours. Framed paintings from local artists hang randomly throughout. The comfortable furnishings are well placed to let everyone see the wonderful view through the large windows. Old fashioned lights give the room a warm glow. It's elegant and rustic in one.

A waiter confirms their booking and shows them to their table. Christian pulls Katy's chair out for her and she sits down. When he sits down next to her, she shuffles her seat over to be closer to him. The waiter takes the drinks order and leaves. Katy reaches out and touches Christian's leg under the table and smiles. "Are you OK now?"

Christian stares into her eyes. For a second, he is lost for words. Floating peacefully in the beautiful depths. She squeezes his leg again and he is tenderly brought back into the room. "Yes, I'm fine beautiful. I'm really sorry about yesterday. You must think I'm crazy? Acting like that and then running off."

"Not at all handsome. I did see what you were lookin' at on the news though. The story of the politician and all that stuff he's accused of. It's bloody horrible mun. And you must see that kind of stuff in your job all the time. I bet it must be really hard to switch off from it all. I dun think there's many people at all, that could just leave it in work and not let it affect them. Anyway, if it was me doin' your job, I'd be exactly the same I reckon."

Christian smiles and kisses her on the lips. Suddenly there is cough from nearby and the moment is broken. Christian looks around and sees Mikey and Steph looking at them. He'd forgotten they were there again.

Mikey smiles at them. "You two ready to order some food or do you want us to leave you too it?"

"I'm happy either way," Katy answers.

Steph laughs at her friend. "Well I'm bloody starvin'. And I didn't get all dressed up for nothin' so I'm orderin' food."

"Yeah, food sounds good," Christian says picking up the menu. He takes a second or two to look at it and then places it back down.

"You picked already?" Katy asks.

"Certainly have. I'm going for the bruschetta to start and the 10oz sirloin as a main."

"That sounds good. I think I'm having garlic mushrooms to start and the beef medallions in peppercorn sauce."

"Ooh, that sounds even better. I think you may have thrown a spanner in the works with that one." Christian picks up the menu again. After another second he places it back down. "I'll have the same."

"Don't you think it's a bit of a waste, coming into a fancy place like this and ordering the same stuff we usually would down the pub? I kinda feel like I should be more adventurous. A bit more posh like." Steph says.

Katy looks at Christian. "What can I say. I like what I like."

Steph sighs and places the menu down. "Yeah, who am I trying to kid? Steak it is."

"Well, who am I to go against the grain. Steaks all round please Gastón," Mikey adds.

Christian gets the waiter's attention, places the food order and asks for two bottles of Chilean red wine to be brought over. A few minutes later, the red wine and conversation starts to flow. Christian and Katy sit quietly as Steph chats to Mikey about what's happening between her and the father of her kids. Every now and then Katy would jump in with; "He's such a prick," and "You're better off without that prick."

Once she's finished her story, Mikey smiles. "Well, you know one of the perks of being a policeman is that you get to meet a lot of bad people. If you like, I could introduce him to a couple of very dangerous ones. Maybe he has an accident or disappears for a while. You know, just to make him see sense." He looks at Christian. Christian stares back with a look of refusal in his eyes. Mikey laughs.

"Thanks for the offer but it's fine. He doesn't scare me anymore," Steph answers. "I just want him out of our lives now, that's all."

"Well, all you gotta do is ask. I deal with bullies like him all the time, so it's no bother."

Steph smiles at Mikey and her hand reaches out for his. Their eyes lock and they smile. Katy looks at Christian and giggles. "They seem to be gettin' on. He's not another knob head, is he?" She whispers.

"He has his moments, but he's got a good heart. He'll be an improvement on the last guy at least."

"God, I should bloody hope so."

When the waiters bring the starters over, the conversation stops. The cutlery is grabbed, and all concentration is placed on the food. The smell makes their mouths water and it isn't long before the starters are done, and the mains are brought over.

"You girls have a healthy appetite don't you," Mikey says.

"Is that a problem for you?" Steph asks.

"No, of course not. I like it. There's no point goin' out to a fancy restaurant if you're gonna have a piece of bread and a glass of water is there? You might as well get it down you and go all out."

"Exactly. You're only here once so make the most of it." says Steph.

After two hours, three courses, a cheese board, five bottles of wine and four brandy coffees, the bill is payed, and the foursome are walking out into the fresh salty air. After a while, Katy takes her shoes off, hands them to Christian and jumps the small wall that leads down onto the beach. Christian and the others quickly follow.

"You can feel the weather turning, can't you?" Katy rubs her arms. "It's getting darker earlier and it's colder in the nights. It won't be long until winter's here."

"Yeah, I know," Christian answers. "I hate winter. I really hate it. It takes so long for the bed to warm up and when it does, you're too scared to move in case you catch a cold bit."

Katy laughs. "Well, you'll have someone there to help you keep it warm now anyway."

Christian puts his arm around Katy and kisses the top of her head.

"I hate the mornings," she says. "You know, when you're lying in bed and you can hear the rain lashing against the windows outside and you're all cwtched up in bed. Your alarm goes off and it's still pitch black and the wind is howling."

A shiver runs through Christian and he wriggles it loose. "Ooh yeah, I hate it too. Bloody awful it is."

Katy tries to continue but Christian squeezes her shoulders. "OK, stop it now, you're making me feel cold."

Katy laughs. "OK, I'll stop." They walk hand in hand and talk about everything and nothing in particular. The waves wash on the shore and the stars begin to twinkle in the sky. They watch a fisherman casts his line deep into the encroaching sea. A plethora of hooks and lures are attached to his well-worn jacket. They shimmer and sparkle in the fading light. A small mongrel dog carries a stick that is twice the length of its body. Its head tilting under its weight. Its frothing tongue hangs loosely out of the side of its mouth. Its owner and the love birds laugh at the sight. Then suddenly Katy turns around. "Hey. where have they got to?"

"Who?" Christian asks.

"Steph and Mikey. Who do you think?"

"Oh yeah. I forgot about them. They're just..." Christian turns around to see where Mikey and Steph are, but they are nowhere to be seen. "I dunno. They were there the last time I looked."

"Which was?"

"I dunno. By the restaurant I suppose."

"Yeah me to." Katy laughs. "What shit friends we are. They could be in a sand ditch or mugged or anything."

"More than likely back on the path. Mikey's not one for nature in his toes."

"Neither's Steph. They've probably gone back to her place to have that drink. We'll just head there is it?"

"Yeah, OK. A night cap sounds good."

They walk along the beach for another twenty minutes, then cross over the road to Steph's place. Katy knocks on the door. "Well, the lights are on so someone's home." A few seconds go by but nobody answers, so she opens the door and begins to giggle. Christian pokes his head in behind her and as soon as he does, he hears the moans and groans of a woman having wonderful things done to her. Katy places her fingers to her lips and creeps up a few stairs toward the bedroom. Christian follows behind just as sneakily. They reach the top of the stairs and Katy pokes her head around the banister. Immediately she has to hold her hand over her mouth to stop herself from laughing. When Christian looks, he sees Mikey has his shoes and socks on, his trousers around his ankles and his arse is going like the clappers.

"Go on Steph girl. Give him hell," Katy whispers.

Christian gives Katy a funny look. "Give him hell? Jees. I think you're more of a lad than me."

Katy's face turns red. "Sorry. I do have got a bit of a Jack the lad in me." Her eyes roll to the top of her head while she thinks. "Make it a wonderful experience for him Steph. Is that better?"

"It's a bit girly like, but yeah, it's a little bit better."

Christian kisses Katy. "Come on. I don't want to see any more of that nonsense. It's burnt into my memory forever now."

"What did you think you were going to see when you looked? A bloody puppet show?"

"Well, to be honest, I was just enjoying the view of your behind." Christian smiles. "I mean from behind." He chuckles. "I mean, I dunno."

Katy slaps him on the arm, and they creep back outside. She

closes the front door behind them and locks it with her key. Even with the door closed it seems the noise from the sexual encounter can no longer be contained within the room.

"Bit noisy ain't she? She'll wake the whole bloody street up now."

Katy nods her head. "Yip. From what I've been told about Steph, you're mate Mikey's in for a real treat tonight. I had a friend she used to go out with. He was a bit of a shagger too and he couldn't keep up with her. He had to finish it in the end. She nearly broke him."

Christian laughs and looks up at the room. "Well, good luck Mikey son. He could do with some good loving in his life." He takes a step toward Katy. "Speaking of which." He leans in and kisses her on her strawberry flavoured lips. "He's not the only one who needs some TLC. I'd like to put them to shame tonight. Do you think we can?"

Steph jumps up and wraps her legs around Christian's waist. "Oh, I know we can. She's good. But I'm better."

SUNSHINE AND SHOWERS

The next morning, Christian wakes to the warmth of a beautiful woman by his side. Her cheek is resting on his chest and her arm is wrapped around him. The soft yellow duvet covers just below her shoulders. He kisses her on the top of her head. She stirs and kisses his chest. "Morning handsome."

"Good morning beautiful. How do you feel?"

"Not too bad. A bit thirsty and tired but I've been worse. You?"

"The same. My head is thumping. You want a glass of water? I'll go down and grab one now see."

"Yeah, if you would please. Make sure you run the tap for a minute though. Otherwise the water's warm and cloudy and tastes funny."

"No problem." Christian kisses her on the cheek and gets out of bed.

"You have a lovely little bum don't you handsome." Katy says giggling.

Christian looks in the mirror and does a muscleman pose. "If you say so. It's not something I really notice."

"Well, you can take my word for it. It's lush. And it can get some good speed up too, which is an added bonus." Katy blows him a kiss.

Christian catches it and pretends to put it in his pocket. "One water coming right up." He exits the room. While the tap is running, he hears Katy shouting down to him. "Your phone's ringing."

He fills the glasses up, downs the contents of one and then refills it before joining her. He hands a glass to Katy and picks up his phone. "It's my boss." Christian presses redial. The phone rings twice and it's answered. "Hey Dave, it's Christian. Sorry, I was downstairs mate. What's up?"

Katy doesn't hear what is said on the other side, but by Christian's reactions it isn't good news. "Can't you just tell me on the phone. I don't see the point in waiting to tell me at your office. I'd prefer to hear it now mate. Please, don't leave me hanging."

Katy hears the mumblings of an answer. Christian gets up and starts to pace the room. "How can they do that. I mean, they don't have any evidence that it was on purpose. He was starting to throw punches. This is complete bullshit Dave."

Christian becomes even more agitated and Katy tries to comfort him. He shrugs her away and continues to pace. "What do you mean legal advice. I have to lawyer up now because some dirt bag tried to attack us. I had to try and stop him mate. He was throwing haymakers around for fuck sake."

There are a few more mumblings from the other side and then Christian stops pacing and places a hand on his forehead. "OK, OK, I'm sorry Dave. But can't you see this is bullshit. Isn't there any more you can do?"

Another mumbled reply and Christian sits down on the end of the bed. His head buried in his shaking hands. "OK, I understand. Yeah, I know you will mate. Thanks anyway."

Christian hangs up. "Yeah, thanks for fucking nothing." He sits on the end of the bed in silence. Katy rubs her hand up and down his back and kisses him. "What's wrong handsome?"

"I'm being taken to court for ABH by a man that was trying to hit me and a colleague."

"What really? How has that happened?"

Christian explains what happened that day and the situation he faces now.

"What a load of bollocks," Katy says.

"Yeah, I know. But the police are saying there's sufficient evidence to proceed to court, so I am expecting them to contact me soon. I'll probably have to go and see them today to start the proceedings."

Christian throws his phone down and leans back on the bed. Katy is quick to try and comfort him. "Is there anything I can do?"

"Not really. Well, I suppose you should prepare yourself to be around a grumpy bastard for a while though."

"I'm sure I can cope with that." She kisses him on the shoulder. "And if there's anything else I can do, just let me know." She leans over him and kisses him on the mouth, but after one quick peck Christian pulls away. "I'm sorry. I'm just a bit stressed right now. I think I'm gonna head home and have a shower so I'm ready for when the police contact me."

"Do you want me to come with?"

"No, it's fine. I just need to be on my own for a bit."

Christian gets dressed and Katy follows him downstairs. When he arrives at the front door there is a newspaper sticking halfway through the letterbox. Christian pulls it out, hands it too Katy, but when he sees the headline on the front page, he pulls it back. He unfolds the paper and his face turns grey. He starts to lose his balance and has to prop himself up against the door. Katy grabs him and leads him into the living room to sit him down. "What is it? Christian what's wrong? Please Christian, talk to me."

Christian throws the paper to the floor and Katy picks it up. "Outrage as politician avoids questioning over historical abuse claims due to medical condition." Katy looks at him. "It's that same guy isn't it? The guy from the TV the other day. Why does this bother you so much? Please Christian talk to me."

Christian gets up and pushes his way past Katy. "I have to go."

Katy tries to block the door and when she sees the tears in Christian's eyes, she holds his head in her hands. "Please, don't shut me out handsome. Talk to me."

Christian drops his head. "I can't. Please, just let me leave. I need to be alone."

Katy moves to the side and begins to cry. Christian opens the front door, takes a step outside and turns around. "I'm so sorry."

"Don't leave. Stay here and talk to me."

"I'm sorry." As Christian walks away from Katy his phone rings. He switches it off and starts to run down the road.

WALLOWING

A few hours later, Christian is assessing how to climb over a six foot wall. He has a bag full of cans in his hand and the beginnings of a really intense LSD trip in his bloodstream. Green moss and grey bricks melt into different shades and shapes before him. His balance is shaky at best. He jumps up, kicks one leg over and wiggles his weight onto the top. Then, he confidently swings the bag of cans over his head. The momentum and weight of his goods throws him off balance. He lands heavily on to the floor on the other side. He rolls around, winded. Stingy nettles scratch his skin, making him feel like he's on fire. He lets go of his beers and crawls around looking for dock leaves. After a few minutes of searching, he gives up and grabs everything that's green to rub on the affected areas. It doesn't work. The pain on his back, neck and arms infuriates him and messes with his high. He grabs a can from his bag, pours half of it onto his skin and downs the rest. Then he makes himself as comfortable as possible on the 'fiery' ground and looks out at his surroundings.

He is laying down on the banks of a river, hidden between two trees on his right and a big bush and stingy nettles to his left. A seven-foot-tall hedgehog is waving at him from the river in front. Christian opens another can. "Hello again, Mr. Hedgehog. How are you?" The hedgehog doesn't answer. Christian closes his eyes and shuts out the madness. When he opens them again a few minutes later he sees the hedgehog is sat on the wall above him. His furry little legs are swinging like a child on a swing.

"You don't look happy Christian," the hedgehog says. "What's on your mind mate?"

"Oh, you know, the usual. I'm torn between hurting someone

and not hurting someone."

The hedgehog laughs and falls off the wall. After it's dusted itself off, it lays down beside him. "Nothing's changed then mate. You're still as crazy as ever." The hedgehog looks out at the water. "Remember when you tried to kill me? It was right here in this very river. Bloody hell." It scratches its chin. "It must be about ten years ago at least. Gosh. Doesn't time fly?"

"Maybe longer." Christian looks at the hedgehog. "I'm really sorry about that mate. I was even more fucked up back then."

The hedgehog laughs. "I'm sorry to be the one to break this to you mate, but you don't exactly look like you've got it all figured out right now either." He ruffles Christian's hair. "I wouldn't worry about that mate. That's all water under the bridge now anyway."

Christian offers the hedgehog a can of lager.
The hedgehog refuses. "I'm trying to cut down on lager mate. Gives me terrible wind." He rubs his belly and laughs.

Christian sits up and looks out over the river. "You said I don't look like I've got it all figured out yet. Well, that's because I don't. You know, I kid myself that I'm this guy that was pushed into doing bad things because of his crappy childhood. And that because I only do it too bad people, that makes me good. But do you know what Mr. Hedgehog?"

"What mate?"

"I enjoy it. Hurting bad people usually makes me feel good. Really good. It was what I was searching for when I came here all those years ago with you in a bag." Christian takes a long drink from his can. "So, I guess that makes me bad doesn't it?"

"I'd say it makes you a bad ass." The hedgehog holds a half-filled whiskey bottle up to toast Christian's bad ass attitude. Christian tries to hit it with his can, but they go straight through each other. Christian falls flat onto his face. When he lifts his head back up the hedgehog is gone. He looks around but he's all alone. He pulls a bag of mushrooms from his pocket, puts a few in his mouth and washes them down with lager. "Ahh, what a bloody day. What a bloody week and what a bloody life."

He rests his head on the ground, closes his eyes and listens to the sound of the birds in the trees and the river flowing by.

"*What are you going to do now then?*" a voice from somewhere asks.

Christian opens his eyes to a darker sky. He looks around but nobody is there.

"*What are you going to do now?*" the voice asks again.

"Who's there?"

"*Who? Who am I? That is a very good question. WHO. AM. I. Am I a man that allows himself to be mistreated by others? Am I a man that allows a child beater to destroy the job that he loves? Am I a man that lets a paedophile escape his rightful punishment? Am I a man that allows his past to destroy his future? To take away his chance for love. Am I all of these things or none of them?*"

"Where are you?" Christian shouts. "Why do you hide in the shadows?"

The voice begins to laugh a loud and hysterical laugh. "*I do not hide. I show myself when I must. I show myself when you need me.*"

"Then show yourself now!" Christian shouts.

The hairs on Christian's neck move.

"*Boo.*"

Christian jumps with fright. He turns around and comes face to face with a flesh eaten, double of himself.

"*Happy now?*"

Terrified, Christian crawls away until his back is against the wall. "What do you want?"

"*I want, what I have always wanted. I want to help you do what you must. We are going to get justice.*"

"But Mikey said..."

"*Mikey is weaker than you. He would never have survived if it wasn't for you. He's frightened now. He's scared of prison and what that will do to him. We don't need him anyway. It is our score to settle and we can do it on our own.*"

"Maybe I don't want to do it anymore." Christian closes his eyes and tries to think happier thoughts. He thinks of a girl with lavender hair and strawberry flavoured lips.

The rotten Christian laughs. *"So, it's the girl is it? You don't want justice because of her. You are becoming weak Christian. What do you think she'll do if you told her your past and your secrets? Do you think she'll accept you once she knows you were once a grown man's plaything? Or if she finds out the violence you hand out to others."*

"I was not his plaything. I was too young. I wasn't strong enough to stop him."

"That may be so, but it doesn't change the fact that you are damaged goods. But that ordeal has made you special Christian. It has made you stronger. It's given you a purpose. You are a hunter now Christian, remember that. You have to end it with her and seek your revenge."

"I am not damaged goods! None of us are!"

The image of Christian steps back and holds his hand up. *"OK, OK, you're not damaged. Poor choice of words. I'm sorry for calling you that. But you are a hunter. A hunter of evil. Be what you were destined to be."*

"I can't." Christian claws at his face. "I won't. I love her." He stumbles to his feet and tries to run away but the ground beneath him is soft and unsteady. He tumbles, hitting the dirt hard. His hands reach up to his head and the last thing he sees is the blood upon his fingers. Light starts to fade, and he loses consciousness. The rotten Christian laughs his cold and evil laugh.

BEGINNING OF
THE END

Christian wakes with a thumping headache and the dizziness that goes along with it. His sight, like his memory is unclear. The white sheets that cling to his body are stained with droplets of blood. He reaches up and touches his head. What is normally a smooth surface of skin is replaced with rough and bumpy with plastic in between.

"It's glue," a familiar voice says. "You've had quite a bump."

Christian moves his head around slowly. Katy's laying down on the bed next to him looking tired but beautiful. "You're in Morriston hospital. A fisherman found you about twelve hours ago. He thought you were dead."

"He's probably not far wrong."

"Brain dead maybe." Katy says while shuffling upright in the bed. "What are you doing Christian? What's going on in that head of yours?"

Christian closes his eyes and rubs his temple as the thumping gets stronger. The light in the room seems to increase the pain. "How did you know I was here?"

"I was phoning you when you were in the ambulance. The medic answered your phone and told me." Katy looks Christian up and down and tears form in her eyes. "Talk to me handsome. Please. Tell me what's wrong."

"I can't. You wouldn't understand." Christian clears his throat. "And if you did, you wouldn't like me anymore."

"I love you, you stupid bastard. Love. Not like. Doesn't it

mean anythin' to you when I say that?" Katy gets up and holds Christian's hand. "You can't keep this secret inside you any longer because it's clearly tearin' you apart. Please trust me. Let me in."

Christian looks at his beautiful girlfriend. She smiles and rubs his cold hands with her warm touch. "Please," she says again.

Christian's stomach begins to turn, and he swallows the water that's flooding into his mouth. "OK, sit down." Katy grabs a chair to sit beside him.

"OK, well I suppose I should start from the beginning. When I was younger..." suddenly a sharp pain races across his brain like a shooting star across the night sky. His vision becomes blurred and the room sways. He reaches up and squeezes his temples as if trying to catch the pain and pull it out. Then as suddenly as it started, it stops. He looks at Katy.

"Don't do it! She'll think you're crazy and weak. Don't do it Christian! It is better if she walks away with a broken heart than stay with a broken man. Don't do it."

Christian turns his back on her sweet face by rolling to his side. "I'm sorry. I think you should leave."

The chair beside him squeaks and Katy begins to sob. "I hope one day you'll change your mind and realise you can trust me completely with everything that's happened." She leans over his bed and kisses him on his forehead. "I love you handsome. Never forget that." Katy picks up her coat and walks out of the room. She stops by the door and turns around. "If you need me, you know where I am."

The sound of Katy's high heels hitting the cold hard floor, fade into the distance. Christian's heart thumps with each step. He wants to call her back. His heart longs for her but the voice in his head says no. When he's left in silence, he feels more alone than he's ever felt before. Christian rolls onto his front, buries his bruised and battered face deep into his pillow, and cries

*

A little while later Christian is startled by the sound of someone knocking at a window.

"What a bloody mess."

Christian opens his eyes. "Hey Mikey."

"Hey dumbass. How you feeling?"

Christian holds his head in his hands. "Like I've just been found in a ditch after hitting my head."

"Not great then." Mikey pulls a mars bar from his pocket and places it by Christian's side. "The shop was about to close and that's all I could grab. Anyway, I've heard a Mars a day keeps the doctors away."

Christian smiles. "I'm pretty sure that's an apple, but thanks anyway mate."

"Really. I thought apples was for dentists? Anyway. I just seen Katy crying outside. What have you done?"

"I'm pretty sure we just broke up."

"Oh, you're a tosser Christian. Seriously. Why mun? I thought you loved her."

"I do but..." Christian gets up in his bed. "I can't be the man she wants. I'm too messed up. I can't get revenge out of my head. I can't let him get away with it."

"No Christian, you won't let yourself be that man and forget your past. I get it mate. Really, I do. But you're an asshole, just like me. Look at what this is doing to you. It's ruining your life." Mikey pulls up a seat and helps himself to the drinks and grapes that are beside the bed. "I'm not goin' to let it ruin mine anymore."

"What do you mean?"

"I mean, I'm going to open up to someone other than you."

"Who? Steph?"

"No, not Steph." Mikey spits a grapes pip onto the floor. "Not yet anyway. It's that reporter chick. All of her witnesses have been met with skepticism because of their dubious backgrounds. The lawyers are sayin' that they're of questionable character." Mikey takes a deep breath. "So, I'm gonna give my story to her. Let them know that one of their own was abused. It may help to kick start things again."

"Why?" Christian asks confused.

"Because I'm tired Christian. I'm tired of luggin' that shit around with me all the time. It's exhaustin'. I need to let it all go. It should have stayed in that place when we ran away."

"That's easy for you to say Mikey because you got your revenge. You got your justice when you cut that man to pieces. Where is my justice Mikey? He's walking the streets right now like he's bloody untouchable. I can't allow that. He has to pay."

Mikey throws a grape at Christian that hits him in the eyeball. "First of all, numb nuts, cutting one guys dick off doesn't even come close to evening out all the abuse I had in that place. I had months of that shit. Dragged out in the middle of the night and taken to parties to be passed around. Fuckers walking into my room at night and doing whatever they fuckin' wanted. Months of it. So, don't even go there." Another grape hits Christian's head. "And secondly, pay how Christian? How are you gonna make him pay? Are you gonna kill him? Is becoming a murderer gonna help your sanity?"

"I don't know. Maybe." Christian rubs his forehead and sighs. "No, probably not OK. I just know that I have to do something. Even if it's to make him look into my eyes while I tell him the pain he's caused me. I need to make him understand that he's ruined my life. I need to do something."

Mikey puts the grapes down and stands up. "OK, Christian. If you gotta do this, then I won't stop you. We've been through too much already for me to stand in your way. In fact, I'll even go one further. I can't go with you on this one, but I will help. I'll get his address and whatever info I can."

Christian smiles. "Thanks Mikey. You're a good friend."

Mikey sighs. "No Christian. A good friend would make you see sense, but it looks like I'm too stupid to do that." Mikey taps Christian on the leg and Christian yawns.

"I'll leave you get some rest then mate. Looks like you need it." Mikey turns and walks away. When he gets to the front door he stops. "When I get what you need, I'll be in touch. But I want you to think very hard about what you're doing. It's not too late until it begins."

Christian nods. "Trust me, I will. It's all I ever think about."

THE MAN IN BLACK

Strong gusts of wind batter tall, orange-leafed trees. Rain drops pool on an already sodden earth. A man studies an eight-foot wall that encircles a large, stately home. He has been there for over an hour and he was there for three hours the day before and most of the night before that. He is calm and sober. In preparation for tonight he's been living on smoothies and soups for two weeks. He's exercised every day and shaved every inch of his body. The black gear he's wearing is new and bought with cash and the bike is stolen with fake plates. He's confident that nothing can be traced back to him. His mind and body feel as sharp as the blade in his jacket and as strong as his desire for revenge.

Inside the house is the man that has tormented his dreams for as long as he can remember. A man that abused his position of power and influence for decades. Now he hides behind old stone walls that have been standing for as long as the parliament he served. The walls of the house make it look like a castle. The man inside probably feels like a king. All powerful and untouchable. That is about to change. That man is about to discover that power and influence cannot stand up against the might of justice or revenge. These are the things that Christian seeks.

Large windows on the ground floor illuminate the garden below. An unmarked police car is parked at the front gate. Christian double checks the pieces of his plan. "*Access point.*" With his binoculars he scans the wall again and stops two hundred meters away from the police car. Ivy has climbed the wall and can be grabbed easily from the outside. He scans up and down the street for cameras. "*Six hundred meters away. One camera, cur-*

rently looking in opposite direction." The ground he has to cover, from where he is hiding, to the house, is approximately two hundred meters. There's a mixture of bushes, trees and shadows for cover. After that, fifty meters of open ground and twenty-five meters across the road to the wall. He makes one final check that his items are in their correct place and nothing can reflect light or makes a noise. His heart beats faster. He takes one deep breath, holds it for a five seconds and exhales. "*Well...let's get on with it.*"

He steps out from under a camouflaged net and begins. His feet slip on the damp autumn leaves that litter the ground around him. When he hits open ground, he crouches down. He makes one final check left and right, before sprinting to the street and hiding beside a parked car. A glance at the camera and police car ensures they're facing away from him. He cleans trapped earth away from the tread in his boots and gets set. "*Three, two, one, go.*"

Strong muscles in his legs push him across the road and toward the ivy. He leaps up and with a one big heave he is through the perverts first line of defence. An untidy bush becomes his cover while he catches his breath.

The enormous house looks intimidating. It's large, arched windows and thick stone walls make it look every bit like the castles of old. The six windows that have lights on become the objects of his attention. Any movement or a flick of a switch will make his plans change but he's confident there won't be any. Not yet anyway. Nobody has entered or exited the house during his observations and Mikey said every member of staff handed in their notice after the allegations.

A light goes off and Christian checks his watch. "Half eleven. Bang on Q." He waits for another five minutes to check his theory. When the clock says 23.35pm, another two lights switch off. 23.45pm the house is in darkness. It has been the same lights, at the same times, in the same order the last three nights. This makes Christian believe they are all on timers. He looks up at the dark walls that protect his tormentor. His hand feels for the blade at his side. *"Let's do it."*

The bush rustles as he steps out and he runs to the door as quietly as he can. He twists the handle. The door opens to a dark dining hall and a spider's web spans the doorway. *"Must be our lucky day Christian. Didn't even need to pick the lock. We've always said overconfidence will bring the mightiest of people down."* He snaps the web, steps inside and a strong smell of stale food assaults him. It tickles his throat and steals his breath. Christian covers his mouth and nose until the sensation to cough disappears.

The room has the type of furnishings that one would expect in a house of this extravagance. Sixteen dusty leather chairs surround a large, wooden table and antique looking décor finishes the look. A large painting of the pervert hangs at the head of the table. Christian fights the urge to put his fist through it. He holds the sleeve of his jacket over his mouth and closes the door. Silently, stealthily, he walks toward a light that shines at the bottom of a door. He presses his ear against it and opens his mouth to amplify any sound. After ten minutes, he's sure the coast is clear and silently opens the door a jar. He enters a dimly lit hallway with wooden cladding on the walls and animal heads placed randomly throughout. *"I'd like to put this pricks head alongside these poor bastards."* Christian's hand feels for his knife again as he creeps through the corridor. The smell of rotten food amplifies with each step and when he reaches a door where it's at its strongest, he pokes his head in. Buzzing flies, whizz around, Dirty crockery covers the work tops and spill out from the sink. A large black bin in the corner is overflowing with rotten food and plastic packaging. This image and the smells confirm to him that the house keepers have left. He finds comfort in that fact. Now, it's between him and the bad guy.

Leaving the stench behind, he heads to the stairs. He keeps his weight near the wall, in case a step is loose or a board is broken. Each step moving him agonisingly close to his target.

At the top of the stairs, Christian gets another whiff of food. This time it's fresh. His heart starts to race. He follows his nose through the dimly lit corridor until the sound of applause stops him in his tracks. Christian's senses jump to high alert. He listens closely to every sound. A few seconds pass before he can distinguish a female voice. His heart sinks. Suddenly there's clapping and a man's voice shouts. "It's B you silly bugger. Clint Eastwood was in Kelly's Heroes. B not C."

"The bastards watching TV." Christian's heart feels like it's going to explode. His nerves run riot. He pauses until he's composed enough to proceed. After what seemed like an hour, but was more like a minute, Christian continues to the flashing lights at the end of the corridor. His legs shake. His hands tremble. He places a gloved hand on the wall to steady himself. *"Not now Christian. Don't lose your shit now."*

He wills himself on. One step, a deep breath and repeat. Finally, he reaches the door that he has yearned for since he became the hunter. He reaches into the rucksack, removes a bottle and rag and prepares for his revenge.

The questions continue on the other side of the wall. "Which actress plays Clarice Starling in the thriller; Silence of the lambs. Is it A; Susan Sarandon. B; Jodie foster. C; Meryl Streep, or D; Nicole Kidman."

"Jodie Foster. It's B Jodie foster." the pervert next door shouts. *"Yeah, you've got Alzheimer's haven't you. You dirty old bastard. You may have fooled the courts but you ain't fooled us. It's time to get yours. We have come for you."* Christian takes a deep breath. His mind clears and the strength returns to his body. He exhales and enters the room.

The pervert is lying in bed with a tray on his lap and a spoon in his mouth. Christian strides toward him at a blistering pace. The pervert jumps with fright, spilling crockery and red soup over himself. Before he can react in any defensive way, Christian has the cloth over his mouth and is putting him to sleep. Christian pulls a plastic bag from his rucksack and removes a new roll of tape from it. He tapes the monster's mouth and ties its hands and legs to the intricately carved wooden posts on the corners of the bed. Once this is done, he takes a step back and looks at the face that has tormented him for too long. The few hairs that still cling to it have grown longer and greyer. Its skin has wrinkled and sagged. Christian smiles. Time hasn't altered this monster too much and he's now positive he has the right man. Christian could never forget this face for as long as he lives. Satisfied, he closes the door and turns the TV off. Then he pulls a chair closer to the bed and removes the tools from his rucksack.

The pistol, and claw hammer, he places upon the antique looking bedside cabinet. The new roll of sticky tape and plastic bag go back into the side compartment. The bottle and rag that he used to render this predator unconscious go into the opposite side. Then he sits down and watches the old grey animal sleep, while thinking about his next move. *"Go straight for the hammer. Hit him until he wakes."*

"No, that's no good. The initial strike will go unnoticed. I want him to feel every ounce of pain."

"Good point. Wake him and then smash him."

Christian looks at the hand that is tightly bound twelve inches to his left. The hand that held tight over his mouth all those years ago. The hand that touched him, hurt him. The hand that stopped his screams and stole his breath. Christian picks up the smelling salts and hammer. He hovers above his unsuspecting prey and waves the bottle under its nose. When its eyes focus on him, he brings the hammer down. "Wakey wakey, you evil son of bitch."

The body of the beast convulses with pain. Christian holds his hand over its nose to hinder the noise that's attempting to leave. Tears begin to roll down its face.

"This is only the beginning. You are going to rue the day you ever laid a finger on us."

The head and eyes of the monster flick right and see the damage the hammer has done. Wrist bones poke through old, thin skin. Blood drips steadily upon the floor. The eyes move left as if searching the room for a friend or a way out. Christian shakes his head. "There's only me and you." Christian grabs the blade in his other hand and holds it against its throat.

"I bet you're wondering why? Why this is happening to you? Why has someone broken into your room in the middle of the night and attacked you?" Christian peels the tape from its mouth and replaces it with his hand. The monster swallows and its Adams apple bumps the cold steel that touches it. Christian stares into the monster's eyes. Slowly he glides the razor-sharp blade across its throat until thin red line starts to trickle.

The monster whimpers and pleads. "Please, whatever you want just take it. I have cash. I have jewellery. I have art and antiques everywhere. Hundreds of thousands of pounds worth. Just help yourself. I won't tell anyone. I promise."

Christian smiles. "It's not your stuff I'm after old man." He places the tip of the knife to the pervert's eye. "It's you." The old pervert begins to cry uncontrollably and Christian laughs in his face. "Don't you want to know why? Why would anyone want to do something like this? To break into your home. A place where you should be safe and secure. To break in and beat you. To cut you. To have his way with you. Frightening isn't it? The confusion it causes. The feeling of helplessness, fear, pain, anguish. Your cries for help going unheard... or even worse...ignored. Why it's enough to turn a person insane." Christian places new tape over its mouth, puts the knife down by the monster's head and grabs the hammer. Midway down the monster's bed he raises the hammer high. The monsters head sways from side to side. Its eyes close. Its muffled protests are pitiful. Christian brings the hammer down. The monster screams. A loud and sickening scream but the onslaught of pain doesn't happen. When the monster opens its eyes, it sees Christian laughing. The hammer, inches above its skin and bone. The monster breathes heavy and laboured sighs of relief. After thirty seconds of staring at the beast, Christian raises the hammer again and crashes it down upon its bones. The agony it causes sends mixed feelings around Christian's body. He tells himself again and again that it's what the monster deserves and it's the only punishment he would get.

Christian places the hammer beside the monster's head and

takes a seat. He kicks his legs up onto the bed, yawns and stretches out. *"How much should we tell him?"* Christian opens his eyes and sees the hedgehog standing in the corner, swinging a rope around that's attached to its feet. *"Should we tell him why this is happening to him?"*

"Well, I suppose that depends on whether or not we're going to kill him."

"Are we going to kill him?" the hedgehog asks.

"No. I promised I wouldn't."

"Isn't that what you've been searching for? To get the pain out of you and on to something else. What better way than to kill the beast that hurt you the most?"

"No. I promised."

The monster turns its teary face to look at Christian.

"We'll make sure to do the job properly though. We'll go as far as we can."

"OK, well if we're not killing him, remember. If you say too much and he lives, then he and the police will be able to find us easily. Keep the silence. The unknown can be a torture all on its own."

"OK, I will." Christian takes a throw away phone out of his pocket and puts on YouTube. "You know since I saw your face on TV, I've taken a rather keen interest in what you actually did to warrant your job in parliament. You know what the first thing I saw was?" Christian shows his phone to the monster. "It's this." The video shows four politicians sitting on the same row on wooden seats on the middle of the houses of parliament. All four are fast asleep. "Is this what taxpayers pay you for? So, you can find somewhere to get your forty winks in." Christian puts his phone away in his top right-hand jacket pocket. "Now, I'm not saying that this is the reason I'm here, but it is kind of the icing on the cake. Taxpayers giving their hard-earned money to wealthy wankers like you. Wealthy wankers who squander it, when..." He raises his hands up toward the ceiling. "When you're already doing alright for yourself. I mean you were born into more money than most people can only dream of. Along with a title and land. You had everything you could ever ask for and what did you do with it?"

The monster shakes his head. His runny nose trickling down its face.

"You did whatever your filthy little mind thought it could get away with, didn't you?" Christian, stands, picks up the hammer and walks slowly down to the foot of the bed. As he raises it, the monster shakes his head violently from side to side. Silently pleading for the justice to stop. Christian laughs. "Have you ever seen the film Misery?" He asks, before landing a heavy blow onto the left ankle of the beast. The beasts back arches. Its head twists from left to right, over and over again. Christian watches the colour drain from its skin. Sweat beads form on its brow. The veins and ligaments in its neck look like they are about to break free. Christian stops thinking about his next move and places the hammer down. Something about this reaction stirs mixed feelings in him. Like an alarm bell that rings somewhere at the edge of hearing. The eyes of the monster roll in their sockets. Froth foams in its mouth. The alarm bell is heard. *"Fuck! He's having a heart attack."*

Christian panics and cuts the beasts left arm free. It rolls to his chest. His fist clenches.

The hedgehog vanishes, leaving Christian alone.

Christian's mind quickly adds up his options as the heart attack unfolds it's agonising symptoms in front of him. He peels the tape from its mouth and takes a seat.

"Help me," the monster pleads. "Help me please."

Christian takes off his balaclava. It's clear in the pervert eyes that he knows no help will be offered. "You recognise me, don't you? You know my face?"

The perverts face contorts as intense pain streaks through his body. "This is your Judgment day. I have dreamt of this moment for many years and now that it's here" Christian leans in and smiles. "I think it was worth the wait. You look like you're in so much pain." He picks up the hammer. "Even worse than what I could do with one of these." He throws the hammer inside his rucksack and leans back with his hands on his head.

"Help me please," the monster pleads again.

"No. If I were to relive these moments a million times over, the answer would always be no. This pain is yours for what you did to me and god knows how many other helpless children in your lifetime." Christian leans forward until he's a foot away from the pervert's face. "You know, I didn't want to kill you when I came here. In fact, I gave a promise to someone that I wouldn't. But I suppose I knew there was a chance it would happen due to your age. It was never part of my plan though." Christian shrugs his shoulders. "But if it happens, well, who am I to stop it."

Christian gets up and begins to place the rest of his items back into his rucksack. Stopping every few seconds as the violent spasms of pain, shoot through the beast's body. When he pulls out his knife, the monsters back arches and its eyes roll up into its head. Once the body relaxes, Christian removes the tape from its arms and legs, packs it into his rucksack. The knife he slides back into its sheath. He double checks the room in case he has forgotten anything. *"The bed? Clear. The cabinet? Clear. The floor?"* Christian gets on all fours and checks under the bed. Apart from a dirty spoon, a bowl, a few odd, stinky socks, it's clear. When he gets back up onto his knees, Christian sees the lifeless body in pyjamas. He looks into its cold dead eyes. Guilt crashes in. "What have I done. What the fuck have I done."

"You've killed the man that abused you. You've got your justice."

"I'm a murderer. I'm nothing more than a piece of shit murderer."

"That man was the piece of shit. Not you. Not us. He deserves what he got. He deserves every ounce of pain and he deserved to die because of it. Fuck that guy!"

"It's not as simple as that is it? You say that he's got what he deserved. Well, what do I deserve now? Murderers deserve prison, maybe, even death. That's what we think isn't it?"

"What the fuck are you talking about. This ain't cold blooded murder. This is revenge for ruining fuck knows how many lives."

"It's still murder! No matter how we try to dress this up.

There's a dead guy in the bed, two feet away from us." Christian stares at the greying form. "Fuck!"

The voice in his head chuckles. *"What did you think would happen, hey? You smashed this old bastard in the limbs a few times with a bloody hammer, Christian? You must have known there was a chance his heart would bloody pop."*

"Of course, but..." Christian rubs his wet forehead and wipes the sweat in his top. "I guess...fuck. I was just so focused on getting in here and getting it done that I pushed that to the back of my mind."

"Well, keep pushing it. Push it away and bury it because we've got to get out of here before we're caught. We're not doing time for this asshole. We've got too much to live for. He's dead because he fucked with the wrong person. That's all there is to it."

Christian takes a minute to think about his options one last time. He could hand himself in. That's what the law of the land would have him do. To face the justice of his actions. To stand up in front of his peers and plead for their mercy after taking the law into his own hands. But those same laws failed him. They failed to bring the grey dead monster to trial and punish him for his evil doings. They failed him and countless others. Christian's stomach steadies as he makes peace with his darkened conscious. He takes one last look at the monster and walks out of the room.

When he reaches the door that leads into the garden, reality kicks in. His mind switches into escape and survive mode. He checks the coast is clear. A bat squeaks just above his head. The trees blow in the wind. He takes a deep breath and sprints as fast as he can to the vines. With one big heave he lifts his weight over the wall and prepares to drop to the other side. A noise pulls his attention to the police car. A door opens. An orange flame illuminates the policeman's face as a cigarette burns. Christian hugs the wall as tight as he can. He keeps one eye on the smoking copper and one eye on his escape. Then he hears a noise. An engine approaches. Deep and grumbling engine. Followed by car lights. The car turns a corner and the headlights creep along the wall he's straddling. He keeps his nerves in check. Slow, controlled breathes. His eyes follow the Aston Martin DB9 until it's past him. His surroundings turning blacker and safer with every meter. When the DB9 reaches the police car, it stops. Christian curses his luck and trains all his senses toward it. A window is wound down. Words are spoken. There's laughter. As the seconds tick by, Christian can feel the blood begin to pool in his legs. His feet throb. Pins and needles stab at the muscles in his legs and the tips of his toes. He curses some more. After what seemed like an hour, the DB9's petroleum horses came to life and wheels began to squeal. Seconds later, all that's left, is white smoke and black parallel lines on the tarmac. The smoking policeman got back in the car and the windows are closed. Christian began to move his legs. Ever so gently. Ever so slowly. Twisting his feet around in a clockwise motion to release the pain. He waits until the night is completely still, before lifting his left leg over to join his right. Then he drops. Either the speed of the fall, the weight of his rucksack or the stiffness of the muscles cause his legs to buckle. His left knee twists under him and he screams. Christian gasps for breath and wills himself up. As he struggles to his feet, torches shine on his blackened frame and voices shout.

"Police. Stay where you are!"

Christian pumps his injured legs as fast as they can go. They burn and throb but he pushes them on. The policemen shout again. A single torch light follows him. When he reaches his bike, he can see the torchlight in the distance. It moves toward his direction. Scanning from side to side. Following his tracks like a bloodhound in the hunt. In a few minutes the copper will be on top of him. He knows others won't be far behind and then they will close the net completely. Christian quickly lifts the camouflaged net from the bike and rams it into its compartment. Seconds later he hears police sirens in the distance. *I suppose that means they've found the pervert.* He mounts his bike and as blue and red lights start to illuminate the woods he starts the engine. Immediately he's spotted. White torchlight zone in on him. He pulls the throttle back and wheelspins off. After a few zigs and a couple of zags through the trees, the white and blue lights are left far behind. However, that is not the last of the police. All around him, dozens of multi-coloured lights illuminate the woods. The net is cast. Fortunately for him they remain by the side of roads or on foot. He stays in the woods until he can break through their lines. He scrambles up banks. Jumps over streams and navigates through farmer's fields. Mile after mile. Minute after minute. Finally, all seems clear and he can get onto a road. When he sees his first street sign for forty minutes, the rain starts to hit hard against his visor. Strong gusts of wind threaten to blow him over. He quickly gets his bearings, pulls the throttle back and wheel spins toward home.

He sticks to the speed limit so he doesn't arouse suspicion and keeps to roads that he could lose the cops on if he's spotted. All was going well, and Christian felt confident about his escape. When he reaches the M4 a patrol car pulls up by his side. He drops his speed to sixty-five miles per hour and tries his best to remain calm. He can feel the eyes from inside the car upon him and the mud-covered bike. Even in this rain it wouldn't take a genius or the eyes of a hawk to see the bike has been off roading recently, but he hopes his cool head may sway it for him. After five minutes, the police car pulls thirty meters in front of him. Christian thinks his coolness has actually worked. Then he sees another three cars pull up behind him, blocking off all the lanes. As the blue lights flash, Christian guns the throttle back and tries to get around the car in front before they can block him in. It swerves to the right to stop his move. Christian quickly leans to his left and onto the hard shoulder. He sees the Severn bridge up ahead and gets up to full speed. Lights from cars whizz by as if they were standing still and it isn't long before he reaches the bridge. He lowers his speed to give himself time to work out his next move. When he sees a lorry overtaking another, he aims for that. He times it so well that as the lorries block valuable lane space, he's able to jump in front, leaving the police cars stuck for valuable seconds behind him. He quickly plans his next moves.

"Get off the motorway as soon as we can and ditch the bike. There's a track near Chepstow that we can get onto and use it to lose the police for good. Once that's done, we can ditch the bike and hide out until we can get hold of Mikey." Once the details are finalised, he starts to feel better about the situation, but when he sees the row of blue lights up ahead, his heart sinks. His wrist flops. His hand loosens its grip. He slows down until he's crawling. Blue lights shine in his mirrors. *"Trapped. The coppers have us trapped."* He looks around frantically. Behind him, in front and from left to right. *"Trapped."* He gets to within one hundred meters of the police in front of him and stops. The cars behind him stop forty-five meters away.

"Put your hands above your head and step away from the bike." Somebody, somewhere shouts.

He looks to his front and sees at least a dozen armed cops waiting there. More are appearing to his rear. He curses himself for not ditching the pistol while he had the chance. Being caught with that is at least five years behind bars. Adding the pervert's death in with that, he's looking at a long old stretch in prison. Christian pulls back the throttle and wheel spins to find another way out. The police cars move together well, closing all possible escape but they keep their distance. Christian's blood boils but in his heart of hearts he knows the gig is up. He screams up at the heavens and moves over to the side of the bridge. While he's on the move, he opens the compartments that are attached to the bike and launches them over the side of the bridge. Then he pulls the brakes and dismounts. Several armed police jump out and follow thirty meters away.

"Put your hands in the air and step away from the bike," the copper in front says as he kneels down on one knee and takes aim.

Christian steps up onto the barrier. The lead copper holds his hand up to stop his colleagues creeping closer.

"Sir, please come down from there and step away from the side of the bridge. Whatever it is you are thinking of doing, please rethink it. It's not worth it. We can work this out. Come down sir. Please."

Christian climbs up onto the slippery railings and looks around at the impossible situation he faces. Scores of police creep forward. A spotlight from a helicopter shines above him. He turns his back on them and looks down at the life-threatening situation below. The dark and deadly water passes by at an incredible pace. Just the look of it makes him shiver. He looks back at the cops and back to the river. Wild winds threaten to make his decision for him, and he has to hold on tight. While battling the wind and slippery conditions he thinks about the things he loves. His job. *"They would never accept us back with a criminal conviction."* Christian could never do a job that wasn't helping people that need it. He thinks about the girl of his dreams. The beautiful girl with strawberry lips and lavender hair. If only there was some way he could have opened up to her. Before he left, he wrote a txt on his phone. It's the lyrics of the first song they bonded over. Katy danced to it on the first night in the bar. It was Romeo and Juliet by Dire Straits. His finger had hovered over the send button until it became stiff. He never had the courage to send it. Right now, he wished he had.

The next thought is Mikey. The friend that was with him through the best and worst of his life. He feels guilty because his lasts words to Mikey ended up being lies. Killing that monster made him a lying murderer. How could Mikey forgive him? More sadness and more guilt brings Katy back into his mind. *"Would she actually have loved you once she knew who you really were? A man that has lied to her. A man that has such a violent secret."* His eyes fog over. Tears start to roll. "I don't know. But I should have tried." He lifts up his visor to wipe them. The possibilities of his future, and the mistakes of his past repeat over and over, until finally his mind is made up. Christian takes his helmet off, adjusts his balaclava and throws the helmet over the side. It disappears with frightening pace into the darkness below. Keeping his back to the police, he sits down, removes his rucksack and holds it over the bridge. A quick check ensures the police haven't sneaked closer to him. He throws the knife and most of the other items into the sea and places the rucksack under his feet. Slowly he removes his jacket, zips it up and ties knots into the ends of the arms to create air pockets. He places the pistol and hammer inside it and throws it over the edge. While he watches it float away, he kicks his boots off and removes his thick leather trousers. Again, he ties knots into each leg in the hope that if he survives the fall, the air pockets inside will keep him at the surface. Finally, he strengthens his resolve.

"*It looks bloody cold mate. Are we really going to do it?*" Christian looks to his left and sees the double of himself. His trench coat flaps uncontrollably in the wind. He fights hard to keep his hat on.

"*Yeah, what is it with you and water Christian?*" Christian looks to his right. The hedgehog walks toward him with a smile on his face. His arms are out as if he's walking a tightrope. "*This will be the second time you've tried to drown me mush. I'm starting to think it's personal.*"

"It's nothing personal lads. We played the hand we were dealt to the best of our ability. Unfortunately, it looks like we lost. I am a murderer after all. Maybe death is what I deserve."

"*So what? You're just giving up now? Is that it?*" The hedgehog asks when it gets to his side.

"*Never had you down as a pussy.*" The double of himself says.

Christian smiles. "I'm not a pussy. I'm accepting my fate and putting it all on the line." The wind whips all around and Christian struggles to hold on. "I'm a murderer. I except that. So," Christian holds on to an upright post and gingerly stands back up onto the railings. "So, if I fall back onto the road. I will be arrested and plead guilty. If I fall into the water I could die. I except that also. Murderers should die. But, if I survive the fall and survive the cold and the currents, then, and only then, will I leave this horrible life behind and start a new one." Christian looks at his two comrades. "What do you think?"

"*I think it's a bloody stupid idea,*" the hedgehog says.

"*I fuckin' love it,*" the double of himself says with his usual evil half eaten smile. "*Fate. It's all up to fate. A man's life and what he*

does with it, is his choice." The evil double gives Christian a hug. *"I'm really starting to like you man."*
Christian picks up his rucksack, looks at the cops behind him and on the top of his voice, he shouts. "Protect the children!" Then he takes a deep breath. Takes his hands away from the barriers that support him and closes his eyes. He sways forward. Then back. From side to side. He fights the urge to grab the post. Then he falls. It's a long fall. Head over heels, into the cold and deadly water below.

LIFE GOES ON

A few days later, a white van stops beside a house in the Sand-fields. The driver, dressed as Spiderman beeps the horn. While he waits for the rest of his superhero team, he reads a newspaper article for the third time in as many hours. It says: A policeman, a fireman and two lawyers, breathe life into the investigation of historical abuse claims; Several arrests have already been made with dozens more suspects being investigated as the ball starts to roll once more. Mikey smiles as the door opens. Catwoman and Wonder Woman jump in. Catwoman takes the paper from him, reads it and gives him a kiss. "You should be really proud of yourself for coming forward. You've showed so many others not to be scared." She kisses him again, throws the paper on the dashboard and squeezes his hand. "I'm so proud of you."

"Yeah," Wonder Woman adds. "It looks like those dirty bastards will actually get what's comin' to 'em now."

"I hope so. There's not much more I can do now anyway." He looks at the girls in their costumes and laughs. "So, are you all set for your day of good deeds?"

"We sure are." Catwoman answers. "I'm not sure why we need these disguises though."

"Well, we don't really. It's just something' we've always done. Christian never liked people to know all the good stuff he did. It was kind of his thing. And I agree with it."

Wonder Woman's head sags and Catwoman gives her a hug. "I'm sure he'll come to his senses soon gorgeous. He's a good man."

Mikey looks at another page on the paper and the article reads: Police give up search for murder suspect after fourth day.

Suspect presumed dead after jumping from Severn bridge during last week's storm.

"Won't he Mikey?"

Mikey's focus is pulled away from the paper and back into the van.

"Won't he what?"

"Christian will come to his senses, won't he?"

"Um, yeah, of course. He's the smartest guy I know. He'll come round before you know it."

"So, have you heard from him?" Wonder Woman asks.

Mikey picks up his phone and checks the messages and calls. "Not for a while, but that's nothin' unusual."

"So, you're not worried then?"

Mikey looks back at the paper and reads: As yet the police have no leads and only a stolen bike as evidence to go off. They are now searching for witnesses and anyone who may have information. He looks at Wonder Woman and smiles. "Nah, I'm not worried at all," he lies. "He'll turn up soon. I'm sure of it."

At that moment, Wonder Woman's phone beeps. She removes it from her bag and stares at it for several seconds. Then she places it back inside the bag. She leans back in her seat, looks out of the window and starts to quietly sing.

"A lovestruck Romeo, sang the streets of serenade.

Laying everybody low, with a love song that he made.

Finds a streetlight, steps out of the shade.

Says something like.

You and me babe, how about it?"

THE END.

Printed in Great Britain
by Amazon

42004342R00127